THE FLIGHT OF THE CASSOWARY

In the middle of the tunnel, I realized something was very wrong.

"Hey, Football Boy," came a voice. "Hey."

"Number forty-four. Here he comes."

"How you doing," I said, and kept walking.

Somebody stepped in front of me.

"How 'bout the helmet? That's a fine helmet you got there."

They had moved out from the wall and were all around me. My mind went entirely blank for a second and then was swept up into a memory that seemed to blend into what was happening to me now.

I was at my uncle's house that previous spring, when a big rat wandered out of the woodpile while my uncle was splitting wood. It was no more than two feet from my uncle, who had the ax raised, poised to strike. Some sort of horror of the rat—some tremendous feeling of repulsion—made both of us watch motionless while the rat crossed between us, then crawled into the woodpile and disappeared.

It wasn't pleasant to make myself into that rat. But a part of me was turned into a rat by their looks.

Not one of them raised a hand as I walked through them.

Out on the street, I was shaking. In my mind I kept trying to reconstruct it. For a moment, it seemed, I had been a rat. I didn't feel like a rat now. But a few minutes ago, I think, I had been one.

Other Bantam Starfire Books
you will enjoy

THE
FLIGHT
OF THE
CASSOWARY

by John LeVert

BANTAM BOOKS
TORONTO · NEW YORK · LONDON · SYDNEY · AUCKLAND

To Cindy

RL 6, IL age 13 and up

*This edition contains the complete text
of the original hardcover edition.*
NOT ONE WORD HAS BEEN OMITTED.

THE FLIGHT OF THE CASSOWARY

*A Bantam Book / published by arrangement with
Little Brown & Company Inc.*

PRINTING HISTORY
Little Brown edition published April 1986

*The author gratefully acknowledges a Fellowship
in Fiction from the Massachusetts Artists Foundation.*

*The Starfire logo is a registered trademark of
Bantam Books, a division of Bantam Doubleday
Dell Publishing Group, Inc. Registered in U.S.
Patent and Trademark Office and elsewhere.*

Bantam edition / July 1988

ISBN 0-553-27389-2

Published simultaneously in the United States and Canada

---

*Bantam Books are published by Bantam Books, a division of
Bantam Doubleday Dell Publishing Group, Inc. Its trademark,
consisting of the words "Bantam Books" and the portrayal
of a rooster, is Registered in U.S. Patent and Trademark
Office and in other countries. Marca Registrada. Bantam
Books, 666 Fifth Avenue, New York, New York 10103.*

PRINTED IN THE UNITED STATES OF AMERICA

O   0 9 8 7 6 5 4 3 2 1

THE
FLIGHT
OF THE
CASSOWARY

I was reading a book about ants. "Even ants," the book said, "have parasites."

"Well, that proves it then," I said to my father. "You're an ant." My father, of course, was not in the room when I told him he was an ant. Earlier in the day, though, he had come into my room to make me get up.

"You sloth," he had said. "Get up. Are you going to lie in that pigsty you call a room all day?"

"Pigs are very clean animals," I had said from my bed.

"All but one," my father said back.

"Well, what am I, a sloth or a pig?" I asked, trying to keep him talking so I wouldn't have to get up.

"Neither," my father said. "You," he said, pointing at me in case I didn't know who he was referring to, "are a parasite!"

"A parasite!" I said.

"Exactly. A parasite — someone who doesn't work, who doesn't help around the house, who doesn't add anything to the common good. That's what you are — a parasite. On me, on your mother, on society . . ."

"On North America, on Earth, on the Solar System, on the Milky Way, on the Universe," I said.

"Get up right now," my father said, and left without closing the door.

But now I knew. If I was really a parasite, then he must be an ant. The more I read, the more possible it seemed. We think we're people, but we could just as well be ants. It's like the idea that the whole world is a speck of dust floating among hundreds of other specks of dust in the air of another, much larger world. Or that all the specks of dust we can see floating in the air when the sun shines in a window are actually whole worlds with people, plants, houses, wars, and everything.

So we think we're people, but we might be ants. Ants — I mean the things we call ants — probably don't know they are ants. The word "ant" in ant language probably means "person," and the word "human," to an ant, is their word for "the terrible thing that squashes us whenever we find jelly to eat." Anyway, we don't know how ants think of themselves. According to the book I was reading, we're still not sure exactly how they communicate with each other. Unless they are like my father and me, in which case why bother.

The reason I was reading the book wasn't to find out whether my father was an ant, though. It was the last Saturday before school started again, the last real day of summer, in other words. It was sunny and hot, and I felt sad that summer was over. I was going into my junior year. Everybody said your junior year was the most important. If you wanted to go to college, you had to get really high grades, because it was your junior-year grades the colleges got to see when you applied. Also, in your junior year, you had to take the college boards, which were supposed to be really hard, and all kinds of other things. I didn't know whether I was sad summer was over because it meant I had to go back to school, or whether I didn't want to go back to school because it meant summer was over.

When I got up, my father was still waiting around to bug me.

"Did you get dressed all by yourself?" he asked.

"Can't I ever sleep late?" I asked. "It's Labor Day weekend, you know."

"What does Labor Day have to do with you?" he said.

He always said stuff like that, but it wasn't fair. I had had a summer job, a really good one, cutting brush and trees for new house lots. It was hard work, but I learned how to use a chain saw and a brush cutter, and I liked it until I got poison ivy and couldn't work for a day. Since I wasn't working, I went to the beach. By the end of the day, the poison ivy had spread all over my body and I had to go to the hospital for cortisone shots. It wasn't my fault that I couldn't work the rest of the summer. Then, when I finally got better, it was time for football practice to start. It always started two weeks before school. A few of the kids who were sure to make the team didn't have to go if they weren't able to, but I wasn't one of them. In fact, I was kind of small for football, but as a sophomore I had done pretty well when they put me in at safety, so I was trying out for that position with the varsity. So this was my last free Saturday before school, and football, and homework, and if the Ant agreed, Driver's Ed, and autumn, and rain, and Christmas, and winter, and more winter, and somewhere in the distant future, if I made it, spring and then summer again.

Even though it was Labor Day weekend, the library was open until noon. Mrs. Dingham, my last year's English teacher, had given out a summer reading list for Honors English, which I was going to take this year, and, since I hadn't read some of the books, I thought I would get a few of them before school started. It was while walking to the library that I began to feel sad about the end of summer. Everything smelled so sweet and the air felt so soft. The birds were singing, and there were about a million yellow jackets buzzing among the rotten apples that had fallen from an old crab apple tree at the end of the street.

Then, when I was almost to the library, I saw these

little kids all crouched around in a circle on the sidewalk. There were three of them, all about seven or eight years old. Whatever they were doing, they were completely wrapped up in it; they didn't even look up when I got to them. There were wisps of smoke and ashes rising from the middle of the circle. I looked down — a few pieces of newspaper were burning over a mound of sand that had been torn apart with a stick. Tiny black burned things were all around. One little kid looked up at me. His eyes were all teary from the smoke, and he had this bizarre grin on his face.

"We're burning ants," he said.

"Oh, boy," I said.

So when I saw this book about ants at the library, I got it. It turned out to be very interesting.

What if you were a giant ant and some snotty-nosed little kid tried to burn you? You could grab him by the neck with your mandibles and then bite his head off. But of course, I wasn't an ant, I was a parasite. My father was the ant. That didn't seem fair to the ants, but if they would take him, they could have him. I read about a good job for him as an ant: in certain species of ants, the book said, they have guard ants to guard the entrances to the nest. These ants are just like all the other ants, but once they become guard ants, somehow their heads grow until they are exactly the same size as the opening they are supposed to guard. Their head becomes the door. They just stand there, and if another ant wants to come in, it knocks on the guard ant's head. The guard ant backs up, takes its head out of the hole, and the door is open. To close the door, it just walks headfirst into the doorway. To slam the door, it runs. If my father was an ant, that's what I would make him. He could be the door to my room. I would nail my Nerf ball hoop to his head and bounce Nerf balls off him all day. Of course, if he were an ant, he could bite my head off for real, not just snap at me as he usually did.

Wednesday was the first day of school.

"Good morning," my father said brightly when I came downstairs to get ready. "Who are you? I hope you didn't disturb my son upstairs. This is the part of the day when he gets his rest."

"I have school today," I said, to keep him from going on.

"Oh," he said. "That's nice. By the way, this part of the day is called the *morning*. It lasts until *noon*, when you usually get up. Ever heard of it?"

I drank some orange juice standing up and left. On the way to school I had to pass the Dohertys' dog, Ken. All the little kids were terrified of him. He was part this, part that, part another thing, but not the best part of any one of them. He was as big as a German shepherd but not smart like one; the color of an Irish setter but without the pretty coat; and he had the energy of a retriever but he wasn't friendly. He also had the lung capacity of Pavarotti. He could bark forever. Sometimes at night he'd get started and you couldn't make him quit. Bark, bark, bark, bark, hour after hour, with you lying in bed thinking you were about to go crazy. The Dohertys didn't care, just as they didn't care that he barked at all the little kids going to school every morning. He didn't actually bite any little kid, but he would go right up to them, barking his head off, and they would have to keep their hands in real tight to their chests to get around him. And then one little kid would be too afraid to move, and Ken would stand right in front of him or her, just waiting while the little kid would be crying and shaking, and the other little kids yelling but too afraid to come back and help. Every day this happened.

I hated him. If I was going at the same time the little kids were, I always chased him away for them. They felt safe when I was there, so they would laugh when Ken ran away. I didn't feel that safe, though. Ken knew the difference between a little kid and a big kid. He was willing to bite a big kid. The thing about dogs, though, is that they all know about rocks. Any dog in the world, if you start to throw a rock at it, will run away. Even if nobody has ever thrown a rock at it before, it knows what you're going to do. And Ken had had plenty of rocks thrown at him. All I had to do was bend down and pretend to pick up a rock — I didn't even have to really pick one up — and Ken would retreat. He'd get back to his own yard and start barking twice as loud, but if he started creeping up on me, I'd put my arm up as if I had the rock to throw and he'd back up again. Whenever I could, though, I didn't pretend, I actually got the rock and plugged him.

You know what Mrs. Doherty said? "Those kids are always teasing Ken, so of course he's going to bark at them."

So on the first day of school there was Ken, right where he had been on the last day of school. He wasn't barking, just looking at me from his yard. When you walk past a dog that's looking at you, you never know whether to look back or to look away. Sometimes if you look away, like you don't even see him, or his yard, or his house, he lets you go. Sometimes he doesn't, though. In fact, sometimes he waits until you have already passed his property and he knows you mean no harm, and then, like a big shot, he chases you away. Which is what Ken did. Which is what I knew he was going to do. I already had the rocks in my hand, but I bent down as if I was picking one up, so he would stop his charge. He came to a screeching halt, and for one second he was a sitting

8

duck. I nailed him right on the top of the head, then got him in the side as he started to run away. The third rock hit the Dohertys' aluminum storm door. The noise made Ken veer to his left instead of going up by the front steps and turning around again to bark, the way he usually did. He went right around the back of the house.

I planned to do the same thing the next day and the day after that until Ken ran around to the back of the house whenever he saw me coming. If I was lucky, I could train him to go to the back of the house whenever he thought it was time for me to come, even if I wasn't there yet. That way, maybe the little kids would get some peace, too.

It was very satisfying. It wasn't that I didn't like dogs. I liked them a lot. But Ken was like the school bully. They always tell you if you get picked on by a bully, just stand up to him and punch him in the nose and he'll back down, because bullies are always cowards. That, of course, is a good way to get yourself hurt, because bullies aren't always cowards, they are usually big kids who know how to fight, and there is nothing they like better than to have some kid they are picking on try to fight back. Then they can beat the crap out of him instead of just pushing him around or ripping his shirt. Also, they tend to have friends who are also bullies, or else training to be bullies, so your gentlemanly sock in the nose is likely to bring them all down on you.

But Ken was the way bullies are supposed to be. He was stupid and a coward and didn't have any friends. So I had outwitted him and sent him away howling. If people were more like dogs, life might be easier.

I was in Homeroom 260, along with my best friend, Jerry Raynor. He was already there filling out his schedule card when I sat down next to him. The year before we had been in the same homeroom, too, but the teacher had made us change our seats away from each other because we laughed too much. Some of the kids called Jerry "Jerry Bummer," not because they didn't like him — in fact most kids did — but because he got in so much trouble. If you were with him, you got in trouble, too. He just rubbed the teachers the wrong way.

"Who do you have for English?" Jerry asked.

"Wells," I said. "You?"

"Mrs. Dingdong."

Mrs. Dingham was famous for her recitations of poetry in class, especially her dramatic reading of Robert Frost's "Mending Wall," complete with New Hampshire accent and whistling through her teeth on the "s" words. She also did a good "Chicago: City of the Broad Shoulders" by Carl Sandburg, and, if there weren't any black kids in the class, she'd give a whole reading, complete with sound effects, of Vachel Lindsay's "The Congo." I had her the year before for Sophomore Honors, and she was in the middle of "The Congo," rolling her eyes, going "Oompa, Oompa," when John Robbins, who's black, started moaning and rocking in his seat, moving his feet and drumming on his desk. He was kidding her, but she thought she really had him going, that she had started up the ol' Spirit deep inside him or something, so she stopped. She didn't want to be responsible for him reverting to being a cannibal like his ancestors.

"Is she a hard marker?" Jerry asked.

"No," I said. "You have some papers, but mostly she makes you write journals of what you're thinking about when you read the book. But you have to be very sincere."

"Uh-oh," said Jerry. "Did you keep yours from last year?"

"No, but anyway, you probably won't be reading the

10

same stuff. She's okay. Just don't do anything stupid when she reads to the class."

"It doesn't work," said Jerry. "I always look down at my desk, but they can read my mind. They always call on me right when I'm trying to think of something else so I won't laugh."

Just then the bell rang, and the morning announcements were read over the loudspeakers to the whole school. First Mr. Feininger, the principal, welcomed us back to school and wished us a good year and told everybody to come root for the football team in our first game Saturday; then some kid got on and announced tryouts for *The Fantasticks*; then Kurt Herter of the Meteorology Club told us the temperature and wind velocity; then school started for real.

At practice after school, Coach Sisskind divided us up into two squads. It was the cut: we knew that everybody in squad B was going with Mr. Margolis, the junior varsity coach. I was standing with Moose Duval when Coach Sisskind said, "You two, over here," and I knew I had made the cut. I don't know why Moose's nickname was Moose. Most kids are nicknamed Moose because they're so big. He wasn't that big. He was that strong, though. He played tailback and safety, the same positions I did. Last year he had been the only sophomore starter. This year everybody expected him to be great. So it looked like I might be his backup. Certainly I would get to play on defense when they gave him a rest. Also, they needed somebody ready in case he got all D's and was declared ineligible for the Thanksgiving game, like last year.

When tackling drills started, Moose and I lined up against each other, as we always did. Some kids really cracked helmets, but Moose and I had it down. We would both fire off the line, but when we hit, we would sort of

11

slide off each other, with the runner falling forward and the tackler going down sideways nice and easy. We both grunted and did a lot of digging and stomping with our feet, but somehow, even though Moose always made about a yard on me, he never got through; and, even though I always made about a yard on him, I could never break away. We had never planned it that way. We never talked about it at all. In fact, of all the players on the field, Moose and I were the only ones who weren't acting like mooses. All the others would come up butting heads two or three times before going down.

As Coach Sisskind walked down the line, he yelled. "That's it! That's how to hit! Be an animal on the field." Be a nanimal it sounded like when he said it.

Tommy Hanes and John Robbins, both tackles, lined up opposite. Coach yelled "Go!" and all four hundred and sixty pounds of them cracked heads. Tommy Hanes knocked John back about three yards and then John knocked him back about three yards. Neither of them used their shoulders or arms or anything, just their heads.

"That's it!" Coach said. "Look at this kid! A nanimal! All right, everybody watch this. Do it again."

They were both willing. Here were two mooses for real, stamping, pawing the ground, grunting. This time, though, when Coach yelled "Go!" they missed. Like two trains on separate tracks, they roared right by each other. Both of them ended up face first on the ground.

"Rhinoceroses," I whispered to Moose.

"Huh!" Moose said.

"That's okay," yelled Coach Sisskind. "Way to try. Good effort. Be a nanimal when you tackle."

In the locker room, Tommy Hanes was using a towel to round everybody up into the showers. "Okay, you animals, get up there, move along," he yelled like a cowboy.

"Hey, I'm no nanimal," said Moose. "I'm a humid being. Lemme in the shower."

After I was dressed, Coach called me over.

"I don't know how much I'll be able to get you into the games," he said, "but don't worry, you'll play. I like you 'cause you're smart. Sometimes you need some smart players out there, too. Being smart can make up for lack of natural ability. So you keep trying. I like your effort and I like that you play heads-up. You don't have to be an animal to play football, you know."

I went home very proud, even though Coach made it sound as if the only time I'd get into a game was if the referee decided to give us a quiz. It was a lot better than the last time he talked to me.

"You're just too small," he had said. "You play your position well, you try hard, but one of those big bulls is gonna end up killing you." That was after we had a one-on-one blocking drill, linemen against backs, and I had drawn Tommy Hanes. All the other coaches stopped what they were doing to see what was going to happen to me. Just before I was pulverized, I dropped at his feet and let him run over me. I got tangled up in his feet and down he came. As he landed on me, I put my good arm — the one that wasn't already numb from the impact — around his legs. It looked like I had tackled him.

"Good job," Coach said. Tommy Hanes wanted to do it again, but I just staggered over to the other backs and tried to regain my wind.

That night at supper, my father asked me how school had been.

"Okay," I said. "By the way, I made the football team."

My sister, Jessica, who was in the seventh grade, said, "Oh, wow. Can I wear your letter jacket?"

"You don't get it until the season's over, and you have

13

to play a certain number of minutes before you get one. And, anyway, it wouldn't fit you."

"That's all right," she said. "I want to. It's not like you have a girlfriend or anything to give it to. You might as well let me."

My mother told Jessica to be quiet. She thought talking about girlfriends embarrassed me. I don't know if it did or not.

Then my little brother Luke said he hated the meat loaf. Six-year-olds are the worst eaters. He didn't like the potatoes or the peas, either. Salad made him cry.

"Don't eat the meat loaf if you don't want it," my father said, "but don't talk about it."

"Can I still have a treat afterwards?" Luke asked.

"If you eat the meat loaf," my father said.

"It's horrible," said Luke.

"Don't talk about it. Just eat it," said my father.

Luke started to cry.

"Then don't eat it!" yelled my father.

"Can I still have dessert?" asked Luke.

"Eat some of the meat loaf," said my father.

"Just one bite," said Luke.

"Half of it," said my father.

"Two bites," said Luke.

"All of it!" said my father.

Luke started to cry again. My mother took his plate and divided all the food into two piles: one pile he had to eat, the other he could leave. He just sat there sniffling.

It was always like that at suppertime. It drove me crazy.

Then it was time for us to have our nightly fight about the milk. I was trying to gain weight for football. Also, I was hungry at suppertime, and I liked milk.

"Take the milk carton off the table," my father said. That's his standard opening, like Pawn to King-4 in chess.

My move. I got up from the table, put the milk carton back in the refrigerator, sat down again, drank all the milk in my glass, got up, took the milk out of the refrigerator, poured another glassful, put the milk back, and sat down. I ate a bite of meat loaf while he considered his next move. He already knew what I would do when it was my turn again.

"Pass the salt, please," he said to me. Then, in a very nice voice, he said, "Luke, eat up now — if you want dessert."

A very safe move on his part.

He was waiting for me to play.

I took my time. I ate another bite of meat loaf. I drank the milk. I didn't get up.

My father said something to my mother. Obviously, tonight he wasn't going to be the aggressor. He started to eat, warily.

Me to play. I picked up my milk glass, got it halfway to my lips, discovered to my surprise there was nothing in it, and got up to refill it.

"That's a dollar's worth of milk you've drunk already!" my father yelled.

"It's only three glasses," I said. "If you'd let me leave the milk on the table, it wouldn't be such a big deal."

"You'd think we owned a dairy farm," my father said.

My mother said that if I wanted to drink that much milk, I probably needed it. She always said that. Sometimes she said it was better for me to drink too much milk than to be a heroin addict or something. My father could never see the connection. Neither could I actually.

"I don't care how much milk the kid drinks," my father said. "If he wants it, let him have it. But all this up and down, up and down, every suppertime. And he doesn't seem to realize that milk costs money. Food costs money. He should realize when he sits down and drinks a gallon of milk like it was water that I worked to put that milk on the table."

I finished my milk. I knew that whenever my father started calling me "he," as if I wasn't in the room, that my mother had managed to get the heat off me and onto her. But I also knew enough to wait before getting more milk.

"Look," my father said, as if it was my mother who didn't understand that milk costs money, "I don't begrudge him his football, or his other school activities. I wish I had had the same opportunities when I was a kid. But we were expected to help out. We all held some kind of job, after school or Saturdays or something. I can remember my father asking my older brother Billy — your uncle Billy," he said, looking at me so I couldn't get up, "at the dinner table, saying, 'Billy, did you work today?' And when Billy said, 'No, Dad, I didn't,' my father said, 'Then take your hands off the butter.'"

He had only told this story about a thousand times before. The only one who wasn't tired of it was Luke. He was always being told to take his hands off the butter, too. He probably thought if he had a job he'd be allowed to play with butter all he wanted.

When we had dessert, I got another glass of milk. My father had another glass with his dessert, too. I poured it for him, but there was only half a glass left in the carton.

That night in bed I thought about being an animal playing football. We certainly had some. Robbins and Hanes were animals. Mooses? They were too low to the ground for mooses. Bears? Eddie Sarodny, who played middle guard, was a bear. One swat of his paw and you were like a salmon knocked out of the water. Robbins and Hanes were more like charging rhinoceroses. Robbins was pretty smart — he was in Honors English with

16

me — but Hanes was a little like a rhinoceros off the field, too. He didn't mind kidding, but if he thought you were laughing *at* him — and the thing was, he couldn't always tell — watch out. Just like on "Wild Kingdom," where the rhinoceros charges the jeep. And if you didn't have a jeep, you were in trouble, because he could run fast, too. All he needed was one of those birds to perch on his head.

Then we had a gorilla as linebacker. This was true. This kid, Laurie Wakes, was built like a gorilla. He was always doing push-ups and lifting weights. In gym class, he could go up and down the rope seven times using just his arms. He was kind of grotesque. He thought he was body beautiful. What was Moose Duval? A horse, maybe. When he started galloping up the field he was like a horse. Boy, could he run. And when you tried to tackle him, it was like tackling a horse. It didn't work.

Maybe the whole team was made up of horses. Big draft horses in the line, thoroughbreds in the backfield, a few tough mules as linebackers. What was I, then? A donkey among the horses! A Shetland pony? Coach said I was smart. What animal was smart, not too big, quick, and tough? And cute. A weasel. No, I didn't want to be a weasel. A cat. I would be like a cat out there. Then I fell asleep.

2

Saturday we had our first game. I did pretty well except for the punt that bounced off my head. Moose Duval had gotten the wind knocked out of him a few plays before, so Coach Sisskind sent me in as deep man when the other team had to punt.

He grabbed me by both shoulders. "Let it go if it's too deep," he said. "Don't try a fair catch. If you can't run with it, run away from it. Don't let it touch you." Then he shoved me onto the field.

The ball was snapped, the lines charged, and their punter kicked the ball right into outer space. It hung up there near the moon for a minute, then began its reentry through the atmosphere. First it was a speck, then it was the size of a dime, then a quarter, then you could make out that it was a football plummeting at incredible speed toward the earth. I was getting ready to catch this space-shuttle football when I noticed the ground seemed to be shaking. As anybody who's ever watched an old cowboy movie on TV knows, that can mean only one thing: buffalo! I looked upfield and, sure enough, there was a whole herd of stampeding buffalo, and they were headed right for me. Meanwhile, I lost sight of the ball. I still had my hands up to catch it, but it hit right off the top of my helmet and bounced toward our goal line. I was standing stock-still, like you're supposed to, and, just like in the movies, the herd of buffalo miraculously parted. I was left untouched, but the buffaloes recovered the ball on our three yard line.

I was burning with shame as I ran toward the bench,

but Coach waved me back out to play safety. They tried four straight plunges into the line. From where I was, near the goalpost, it didn't look like football. It looked like a whole bunch of hogs fighting at the trough. Three times these big porkers bellied up against each other, made horrible grunting noises, then sank down to rest. On the fourth try, I ran in and jumped on the top of the pile, where I met the ballcarrier, who was climbing up from the other side. I gave him a little push, and he slid back down his side.

"Well, that saved a touchdown," Coach said when I ran off the field. "Excellent play. That makes up for the other one."

On Monday, we watched the game films. We always laughed when Coach ran them backwards to show us a play a second time. The punt flying off my head way up into the air and landing so delicately on the kicker's toe was one of the highlights. We had won the game, so Coach thought it was funny, too. As a special treat, he showed Moose Duval's eighty-yard run backwards. He was like a magnet: he would leap backwards over a fallen player, and the player would fly up onto his feet again and run backwards along with Moose, until pretty soon all the scattered players were converging backwards on Moose, who then hopped backwards through the line and let go of the ball, which flew into the quarterback's hands and was shoveled like a hot potato under the center, and suddenly Moose and everybody took a big bow and stayed still in their three-point stances.

We laughed so hard we couldn't stop. All the coaches were laughing, even though I'm sure they can see this sort of thing anytime they want when they look at films by themselves, and Laurie Wakes actually fell out of his seat, he laughed so hard. He wasn't faking, either.

"Okay, you monkeys," Coach said. "Tomorrow, full-contact scrimmage. Next week's opponent is tough."

Monkeys? These apes aren't monkeys, I thought. They're nanimals.

On Tuesday I had biology with Jerry Raynor. It was the only class I had with him, except for homeroom and one study hall.

Before class he asked me, "How's your head?"

"What do you mean?" I asked.

"I saw you catch that punt Saturday."

I started to turn red and shrugged my shoulders. "Do you think anybody else saw it?" I asked him.

"Only about three thousand people. I told everybody around me that it was you. I spelled your last name so they could remember it."

Class started. Mr. Fideles started right in. "Most biology classes start with plants and work up to animals, but this year we'll take it the other way around. All animals are essentially alike. In other words, all animals, no matter how dissimilar they appear to be, have more in common with other animals than they have in opposition to them. The thing to remember is that we, too, are animals. We are composed of the same basic cellular structure as the amoeba, and we have the same basic response mechanisms — the same desires, one might say — as the protozoa, the earthworm, the frog, the ape. Some of our parts — most especially our brains — are much, much more highly developed than those of other animals. Some are less developed. But essentially, we are all animals, and are closely or distantly related to all other animals."

I looked at Jerry. He was doodling, but I knew he was listening. He was always pretending not to pay attention, but he always was. I could barely wait to talk to him after class. Mr. Fideles was saying exactly what I had been thinking for the last week or so. I hadn't thought about it in any clear way, but the way Mr. Fideles said it, it made sense. People are animals. They have elements of all different animals in them. Sometimes you can actually see that.

After class I grabbed Jerry. He had some of the same interests as I did, including liking to read books about nature and animals. He read a lot about paleontology and evolution, too.

"Jerry," I said. "We're really all animals."

"Everybody knows that," Jerry said.

"Oh," I said. "Well, I never really understood it before. What I mean, though, I don't know if Mr. Fideles meant this exactly, is that inside us we have parts of all animals. Like with your ancestors: a person is part Irish, part French, part Jewish, and so on, so you have some of the characteristics of all those countries."

"Jews aren't a country," said Jerry. He was Jewish.

"You know what I mean," I said. "Anyway, the same thing with evolution. We're descended from apes, who are descended from reptiles, who are descended from amphibians — I forget how it goes. But, anyway, those are your real ancestors, so people have inherited some of the characteristics of all those other animals."

"Yup," said Jerry.

Still, in spite of Jerry, that idea seemed to go a long way toward explaining why it was possible to see people as rhinoceroses and horses and ants. I wondered what the dominant animal gene in me was.

Life began to take on some of the same rhythm it always does after you get used to being in school again. School, practice, supper, homework, bed. The days were still warm, but the mornings were cold. Now I wore a jacket to school and carried it home. We had our first paper to write in English and our first biology quiz. We won our second game in football.

I had to tell the grade-school kids not to throw rocks at Ken. For a week I had peppered him every time I saw him, not being mad or anything, just making sure he got the point. Now he just sat in his yard and watched everybody going to school. He didn't bark or get up or anything. Sometimes Mrs. Doherty opened the front door and watched us go by. She and Ken had the same expression: they were both mad, but neither of them dared to bark.

My father, of course, still barked. On the Sunday after our second game, I was lying on the sofa watching some program where they had kids bowling. I had already watched "The Armenian Hour," which I liked, and "Faith of Our Fathers," which I didn't. I was sore from the game the day before. I had played almost half the defensive plays, and I thought this would be a good way to recuperate. My father had walked through the room during "The Armenian Hour," watched it standing up for a minute, and looked at me with a face. He himself was a pretty good TV-watcher on Sunday afternoons. Often, he would lie exactly where I was lying and watch two football games in a row, and you would find him, with the room growing dark and some show about animals in Africa on the TV, still there, snoring. But me watching TV Sunday morning evidently was too much for him.

"I'm sick of seeing you lying around the house doing nothing. It's time you started helping out around here. Go out and rake the yard."

"Dad," I said. "I can't."

"No back talk. Just do it. Now."

"Dad," I said. "We don't have a yard. We live in an apartment."

He was so mad because he forgot we lived in an apartment, he didn't know what to do.

My mother came in. She went over and put her hand on his arm and looked at him with this sincere expression on her face.

"Pa," she said, "the boy's right, you know. There's no yard here."

He was really mad now.

"What is this, 'The Waltons'?" he said. " 'The boy's right, you know!' First of all, my name is not 'Pa.' What's the matter with you? Second of all, stop sticking up for him. You won't think it's so funny when he's thirty and you're still picking up after him and I'm still supporting him and you can't get the new couch you want because you can't pry him off the old one. And third of all, let him rake somebody else's yard if we don't have one. Let him do something, for God's sake, besides eat and sleep. He's a kid, after all, not a pet."

But, once again, my mother had saved me, like in the movies, by throwing herself on the grenade. Now, he exploded at her instead of me.

"By the way," he said, "there's no milk. I thought you did the shopping yesterday."

"We must have drunk it all," my mother answered.

"There's also no orange juice and no cereal," he said accusingly.

"There's plenty of cereal," my mother said.

"There's none of the kind I like," my father said. "There never is!"

He stomped out, but came back in five minutes.

"Where's the magazine I brought home from work yesterday?"

"How should I know?" said my mother.

"I left it right on the bureau," he said. "'Dammit."
And he left again.

23

A few minutes later, I heard him go into the bathroom. A second later, I heard the door fly open and then two crashes as something was thrown at my bedroom door. I must have left my sneakers in the bathroom. Then two more crashes against my parents' door. My mother must have left hers in there, too. Then my father's footsteps as he walked into the bedroom, opened his closet door, and, I think, hung something up. He must have left some stuff in there, too. Then, back in the bathroom, sounds as if he was dismantling the place. That was his way of hanging up the towels. It was his way of telling my mother that he thought she should have hung up the towels. "Goddamn dump," he was saying to my mother, three rooms away. It went on like this until dinner.

Dinner was the usual.

"Stop kicking me under the table, Luke," Jessica started.

"I'm not kicking you. You're kicking me," said Luke.

It was my father kicking them both under the table. That was his way of joking to make up for being nasty all day. I had my fork ready under the table in case he decided to fool around with me, too, but he didn't.

I had a paper due on Monday for English, so after dinner I went to my room to write it. It was on "The Metamorphosis" by Franz Kafka. It's a story about this man who wakes up one morning to find out that he has turned into a giant cockroach while he was sleeping. He has parents and a little sister and everything, and when they find out what has happened, they don't know what to do. For a long time they keep hoping he'll turn back into himself, but finally they get tired of him being a cockroach, and they kill him.

We read the story in class, and some kids just thought it was weird, but some really liked it. I did. In the paper, we were supposed to forget that such a thing couldn't really happen, and write what we thought could have

24

made him turn into a cockroach. In class, we all agreed it was his family. The story doesn't say very much about them, but you can tell. I tried to explain how it *could* happen. Inside Gregor Samsa, I wrote, was the potential to become almost any animal. Since we have evolved from lower animals, we have remnants of their instincts within us. Gregor Samsa's family brought out the cockroach in him. Perhaps a cockroach was the kind of animal that could best survive in that situation. So probably, without him knowing it, his cockroach instincts began to emerge. I didn't think, as someone said in class, that he did it in order to get back at his parents. Rather, it was his natural response to his environment: it was the best way to deal with the situation.

Gregor Samsa did what seemed the best thing for him at the time. He did not become the thing that people treated him like — that was Mr. Wells's suggestion. He became the thing that was best adapted to that environment. I ended my paper with a flourish, even though Mr. Wells didn't like flourishes: "Unfortunately, in becoming a cockroach, one risks getting squashed like a bug. Gregor Samsa could have, and should have, become an eagle."

3

Jerry Raynor and I were making cow sounds in study hall. He had his math book propped up in front of his face, while I was resting my head on one arm, hiding my mouth behind my cupped hand. We lowed "Moo-oo" quietly, like cows waiting to be milked, each time a little louder. Janey Boudreau was sitting next to Jerry, looking very irritated, and shooting dagger eyes at him. At which point, Jerry produced a full-scale moo that broke in the middle from a low to a high register, then trailed away to a cowlike pleading. Too late, she decided to ignore him. "Jane-ey," he mooed. "Ja-ney." He was driving her crazy, and he knew it. I had stopped mooing and was dying trying to keep from laughing. Karen Cleary, on my left, was looking very superior but she was trying not to laugh, too. Then Jerry had an inspiration. He mooed "Ja-ane" again and then did a great, fat, slobbery sneeze, a huge snort. Just like a cow. It was so wet you could feel it as much as hear it. Janey Boudreau turned beet red. At the same time, Jerry and I both realized how quiet the room was. I for one had no idea how long Jerry had been mooing in that silent room. Jerry and I both looked up. Miss Moran was staring at him — staring at him as if she had been staring for quite a while.

"Mr. Raynor," she said. "Go graze elsewhere."

Jerry closed his math book, sighed, and left the room without looking back. He opened the door nonchalantly and flung it shut behind him. Unfortunately, the glass pane shattered. He just kept walking. Once again, through no fault of his own, Jerry was in the shit.

"What happened?" I asked him after school.

"It's not that bad," he said. "Pay for the window, apologize to Miss Moran, probation till marks come out."

"No suspension?"

"No, but they called my house. They got my grandmother on the phone, so by the time I get home, they'll think I burned the school down. I tell them all the time, don't talk to my grandmother, she doesn't speak English. They know she gets hysterical, that's why they do it. She's probably calling my mother at work right now. After that, she'll call my father at his work."

"What'll your father do?" I asked.

"The Recidivist, he calls me. Now you're sentenced to your room for another week. Last time he punished me, I asked for a jury of my peers. He said if they ever assembled a jury of my peers, the cops would disperse them."

So Jerry went home to calm his grandmother down, and I went to football practice.

Nobody dressed on Monday. First, as usual, came last Saturday's game films. I couldn't take my eyes off myself. You know how, if you find a trail of ants, you see hundreds of ants going in both directions, all hurrying in two lines like nonstop traffic, some of them hurrying to get stuff, others carrying stuff back to the nest, and then you notice one ant wandering off in the complete wrong direction? That was me out on the field.

"Look at you," Coach Sisskind said. "You're hesitating. Don't hesitate. Commit yourself. Don't wait for them to come to you. That way they'll get their downfield blocking organized and run right over you."

On one play, a reverse, our whole defense was fooled by the flow of the blocking, and the runner turned the corner all by himself. I made the tackle alone, having been fooled before the play turned into a reverse.

"That's better," Coach said. "That's how to react. As soon as you see the play developing, pounce."

Pounce? That was like telling a dog to pounce on the car he's chasing. I was too small to pounce. Pounce and get bounced, I thought. Yet actually, it wasn't a bad metaphor. I should stay back, see the play, then pounce — not like a dog, like a cat. Okay, I'd do it.

After the lights were turned back on, Coach told us about our next game.

"The team we're playing," he said, "they're all black."

"Even their teeth?" asked Moose.

27

"I mean all the players are black. It's a school for colored people."

"I thought they did away with them," John Robbins said.

"What? Colored people?" said Bennie Williams. He was black, too, like Robbins. He was a wide receiver.

"No," said Robbins, "schools for them."

"All right, stop," said Coach Sisskind. "That's enough." He was a little embarrassed at having used the word "colored." "What I'm trying to say is, I mean . . . You know what I mean. You don't have to be scared of them."

"Coach, I'm scared of them," said Robbins. Coach raised his eyes to the ceiling.

"No, I'm serious. Those dudes are bad. They're gonna pick on me. Man, what if they make me play for them 'cause I'm black? Coach, I don't want to play for them. I want to play for us. I don't even know their plays."

"Maybe they don't even have plays," said Williams.

"That's right, Coach, they probably don't even have plays. What are we going to do?"

"We're going to play one-on-one football," said Williams. "That's the ghetto way."

"No defense," said Robbins.

"We'll play half-field, winners out," said Williams.

"That's right," said Robbins. "Schoolyard football."

"With the blood."

"No bones about it."

"Except maybe a token toke."

Most of the kids were laughing a little, but not too much. Williams and Robbins were talking jive. They were laughing, but they were pretty mad.

"Okay," said Coach Sisskind, "enough. What I mean is, they're a tough team. They're very good. But you shouldn't be afraid just because you're playing an inner-

28

city team. You're good, too. All you have to do to win is execute."

"That's right," said Robbins. "Execute. Kill 'em all. Except me and Williams here, we're on your side. We're good niggers."

"Robbins," said Coach, "you're making a lot of trouble over nothing. I'm sorry I said the word 'colored.' I didn't mean anything by it. Now let's just try to play football and forget about it." Then he left. He was mad, too.

After that, we had the whirlpool and heat and stuff for people who had gotten hurt last Saturday, and the rest of us got out early.

It must be hard to be one of only a few black kids in a mostly white school. They stuck together a lot, but there wasn't really any trouble between them and the white kids. Remarks, of course, which you're always going to get, I guess, but no real fights. I think everybody knew that if a white kid and a black kid got into a fight, even if it had nothing to do with race, it would end up being a racial thing. Even if the race part began just by the way somebody told what had happened: the black kid beat the white kid or the white kid beat the black kid. And then people's buried prejudices would come up, and they'd start talking that way. I think all the kids felt that, no matter what their feelings were, that particular thing was something to be avoided.

Robbins against Hanes would have made a good fight, though. Our two All-State tackles. They always had their pictures taken together, very impressive in their jackets and ties, two high school athletes, one white, one black, holding the plaque between them, or shaking hands with the speaker at some banquet. Whenever one of them put on a tie, he looked like a tree some kid had tied a little string around.

They didn't like each other very much. A lot of times

in practice their blocking drills turned into fights, and the coaches had to make them stop. Then they'd bump into each other a lot for the rest of practice. Off the field they left each other alone.

Robbins was all right. He always walked slow and talked slow, but underneath he was pretty quick. He was good in math and very good in English. Hanes, on the other hand, flunked typing. He said it was because he kept hitting two keys at once because his fingers were too big. After a while he'd get frustrated and just start pounding the whole machine like a bear pretending to type.

Robbins was the only one of the black kids I knew really well. Williams I covered in practice and he never juked me too bad, and about all we ever said to each other was "nice move" or "good tackle." The only thing about the black kids was when they all hung out together after school. I couldn't blame them for that — I couldn't blame them for anything, after all — I mean, I guess I'd do the same thing, if I was in the same situation, but sometimes, they'd act so private and cool, they'd look like a bunch of cats watching a dog go by. Cats always looked like they expect you to envy them. They come back to the house with their heads so high, carrying a dead mouse or a bloody little bird in their teeth. They know you will be disgusted, but they look at you as if to say, "Disgusted or not, let's see you catch one." A cat's whole act is to hint at the terrific things they do when you're not around, or that they can do that you don't know anything about. That's the way the black kids acted — as if they were cats — Mysterious Creatures of the Night. They treated the white kids like dogs — I mean the way cats treat dogs. The white kids were big, clumsy, potentially dangerous, maybe, but the idea was — "Come too close, Rover, and you gonna get scratched."

Anyway, I was neither a dog nor a cat. When I got home, I was just a kid with things on my mind.

The first thing was Karen Cleary. In study hall, she thought Jerry's mooing was pretty funny, or at least she thought his mooing "Janey" was pretty funny, which it was, and you could tell that when he got kicked out of class she felt bad for him. She was kind of quiet, but had a good sense of humor. I used to talk to her before English class the year before, and once she did a pretty good imitation of Mrs. Dingham reading Emily Dickinson. She was also really good-looking. But her brother had been co-captain of the track team before he graduated, and she mostly went out with seniors. I really liked her, but I couldn't see any way. I didn't know how to ask her out. I thought of calling her up and asking her about homework, but that's stupid. She'd know I wasn't really calling her about homework. She'd know I wanted to ask her out but was too scared to do it. She'd think I was a real nerd. It was possible she thought that already. I could just picture her tomorrow on the bus to school telling everybody, "This little creep in my English class calls me up last night and says he wants to talk about the homework." Ha, ha, ha, all the girls laugh, "Who was it?" And then she tells them who it was and they laugh harder. Or worse — this could happen, too — Karen Cleary tells everybody my name and they all laugh, and then Linda Farmer, who's my sister Jessica's best friend in seventh grade, pipes up from the back of the bus, "Don't say bad things about him. I love him."

But even if that didn't happen, I still decided against it. Even if she was nice, it would be stupid. I knew what the homework was. I always did. Anyway, we only had one phone, in the kitchen, so there was no way to call in privacy. There was no way I was going to make that telephone call with my mother in the room, or Luke coming in to ask for something to eat, or my father yelling so she could hear, "What's that — some girl he's talking to? Get him off the phone!"

I just didn't know how to ask her out, that's all. Her or any other girl. Some guys just did it. They'd just walk up to a girl's locker and ask her out right in front of everyone. It put them on the spot, but in a way it put the girl on the spot, too. She had to say just the right thing or she'd look like the fool. The guy had been right up-front about it, now it was up to her. She couldn't mumble, she could say no, but she had to do it just right. She could say yes, but she had to do that just right, too. Usually, everything was said in a joking way, so nothing had to be decided then, but then later, the guy could call the girl, since they'd already talked about it, without having to make up something like homework. Or the girl could bring it up again if she liked him. And if nothing got started, the guy would just hop over to another girl's locker and talk to her.

Actually, the whole ritual reminded me of birds. Once, on a Saturday when the baseball game was rained out, they showed a program called "The Courtship Rituals of Birds." Always the male bird has to attract the female. The male bird always has the bright colors, while the female is usually just plain-looking. Like, for example, the male cardinal is bright red, but the female is just a drab sort of gray. Pheasants are the same way — the male has the ring and the bright feathers; the female is plain brown. So the males fly around, show the females how handsome they are, puff themselves up to look bigger, and strut around while the females just cock their heads and watch. The males have to show off and pretend to fight, and whoever is the best show-off gets the female. That doesn't bother the other males, though. They just go find another female and show off in front of her. They don't seem to care at all about being rejected. The funniest part of the program, though, was seeing the birds dance. A female bird would be looking at a male bird, and he'd be bobbing his head up and down at her as if he was saying really smooth things, then all of a sudden he'd hop up and do a rumba right at her. Then, he'd stop and start nodding to her again. Or else there'd be all these males standing around and suddenly one of them for no reason would start hopping up and down and another one would start, and the two of them would boogie across the floor to each other, bump bellies, and sit down again. Then two more would do it.

I couldn't see the difference between that and the hallway between classes. The boys preened and showed their rump feathers, while the girls just kept their distance and watched. We had our thumpers, our chirpers, our hoppers, our wing-spreaders. We had drumming contests the way grouse do, we had roosters crowing, pigeons cooing, thrushes singing, mockingbirds mocking, geese honking, and in general a whole flock of male birds doing their ground-stomping dance while the females got their books from their lockers and went to their next class.

The only bird I could see being was an eagle. Not because they are so majestic or powerful or anything, but because of the way they go about it. They don't hop along the ground and peck on each other's head. The male eagle flies up into the air in circles, higher and higher, until it is just a tiny speck in the sky. Then, it folds its wings in and plummets down, faster and faster. Just before it smashes into the ground, it opens its wings and touches down gently. That would certainly impress Karen Cleary. Unfortunately, like most humans, I couldn't fly. But that's the way to do it. Like an eagle.

Another thing on my mind was this game Saturday. I might not have thought about it any differently from any

33

other game, except that the coach had mentioned it. It wasn't one of those games between white and black teams from different parts of the same city, where there's always a real rivalry and a lot of times real hatred. It was two high schools from two different cities, that's all. Still, things weren't as they should be — there was always something going on when a black school played a white school, or in our case, a mostly white school. I was worried most, though, about getting beat deep. "Don't get beat deep" was the first rule for a safety.

While I was thinking about these things, Luke came into my room.

"Daddy wants you," he said.

"For what?" I asked him.

"I don't know. He wants you."

My father was in the kitchen.

"That was Jerry's grandmother on the phone," he said. "I can't understand a word she says. What happened with Jerry?"

"Nothing. He slammed a door in school by mistake and broke a pane of glass," I said.

"That's all?"

"Yeah."

"Were you involved?"

"No."

"Why did his grandmother call here?"

"I don't know. She gets all upset."

"She keeps saying you're such a good boy," my mother said. "If only you could keep Jerry out of trouble."

"He's not in trouble," I said. "He just has to pay for the pane of glass."

"And you're sure you weren't involved?" my father asked. He was looking at me very closely. "You weren't fooling around with him when it happened or something like that?"

"Yes, I'm sure," I said. "We were talking in class, and the teacher told him to leave. When he shut the door, it broke somehow, that's all."

My father was still looking at me closely. "You were talking in class? What class was this?"

"Just study hall," I said, with a sigh and started to leave the kitchen.

"Just a minute," my father said. "That can't be the whole story. All you were doing was talking in study hall and Jerry got thrown out? Why didn't you get thrown out?"

"I don't know."

"There's something wrong here," my father said. The Interrogator. He was always looking for holes in my stories. Even if I said I was going to the bathroom he'd look at me suspiciously.

"Let me get this straight. You were talking to Jerry in class."

"Study hall," I said.

"Study hall. That's all you were doing?"

"Right."

"And then the teacher kicks Jerry out of class."

"Right."

"Without even saying Be quiet, boys, first?"

He figured he was onto something. He was going to drag it out of me inch by inch — millimeter by millimeter — the way they used to drag tapeworms out of people in the Middle Ages. He had a grip on something and he was going to pull until the whole thing came up. Even if it turned out to be nothing. He just liked pulling.

"Dad, it was nothing. We were fooling around in study, and Jerry kept it up, and the teacher didn't like it. Then he shut the door and the glass broke. It was an accident. The school people knew that. Jerry's grandmother's crazy."

"Jerry's grandmother is not crazy!" my father yelled.

35

"Jerry's grandmother is worried about Jerry. As she should be. What about you? You're his friend. He gets in trouble, but you were fooling around with him. You're just as much to blame as he is. Don't you think so?"

"I guess so," I said.

"You guess?" he said. "I know. I think you should pay for half the window he broke."

"Oh, boy," I said.

"What?"

"Okay."

"Okay, what?"

"Okay, okay. I'll pay for half the window. Okay."

"I don't understand you sometimes," he said. He looked at my mother with a frown, and she frowned back at him to show that she didn't understand me either, and the two of them left the room together, frowning.

I stayed in the kitchen, frowning. What an asshole.

My brother Luke was still in the kitchen, too. He had been listening to the whole thing.

"Paul," he said, "will you play a game with me?"

I didn't answer him.

"Will you?" he asked again.

I couldn't answer him. I just went back to my bedroom.

"Mama!" I heard him yelling. "Mom! Paul's turning into the Madman again. Paul's going to be the Madman." That's what he said whenever I got mad. It didn't mean I was really acting like a madman, just that I was being a mad person. He said the same thing when Jessica sulked or got angry. "Jessica's turning into the Madman," he would tell everybody. "Don't talk to her. She's the Madman now."

After supper, I read Luke's bedtime story to him. I wasn't usually the one who read to him, but tonight I felt like it. It was *Mowgli* by Rudyard Kipling. It was too old for him, but he really liked it. It's the story of a boy in India who is brought up in the jungle by wolves. He learns how to hunt with them and how to live like an animal. In the book, Baloo the bear, who is the teacher of all the cubs of the wolf pack, teaches Mowgli the different Laws of the Jungle, and he teaches him the Master Words of the Jungle — how to say "We be of one blood, ye and I" — in the different languages of the hunters, the birds, and even the Snake-People, so that no animal will harm him, since he is kin to all of them. I liked reading it as much as Luke did.

We were reading the chapter called "Letting in the Jungle." After Mowgli is cast out of the wolf pack because he is a human, even though he thinks he is a wolf, he goes to a village to try to live among his own kind. One woman in the village, whose baby was stolen a long time ago by a tiger, thinks maybe Mowgli is her son and is very kind to him. All the other villagers, though, are mean to him. When they see him talking to the wolves, and see the wolves obeying him, they decide he must be a sorcerer or a devil, so they drive him out of the village with stones, yelling, "Wolf. Wolf's brat, go away." Even though the jungle is all around their village, the people don't know anything about it. Then they decide that if Mowgli is a sorcerer-wolf, then the lady who might be his mother must be a witch. They decide to burn her and her husband at the stake. When Mowgli sees how stupid people are, and how cruel, he decides the village has to go. He doesn't want to kill anybody, just erase all traces of humans there. With the help of his brother wolves and Bagheera the panther, he gets his parents out of the village, then he calls Hathi the elephant to destroy it. "Let in the Jungle," he says. So Hathi the elephant and his three sons trample the fields of the villagers and eat all their crops, then destroy all the grain they had stored up in case of emergency. When the villagers finally flee, the elephants knock down the walls. Then the jungle moves silently in, and the whole place is blotted out.

Jessica had come into the room to listen to the end of the chapter. She squealed or said "Oh, the poor thing" whenever something happened to one of the animals, but she only did that because she thought she should, so I ignored her. At the end, I asked Luke what he thought of the chapter.

"Good," he said.

I asked him if he would like to be Mowgli and know the Master Words for all the animals.

"I'd like to know all the things a wolf knows," he said. "But why did they kick him out?"

"Well," I said, "after all, he wasn't really a wolf."

"He was, too," said Luke. "He could be a wolf if he wanted. He can run as fast as a wolf."

"Even so," I said, "that's not all there is to being a wolf. Besides, remember, the wolves called him the Hairless one. He didn't look like a wolf. He looked like a boy."

"Having hair doesn't make you a wolf," said Luke. "You're a wolf if you act like one. He was like a wolf only better. He could be a wolf *and* a boy."

I asked Jessica who she'd like to be.

"I like Bagheera," she said, "but he's so cruel when he hunts the other animals. I guess I'd like best to be a little fawn, but then Bagheera would come and kill me."

"Aiee," I said. She said those things on purpose, the same way she arranged her stuffed animals on her bed when her friends were coming over. She didn't like stuffed animals at all — never had. Going through a stage, as they say. A particularly stupid one, I thought. If there was a bug in her room, she'd get up on the bed, like a cartoon lady jumping on the table when a mouse appears, and start screaming for me to come and kill it. Even a moth. But of course I wasn't supposed to kill it. I was supposed to capture it and let it go outside. Once I opened her window to let a fly out and a wasp flew in. Wasps get mad when you try to let them out. They get even madder when you try to kill them. What they like to do is crawl up and down the windowpane looking for their own way out, and every once in a while make a slow tour of the room at the level of your face, with their legs dangling down, and then return to the window for some more glass-crawling. This one did just that, with me following it around very cautiously with the rolled-up magazine I had wanted to use on the fly. Jessica wanted to leave the room, but didn't dare, the wasp had barred the way. Finally, for no reason at all, it landed on the floor, and I stepped on it.

Anyway, reading *Mowgli* gave me an idea.

"You know what we should do?" I said to Luke and Jessica. "We should dig a big pit in the backyard and cover it with branches. Then we'll lure Dad into it and us kids can kill him with spears."

Luke thought it was a terrific idea, but Jessica looked horrified.

"Don't scare Luke like that," she said.

Then Luke said, "Let's kill him like they do Shere Khan."

"Well," I said, taken a little aback by Luke's ferociousness, even though I knew it was only a game, "maybe we should let him live. He's not as bad as Shere Khan, is he?"

"No," said Luke, "he's not that bad. He may live."

Then he went to bed. From his room, I heard him say in a commanding voice, "Let the Jungle into this place, Hathi. Hathi, let in the Jungle."

It seemed like a good idea to me.

4

My English paper came back A−. "A few sentence mistakes," Mr. Wells wrote on it. "Intriguing ideas. I especially liked the metaphor of real animal identities buried within us." What metaphor? I thought. It's true. In fact, Mr. Wells, it could happen to you.

While we were leaving class, I asked Karen Cleary something about the homework. She looked surprised.

"You were there," she said. "Weren't you listening?"

"Was it read chapters two and three and answer the questions about the main characters?"

"Yeah," she said. "Exactly. So why'd you ask me about it?"

"I wasn't sure," I said.

"Well, next time write it down so you won't have to be asking other people," she said and walked away.

My approach hadn't been quite the Flight of the Eagle. I went to Biology class thinking of things I should have said.

"Arthropod," Mr. Fideles began.

"Absent," replied Jerry.

"Raynor," said Mr. Fideles, "if you are asked to leave this class by me, you will not be allowed back in. You supposedly have some aptitude for science, if your work in general science last year is any indication. I suggest that you use that rather than your perhaps greater aptitude for getting yourself in trouble.

"Now. Arthropod is the phylum that includes insects, arachnids, and crustaceans. The brain of the arthropod — we will take the insect as our example — is more like a switchboard than a brain. For instance, if a fly's eye sees something large coming toward it, the fly takes off. It doesn't think about it, the brain doesn't decide whether it should move or not, it is an automatic process. The reception of the stimulus and the response to it are the same thing. The brain is just the set of wires that connect the parts."

Then Mr. Fideles told us how the brain of the insect evolved into the ganglia at the stem of our brains. The root of the human brain, he said, is the insect sense-receptor apparatus.

Jerry walked me down to French class.

"So underneath all this other stuff," I was saying to him, "we have the brain of an insect."

"Yeah, well," he said, "you can't take it too far. What it really means is that our brains evolved out of the same kind of sense receptors that insects have. Really, those ganglia at the base of our brain — they're *like* the brain of the insect, but they're not the same thing."

"I like the idea that we really have the brain of a fly, and all the rest is just padding."

"HELP ME, HELP ME," said Jerry in a tiny voice and left me at the door to French class.

To me, French sounded like water being squeezed out of the hole in Luke's rubber ducky in the bathtub. Or else like a conversation between Huey, Dewey, and Louie. Madame Garnaud, the French teacher, looked like Julia Child and sounded like Unca' Donald.

She would start talking about *La Belle France* and get all excited and flap her arms around just like Julia Child telling you how delicious eggs with snot in them would taste. Or else she would be making us recite our irregular verbs and start pounding on her French book like Julia Child wrestling a chicken.

41

That day we had the part I found hardest of all: a dicté. Madame Garnaud read a passage from something, then repeated it slowly while we tried to write it down. Then we had to translate it into English from our own French. This one was all about the *Ecole des Bozos*, where the young French of promise attend to apprehend the arts. In particular, those of the painting, the sculpture, and something else. They assist at conferences by professors and study the tables of the great maître d's. In the year one million nine hundred and sixty-eight, the students of the School of the Bozos participated in the manifestations of the students of the Left Bank. In consequence, many reforms of the ancient laws were instituted. Today, students from all the parts of France, along with numerous strangers, continue to grab the art at the School of the Bozos.

I knew I was in trouble with that translation. I could figure out what it meant and what the words should be. Writing it like that was the kind of thing Jerry did. It was funny, but it wouldn't be when she saw it. We started to hand the papers in. I decided to fix mine quick, but suddenly it got snatched away and it was too late. Oh, well, I thought, I knew something bad was going to happen.

In fact, I had had a sense of foreboding all day. Not exactly foreboding — I'm not sure — a sort of restlessness. Like I could feel something in the wind but couldn't tell what it was. I still had it after French class — like a storm was coming. They say that animals can tell coming changes in the weather. If there's a thunderstorm coming, all the birds start darting around lower and lower to the ground, very excited, then you see them lined up all along the telephone wires and on low branches in the trees, like they're waiting for something to happen, very nervous. So even if the sun is still shining, you know there's a storm coming. It seems very mysterious how they know, until you find out that when a storm is coming, the air pressure drops, even before the wind starts or the clouds come, and the change in air pressure makes it hard for the birds to fly.

That's how I felt. I felt the pressure dropping on me, and I could hardly move. I don't know whether the birds know there's a real storm coming, or whether they just think, "Man, I just can't do it today. I just feel bad for no reason at all." I was very agitated — that's the word they use to describe how the birds act when they don't want to use words that would make them seem too human, like irritable or sad. I wouldn't have known which human word to use to describe myself, either, but I certainly felt agitated. Jumpy. Like a storm was coming, and I couldn't fly very well. Was I nervous about the game coming up? Was it something else? Actually, I didn't think about it at all; it's just the way I felt. And acted.

After school I got my stuff from my locker and started to football practice. I was a little late: the whole corridor was deserted, except for Karen Cleary way down the other end at her locker. She was about fifty feet away, and there was nobody between her and me. I started walking toward her, but instead of walking normally, I found myself walking like a duck. The more I tried to walk naturally, the more ducklike I seemed to walk. When I was about halfway to her, I started to tip over. I was listing to the left, so I had to lean to the right and walk flat-footed, with my feet making noises splat splat like a duck's feet. I pretended nothing was wrong. When I was almost in front of her, I said in a nonchalant way, "Hi, Karen." It came out "Haw, Caw," more like a crow, actually, than a duck. She looked up, as if she hadn't noticed me careening toward her for fifty feet, and said in a surprised sort of tone, "Oh, hi, Paul. See you tomorrow." I went on by, trying not to bump into things.

In practice, we concentrated on pass defense. A bad sign.

"They can run and they can pass," said Coach Sisskind, "but they can't do both at once."

"He don't know these dudes," Bennie Williams whispered to me.

"So, we take away the run, and we know they have to pass. You linebackers will be playing up tight to the line. That's going to put a lot of pressure on you defensive backs."

That's what I thought, I thought.

"Your primary responsibility is still not to get beat deep. But you also have to be alert for the short pass in the flat, because the outside linebacker may not be there."

So we practiced having the linebackers pinch in to turn the running plays back into the middle. That left me with about half the field to cover. Bennie Williams beat me shallow, beat me on the sideline patterns, and then for good measure, beat me deep. I felt so sluggish, so slow. I couldn't cover all that territory.

"I don't know if this is going to work," I heard Coach saying.

After one catch, Bennie Williams said to me, "This'd be a good spot for corn." After another one in the flat, he said, "Beans. Maybe cotton."

Finally, after he caught the long one, I asked him what he was talking about.

"Well," he said. "See all this land?" He pointed across the part of the secondary I was supposed to cover. "It looks like some black folks are finally going to get that forty acres and a mule they was promised, and, boy, you are one slow mule."

• • •

I felt the same way at home. In fact, I spilled my milk, something even Luke didn't do anymore. Nobody at the table said anything.

Finally, my father said, "You have a big game coming up on Saturday."

"Yes," I said.

"Maybe I'll try to come if I can make it."

"Okay," I said.

"You sure you want me to?"

"Sure," I said. "That would be good."

"By the way," he said. "Don't make any plans for Sunday. I want you to help me over at your grandmother's."

"Doing what?" I asked.

"Digging a new leach line for her septic tank. It keeps getting clogged up."

"That sounds like fun," I said.

"Well, it has to be done," my father said, "and I can't finish it all by myself."

"Take Luke," I said.

"Yeah. Take me, Daddy. I'll help," said Luke.

"I would," my father said to Luke, "but I don't need anybody smart. I just need somebody strong."

I just sighed. Teasing was my father's way of being in a good mood, just as it was his way of being in a rotten one. And there was no use arguing about helping. If there was one rule in the house, besides never referring to my mother as *She* — as in "*She* said I didn't have to" "Don't call your mother She" — it was everybody had to help out if there was work to do. Since we had moved into the apartment, my father had had a little trouble keeping me occupied, but not for lack of trying. I still had my chores, like doing the dishes every other night, alternating with my sister, but there was no more mowing the lawn or helping paint the house. Still, if my grandmother's house needed work, I was expected to help. Actually, I couldn't complain. For once, I could see his point. Even though, in this case, there went my Sunday.

I didn't feel that much better the next day, when I saw Nino Cappellano flirting with Karen Cleary in the hall. He was a senior and a major stud around the school. He played guard on the football team, was co-captain of both the football team *and* the basketball team, vice president of the senior class, sang baritone solos with the Glee Club, and looked like a god. You know, six feet tall, perfect build, black, curly hair over a classic Mediterranean profile. The Golden Greek. To complete the picture, in track he threw the discus.

He was asking her out in that joking way of insinuating things.

"Come on," he said. "I don't just play football, you know. There's other games I know that we could play together."

He was leaning against her locker looking extremely relaxed. She was smiling up at him.

"Well," she said, "I don't think I know how to play the kind of game you're talking about."

"That's all right," he said. He smiled like he was half asleep and dreaming about something very nice. "I can teach you."

"Well," Karen Cleary said slowly, "when you're a beginner like I am, you don't want to start out picking up bad habits, you know, like the wrong grip or something, that you'll have to correct later. I think I'll wait and get a good coach and learn the right way. But thanks."

That shut Nino up pretty good. He kept smiling, though, all the way down the hall. It shut me up, too. Her dumping on Nino was no consolation. A beginner, she called herself. She didn't talk like a beginner. She was certainly out of my league. Because there I had been a minute before, waiting for Nino to get out of the way so I could ask her about the homework again.

On Friday night, I went over to Jerry Raynor's. He had a Ping-Pong table, so we were probably going to play some Ping-Pong, maybe watch some TV, then I'd go home and go to bed early. When I got there, Jerry was just getting ready to torture his grandmother.

Jerry was Jewish. His grandmother had come over from Poland just before World War II. She still spoke Yiddish when she talked to Jerry's father. Her English sounded pretty funny, and when she got mad or mixed up, she went back to speaking Yiddish, even to me. You could get her mixed up pretty easy by mumbling or talking fast. Jerry would ask her for some money, and she would ask him for what, and he would say in a normal tone but a little too fast for her, "I got to go downtown and pick up some milk and some drugs and some ice cream." Then she'd give him the money, and for a minute you could see her figuring out the words in her head. Then she'd start yelling, "Drug, you said! Oh, you bad boy! Give back the money to me. Back I want it!" Then Jerry would say he was only kidding, he just wanted some bruzzatolines, or something else that didn't make any sense. But she'd figure that was something else bad and keep trying to get the money back. Or else she'd put her hands on her hips and say, "Yes? And what is a bruzzatoline?" pronouncing it exactly as Jerry had.

"Nuzzatoline," Jerry would say. "Not bruzzatoline. Oh, brother." Then they would stand there looking at each other, Jerry's grandmother trying to figure out exactly which trick he was pulling on her, and Jerry trying to think up another thing to horrify her.

"It's like pot," he would say — she knew about pot —

47

"but you don't smoke it, you put it in your grandmother's soup and watch what happens."

Then she'd make another grab for the money, but he'd hold it up high while she jumped for it. She only came up to about his chest. "Up, Grandma, up," he'd say, until finally she'd punch him a few times and give up.

Before the war, when she was a little girl in Poland, there had been a pogrom against the Jews in her town. In order to save the children their parents let them be baptized. Jerry's grandmother had been just a little girl, but she was ashamed of having been baptized. Especially, I guess, combined with the fact that later she had escaped from Poland while so many of her family had been killed. In any case, this was the main way that Jerry tortured her.

"Grandma," he would say if she was bugging him, "go say your Rosary." He had a little crucifix, which she used to ransack his room trying to find, which he would bring out from time to time to wave in front of her. "Jeddy, Jeddy," she would say, shaking her head, "you dun't know what you doink." He never did any of this when his parents were home. And I don't think his grandmother ever told them. His father would have killed him. I mean really, like stabbed him or beat him to death. His father was kind of a tough guy. He sold fruits and vegetables to all the small grocery stores and had one big truck that said Raynor's Produce. He also had a tattoo on his arm that said, "Jake" with a Star of David around it. Jerry said that went over real big with the doctors and lawyers his father met at temple.

Anyway, when I got there, he was trying to get her to go to Friday night confession down at Our Lady's Church.

"Father," he said, mimicking her voice, "forgive me for my sins. For fifty years now I been pretending I was

48

Jewish. I'm sorry. Also, my grandson Jeddy I treat bad."

"Ah, Paul," Jerry's grandmother said to me, "mek Jeddy stop."

She liked me. I don't know why Jerry always started that stuff when I came. He did it to show off, I know, but I didn't like it. I always made him stop. It was awful, especially when she started crying.

"Okay, Grandma, I'll stop," he said. "But don't think I can't hear you in your room every Sunday morning listening to the mass on the radio. And God knows. Yowsah, as you Jewish people call Him."

"Enough already," I said to Jerry.

I liked his grandmother. She thought I was a good boy. She told me so whenever I went there. "Paul," she would say, "Jeddy's a gut boy, he hass for a friend a gut boy like you. Mek from him a gut boy, too."

So when Jerry stopped torturing her for my benefit, she said, "You want someting to eat? Dhere's notink. Jeddy, go get some ice cream, sometink for your friend."

"You want some ice cream?" Jerry asked.

"It's not far," I said. Jerry's grandmother liked ice cream a lot.

So Jerry and I walked down to the store.

"I bought a car," Jerry said.

"Why?" I asked.

"I don't know. It was cheap. Terry McManus said he'd help me fix it up. A sixty-nine Chevy Two. It's all right. Now we won't have to walk everyplace. We can go out on dates and stuff."

"Dates," I said.

"Well, intercept a pass or something and get a girl-friend."

"Is that how you do it?" I asked.

"Yeah," he said.

We got Jerry's grandmother her ice cream and went

back and played some of his video games. Then his mother and father came home and asked me how school was, and then I went home.

"Hey, good luck tomorrow," Jerry called after me. That was an odd thing for him to say.

5

The next morning, we suited up and rode the team bus into the city. My stomach took another route by itself. On the bus, Tommy Hanes started his usual yelling.

"Come on, get up for it, get up for it!" he yelled, walking up and down the aisle whacking people on the shoulder pads. "Big game now! Big game!" He went from player to player giving individual words of advice.

"Get tough now, Paul, get tough," he said to me.

"Moose!" he said. Moose looked up. "Play tough out there, Moose. Play tough."

"Come on, Bennie, time to get tough."

"Be tough," he said to John Robbins, pounding him on the pads.

"Tough," he said to Nino.

Moose and I sat together in the back of the bus. Moose wasn't a great talker in the best of circumstances, and before a game he usually said nothing at all. Most of the kids were chattering away or getting tough. Moose and I just looked out the window during the ride.

The bus stopped outside the walls of the stadium. They had no locker rooms or showers or anything, so we had to wait in the bus until it was time to go out on the field. During halftime we would have to come back and sit in the bus. Coach Sisskind had brought a big drawing board to set up in the front of the bus to diagram plays.

The stadium was right in the middle of the black section. Across the street from where we were parked was a bar. The windows were dark, so you couldn't see inside it, but the door was open. You could hear music coming from inside. Whenever somebody came out, he would stop in the doorway, squint until his eyes got used to the sun, look up and down the street while he pulled his pants up a little, then start walking. Just sitting there, staring out the bus window, I realized, after a few minutes of watching, that every person did the same thing: stopped, adjusted his pants, then walked on. All up and down the street, whenever a guy came out from a store or an apartment or anyplace, he always stopped, pulled at his pants, then went about his business. I wanted to ask John Robbins if all black people did that, and if there was some special reason for it. I knew the kind of thing he would say — They're making sure they Don't Leave Home Without It, or something like that — so I tried hard to remember to ask.

There were a lot of people out, little kids, older kids, women with kids and bundles, and clusters of guys outside the bars and stores. All in all, it was just a busy, noisy city street. I felt out of place, not so much because I was white, but more because I was sitting in a bus with my football uniform on, while in back of me was a busful of white kids with their band uniforms on, yelling and tooting their instruments.

Nobody paid any attention to us except for the real little kids, who stared at the buses. We stuck out so much, at least in my mind, because the people on the street were so oblivious to us. We had nothing to do with these people. This game, which was about to happen, had nothing to do with their lives. Most football stadiums, especially high school ones, are the center of wherever they are. There are parking lots, field houses, concession stands — everything seems to radiate out from the stadium. All the people who are there have some interest in the game. Most people are going to the game, and even the others who might be just driving by, honk their horns at the team bus or something.

But here, there was just a dirty concrete wall with things spray-painted all over it, and some kids playing stickball off it into the street. Otherwise, there were hundreds of people right across the street from it who could care less. It was just one side of the street, with nothing there but a big wall instead of stores and bars and apartments. Nobody even walked on the stadium side of the street.

It was time to get out of the bus. We walked single file under a big arch and through a dark, pee-smelling tunnel. Our cleats made an incredible racket on the cement. On the other side of the tunnel, the sun was shining again very brightly. I stopped, let my eyes get used to it, and adjusted my pants. We all bunched up at the tunnel exit and waited until one of the coaches found out which side of the field we had. Then we all gave a big clap and yelled as we ran across the field. The other team was already out doing their warm-ups. They paid no attention to us.

It was as dirty inside the stadium as it had been out on the street. Bottles and papers all over the place; Cholo, Pistol, The Devil Stars written in spray paint high up on the stadium walls; broken glass around the edges of the field. The stands were made of concrete, with iron rails and wooden benches. Everything but the concrete was busted. Sections of the railing pipes were sticking up in the air, and whole planks were missing from the seats.

Luckily, it wasn't very windy. The field was mostly dirt with just little patches of grass here and there. Not dirt, really, dust. Watching them do their wind sprints was like those pictures of animals migrating across the Serengeti during the dry season, with great clouds of dust being kicked up by the herds. Every once in a while, one of their linemen would do a shoulder roll, and it looked just like an elephant taking a dirt bath. On the sidelines one of their backs, a little guy, was doing sprints by himself. He looked like a pickup truck racing through a construction site, kicking up little puffs of dust behind him, then slamming on the brakes and being enveloped from behind by the dust he had raised.

We took the field to loosen up. It was hard-packed, with no spring to it at all. There were a lot of little sharp rocks in it, and some glass, too.

We were doing up-and-downs, and I said to John Robbins, "Coach said this game was going to be a war. I think they had the war already."

Robbins didn't laugh. "Not everybody grows up with your advantages," he said in the voice of somebody's mother. He said it funny, but he looked serious. Then he went down for push-ups and cut his palm on a piece of glass.

"Shit," he said and wiped the blood off on the front of my uniform.

Before the game, their captains, four of them, came over to our bench. Usually, the captains meet out in the center of the field. They came over, with their helmets in their hands, and stood right in front of our captains. One of them stood in front of Robbins, and the two of them stared at each other with their faces about an inch apart, neither one of them blinking, like you see boxers on TV before a fight. The only way to win a no-blinking contest is to be a snake, because snakes have no eyelids.

So while the other guy didn't blink, Robbins started blinking normally — as if to say, you can't make me stop blinking — instead of the other way around. The other guy was number 88, which made him an end. He was the biggest end I had ever seen.

Please, God, I thought, make him a defensive end. Make him a tackle who put on the wrong shirt.

Then he said to Robbins very quietly, "Have a good game, brother."

Robbins said, "All right," quietly, too, and they shook hands.

Then they walked down the line, telling everybody to have a good game and shaking hands. We shook hands in the businessman's way, not with the thumb-over-thumb grip that kids use and that black kids started. Number 88 shook my hand and said, "Have a good game, little fella," but I think he thought I was a sub.

We kicked off to start the game. The stands were pretty full, mostly black people with little patches of white people here and there. Our band sat all bunched-up right behind us, looking like a bunch of those Have-a-Good-Day Smile faces somehow stuck in the middle of a crowd of real people.

They went into the line three straight times and had to kick. I came off the field untouched. The question of how long it would take them to attack me wasn't one of how smart they were — we knew they were an intelligent team — it was more a matter of how stubborn. First, they would try to establish their running game. If that didn't work, they should try short passes to keep our linebackers honest. On the other hand, they might get mad and keep banging away at the line. John Robbins was playing nose guard. He was going both ways this game. So far, it was as if they were trying to beat him, not us. The second time they got the ball, they went straight at him three more times. "I think they like me," he said in the huddle. Already, he was so winded he could hardly talk.

When they slaughter cattle, they have one steer they call the "Judas." He leads all the other cattle up the plank and into the pens. Then he walks back down again while all the ones who followed him are slaughtered. Here it was just like that, only each time Robbins drew the cattle after him, he got slaughtered and they walked back to their huddle to start again. Still, none of them got loose, either.

At the end of the first quarter, they still hadn't thrown a pass. It looked like they were going to fight Robbins to the finish. Then it started. Suddenly number 88 loomed in front of me, coming like a charging elephant as if to block me, with his arms waving like an elephant's ears; then he stopped, turned around, and caught a little, soft pass directly in front of me. He went down gently, cradling the ball in his arms. Obviously, they had spotted me.

In general, I managed on the football field through a sort of protective mimicry. All the football players had a uniform on; so did I. All the football players had numbers on their uniforms. My uniform had one, too. I occupied the same ecological niche that a football player usually did. But I was like one of those butterflies that looks like a wasp. Wasps stung things to death. I ate leaves. And now I had been spotted by predators.

You're not supposed to think at all out there, but I was having those thoughts. They threw another short pass, this one to the sidelines. I pushed number 88 out-of-bounds, but he was going that way anyway. My face was burning. It wasn't as if they were testing me, not the way they had been testing Robbins. It was more as if they were trying to figure out what I was. "Why, it's just a little butterfly," I could feel them saying in the huddle. If I had only stayed a caterpillar, one of those swallowtail caterpillars with the huge, scary face painted on its backside, maybe they wouldn't have come so close. But now they knew.

An animal, Coach was always saying. Become an animal. What animal? A defensive back is supposed to be a hunter. But even the hunter, all alone, becomes the prey. And, oh, not a hunter, a butterfly. The end of the butterfly is swift and sure in the martin's beak, says one of my old nature books. I'd accept that. Because they were no longer treating me like a butterfly. My death wasn't swift and sure. Now they were snapping at me, isolating me, like wolves separating a calf from a herd of caribou, drawing me out farther and farther from the protecting herd with their sideline passes. Be an animal. They threw again, and I leapt on 88 and dragged him down like a leopard pulling down a Cape buffalo much larger than himself. Somehow, my hand got inside his face mask and I scratched him.

"Hey! Are you crazy?" he said. He touched his face and ran back to the huddle.

On the last play of the half, they threw deep. I was beaten, but Robbins tipped it as it was thrown, and it floated right to me. I knocked it to the ground, and the half ended.

"You could have caught that," Laurie Wakes said as we ran off the field. "You could have had an interception."

It had no more occurred to me to catch it than it would have to take wing and leave the earth behind. For one play I had been a leopard, but otherwise, I was just a little field mouse far from my burrow, and even the ball was one more hawk swooping down. I had just batted the thing so it wouldn't hurt me. I looked at Laurie. He looked like he had just come up from the mines.

"Those niggers aren't so tough," Laurie said.

John Robbins came up behind him and put his hand around the back of Laurie's neck, hard. "I'm gonna tell them you said that, Laurie," he said quietly.

"You can always trust Laurie to say the right thing at the right time, can't you, Bennie?" he asked.

"Always," said Bennie.

This was true. Laurie's mouth was as grotesque as his shaved head, which was as grotesque as his Popeye muscles.

John let Laurie go. Both Bennie and John looked very pleased for some reason, as if this game was exactly what they wanted to be doing. John looked like he had been trampled by horses, and Bennie hadn't caught a single pass. We all stopped on the sidelines to watch their band for a minute. The band was really something. Our band played the school fight song, a couple of old marches, and a medley of *Annie* songs all in brass. But this band really turned it on, with gospel music, "My Country 'Tis of Thee" double time and syncopated, lots of intricate precision marching, and a drum major who threw his baton up farther than I could throw a baseball and caught it behind his back.

"Well, at least we've got the best band," Robbins said. By we, I think he meant they.

In the bus, Coach Sisskind was drawing up some revised blocking assignments for the offensive line. Coach Stahl, the backfield coach, was sitting next to Moose, talking in a low voice to him. Moose was having a rough day. He hadn't made it back to the line of scrimmage yet.

Coach Sisskind spotted Tommy Hanes. "What's the

matter with you?" he said. "You're getting pushed all over the field. Get tough out there."

I looked out the window. There were a lot of people out. There were lots of men standing outside the different bars, groups passing paper bags with bottles in them around, and lots of kids hanging out under the stadium wall.

"Anybody else?" the trainer yelled from the front of the bus. A lot of players had abrasions and cuts from the field.

"Keep it up, defense," Coach Sisskind told us as we left the bus. "You defensive backs — they're going to test you now. Talk to one another out there. Call for help when you need it."

Good idea, Coach, I thought. How about calling a tow truck to haul number 88 away.

Joey Napolitano caught up to me in the tunnel. He was the other cornerback when we were in the umbrella.

"Well?" he said.

"Well, what?" I asked.

"Well, talk to me."

"Hi, Joey," I said.

"No. Out on the field. You're not communicating. If they cross at least yell 'Cross.' If they flood the zone, yell. I'll be there. You're not alone out there, you know." He whacked me on the rump and ran out to do some stretches.

Joey was a great one for talking out there. In fact, he kept up a running commentary of the play as it developed. "Okay, here he comes, little stutter step, one fake, don't leave your feet, follow him, backpedal, ball! ball! Great play, Joey!" I just tuned him out. Otherwise, it was like trying to add up a column of numbers in your head while somebody was yelling different numbers in your ear. It was better when we played single safety, and I had him in front of me. Then I couldn't hear him, but I could still see some of his movements. In addition to talking to himself, he pointed at the ends or whoever was coming out of the backfield, a little like a policeman directing traffic while dodging it, so out of the corner of my eye I could see what kind of traffic patterns were developing in his area.

On our first defensive play of the second half, Joey the policeman got run over by a bus. It was a little screen pass, and a guard pulled out from a side street and knocked Joey right into next week's game. Some of the guys from the other team stood over him in silence while the trainer worked on him. Finally, he got up and walked off the field. As he passed them, different guys from their team gave him a little pat or said "Good going" or something like that.

The next play was an end sweep. Number 88 came out and blocked me into the ballcarrier. All three of us went down together. I landed wrong or maybe got kicked, because my foot was killing me. Number 88 helped his man get up, then turned and pulled me up. "Good play," he said.

The third quarter ended with still no score. On the bench, Joey Napolitano was saying, "Great play, Joey," to himself, but otherwise, both benches were quiet. On the field, players from each team had begun to help players from the other team up after each play. There was no chattering out there, no talking it up.

Then a strange thing happened. Both teams went back to their opening offense — running into the line. The game was still nothing to nothing. Neither team was able to get the ball across the other's forty-five yard line. But as the game got closer to being over, the two teams, instead of looking like two animals fighting, began to look like one animal, wounded, crawling on the ground. Neither team punted. Both ran on all four downs. Since neither team could make a first down, the game was being played in a ten-yard area. There were tremendous blocks, terrifying tackles. Yet the ball moved less and less each play. It looked less and less like a football game and more like some sort of primitive contest between neighboring villages. First their champion grabbed the pig and carried it as far as he could through a line of our men. Then a champion from our village grabbed hold of the pig and butted his way into them. There were no backfields anymore. I was no longer playing safety; I was crouched in the back of the pack, grunting my way into it when the ball was snapped.

Then the ball seemed to get heavier, more difficult to lift. Now it seemed that we were more like a reenactment of How War Started: two bands of semihuman gorillas taking turns pushing a big rock into each other's territory.

Something told me I was getting too close. These were meat-eaters I was cavorting with. They seemed to be ignorant of my presence, but one of them might discover me at any moment. Like a gazelle grazing too close to a sleeping lion, I was suddenly aware of a slight flickering beneath the lion's still-closed eyelids. An imperceptible movement of the tail — what was it? — that pricked my ears up. Number 88 was lined up close to the tackle, as he had been for the last two sets of running plays, but something was different. It was his left foot. The tension on it was different. It was held lightly, poised to sprint. I bolted into flight just as he took off. We went down the sideline, me a half step in front of him, the gazelle fleeing the lion. We veered once, and dashed across the plain. The ball — that great brown vulture — dropped out of the sky to help the lion with its kill. I leapt up and clawed it out of the air, the lion and I tumbled together on the ground, and the game ended.

A great roar went up, and suddenly all my teammates

were pounding me on the helmet and shoulders. Then both teams were on the field, shaking hands, putting their arms around one another. Number 88 found me again, shook my hand, and tousled my hair.

"All *right*," he said.

"Great game," I said. I wanted to say something else, but I couldn't think what.

Eventually, most of the other team gathered around John Robbins. He had played his greatest game. They weren't talking to him about the game, though. They were asking him where his family was from, did he know anybody from this or that street in his old neighborhood, would he come back and play basketball sometime.

We milled around for a while, all the coaches talking together, the players standing in little groups, everybody sort of quiet. Bunches of little kids were running around on the field, playing touch football with their hats or looking up at the football players.

My father came down on the field.

"You played quite a game," he said. "Everybody did. I'll see you at home."

We started walking off the field in groups of two or three. I walked with my father to the spectator's exit, then turned back and started through the tunnel by myself. I kept having to take deep breaths, even though the game had been over for a while and I wasn't winded anymore.

In the middle of the tunnel, I realized something was very wrong. It wasn't the right tunnel. It was dark; at first I only smelled the pot and beer smells, then my eyes adjusted and I could see there were about ten or fifteen kids, maybe my age, maybe a little older, leaning against both walls of the tunnel watching me. This tunnel led to the street, too, and down the street at the other end of the stadium was the bus, but there was no one, from either team, with me. These guys staring at me hadn't come from the game. They had probably been in here all day.

"Hey, Football Boy," came a voice. "Hey."

"Number forty-four. Here he comes."

"How you doing," I said, and kept walking.

Somebody stepped in front of me. "Hey. Can I have your autograph, sucker?"

"How 'bout the helmet? That's a fine helmet you got there."

"Look at them cleats," said another voice. "Look just my size."

They had moved out from the wall and were all around me. I could feel bodies behind me, blocking my way back. One of them reached out to touch my jersey. "Number forty-four. I'd look good in number forty-four. That's a black man's number, anyway." The circle tightened.

My mind went entirely blank for a second and then was swept up into a memory that seemed to blend into what was happening to me now.

I was at my uncle's house that previous spring, when a big rat wandered out of the woodpile while my uncle was splitting wood. It was no more than two feet from my uncle, who had the ax raised, poised to strike. Some sort of horror of the rat — some tremendous feeling of revulsion — made both of us watch motionless while the rat crossed beween us, then crawled into the woodpile and disappeared.

"What if I had missed?" my uncle asked later. "Or worse — what if I got it? Or what if I hit the thing but didn't kill it?"

Yes, something like that, I had thought to myself, but also something about its being a rat. It wasn't like a raccoon, which my uncle was always having to scare away from his garden or out of his garbage, and about which he might have said the same thing about hitting it but not killing it. No, the rat was different. Had it been in the house, my uncle would have swung, never mind the furniture, the walls, me, even — he would have killed it. But somehow, outside, where it wasn't really a threat, wasn't trapped with its teeth bared, it became something repulsive, but something you could let shrink away, like a man on the street who said dirty things to you but kept walking.

It wasn't pleasant to make myself into that rat. But it's easy to say, Make yourself into a tiger. Frighten them away. How do I know what a tiger feels like in that situation? But as much as I hated them, as much as I wanted to strike at them, as much as I knew that what they were doing to me was out of their own prejudice, ignorance, malice, viciousness — a part of me was turned into a rat by their looks.

Not one of them raised a hand as I walked through them.

Out on the street, I was shaking. On the bus, I didn't mention what had happened. In my mind I kept trying to reconstruct it. For a moment, it seemed, I had been a rat. But I wasn't sure. Had I walked on four legs? Had those kids who were about to mug me seen a real rat? It was very strange. Here I was, in my football uniform, sitting next to Moose, riding in a bus that smelled of football players. I didn't feel like a rat now. But a few minutes ago, I think, I had been one.

6 While we showered and dressed, everybody was asking which party everybody else was going to. There were always parties after the games. You could usually choose whether you wanted a quiet one or the biggest one, where most of the guys would be, and most of the beer. I didn't think I'd go out at all that night. I was still trying to figure out what had happened to me in that tunnel. Besides, my foot hurt. The trainer looked at it and said it was a bruised instep and to stay off it until Monday. That would be pleasant news to my father, who expected me to dig a ditch with him on Sunday. Anyway, I limped home only to find Jerry and his 1969 Chevy II on the street in front of my apartment bulding.

"Well," said Jerry, "where do you want to go?"

"How about back to the Demolition Derby and get one that isn't so beat up."

"Come on," he said. "A little body rot, a few little dents. The engine's perfect. This kid I know is going to sell me a hookup for rear speakers, and I'll be all set. So get some money for gas and let's go."

"Where?" I asked.

"I don't know. Someplace."

"I have to be home early," I said. "I have to help my father tomorrow."

I told my parents I was going out with Jerry, and my mother gave me the standard lecture about kids getting killed in cars — drag racing, she said, like it was 1955.

"You could hurt your back trying to drag that thing," my father said to Jerry.

When we got in the car, Jerry said, "Your father said you made a great play."

"I guess," I said. I would have told Jerry about the game, but I didn't want to go into what had happened after, and that was the part that still stuck with me.

We drove around for a while, and then Jerry wanted to go to this party where the girl's parents weren't home, but when we got there, there was Tommy Hanes on the lawn with a beer can in his hand practicing rebel yells, so we didn't go in. We ended up getting something to eat and going home.

"Beats walking, though, doesn't it?" Jerry asked as I got out.

"I just wish people wouldn't point at us as we passed," I said.

"That's 'cause you're famous," Jerry said.

"Me?"

"You certainly are. You turned back the black invasion of the suburbs."

"Oh, Lord," I said. "You know something? Those were good guys out there." I paused. I wasn't sure what I was trying to say. "They were real good guys."

Jerry didn't say anything. He probably didn't understand what I meant, but knowing enough not to think you do understand is very important. He knew something had happened — he could tell that from my mood all night.

"Something happened there," I said.

"Obviously," he said.

"At least to me."

Jerry said nothing. I would have tried to explain more what I meant, but I couldn't describe, never mind explain, what had happened after the game. So I shrugged my shoulders. He nodded his head.

"I'll see you Monday," I said. "Tomorrow I dig a hole for my father."

"The cops'll find him," Jerry said. "They always do."

"It's not that. I wish. It's for my grandmother."

"Oh," he said. "That's different. They'll never miss her. You think you can fit my grandmother in, too? She's about ready to go."

"Aw, Jerry," I said.

"She called me a *chodlum* today. That's a hoodlum for you goyim."

"On account of the car?"

"On account of I left rubber in front of the house and brought her back strawberry instead of Three-Flavors."

"I'll see you Monday," I said.

"If I live," he said and peeled tread halfway down the block.

7

"Oh, boy," my father said when he saw me limping to the breakfast table.

"Don't worry, I'll work," I said.

"You're damn right you will," he said. "You're not going to pull that little trick on me."

"You don't think my foot hurts?" I asked.

"I think it hurts just as much as necessary for you to try to get out of working today. I think it's very convenient that you have a hurt foot."

He seemed to think my life revolved around my trying to put something over on him. He thought it was "very

66

convenient" when I got poison ivy — like I had done it on purpose. Whenever I didn't get home on time, no matter what had happened to make me late, like no bus showing up, or a thunderstorm, it was always "very convenient." And whatever I said, it was never an explanation, it was always an "excuse." In my father's world, things were never as they seemed. Even my drinking a lot of milk was a trick. He told me I was faking being thirsty for milk. Why anyone would do that he didn't say, but he was sure I was trying to put something over on him. "What are you trying to prove?" he kept asking me.

That fall, all the boys were wearing skimmer caps. The first time I wore one, my father said, "What are you trying to prove, looking like that?" It couldn't be because my head was cold. It couldn't even be because I liked the way it looked. Even such a simple thing as wearing a hat had to have another meaning. With the cap, it was pretty hard for him to decide whether I was faking, trying to pull something, or trying to prove something. Maybe all three.

I'll bet about three-quarters of all those teenage suicides you keep reading about take place when the kid has been told that he's faking, that he's trying to pull something, that he's always got an excuse, so often that he can't think of anything at all to do that would be just a simple, straightforward act that nobody, for once, would quibble about.

So: Blammo goes the gun. What do you say now, Dad, am I still trying to pull something? Are these fake brains all over my bed?

Of course, if I ever did a thing like that, my father would take one look and say, "Very convenient, though, isn't it, that your brains just happened to get blown out when you were supposed to be helping your mother put away the groceries."

We didn't speak in the car going to my grandmother's house. Her backyard really stank. She seemed pretty embarrassed about it, her being just one little old lady living all alone and having somehow produced a whole backyard full of stinky poop.

"Start here," my father said, pointing to the place where the waste pipe came out of the house.

"You don't think it's the leach lines, then?" I asked him. The leach lines would have been easy. All they are is pipes with holes in them that let the water drain away in the ground after all the other stuff has already landed in the septic tank. Digging new leach lines was the last job we had done on our own house before we moved into the apartment. I think it was why we moved into the apartment. That was back when I still liked to help him.

"It never ends," he had said to me back then. He had repeated it to my mother, to my little sister, and to Luke, who was just a baby. That night I heard him telling my mother that the house also needed a new roof.

"It never ends," he had said.

"Couldn't we hire somebody for once?" my mother had asked.

"How could we afford that?" he had said. "I'll do it when I take my vacation. Paul can help me."

We never did it. We moved into the apartment, where stuff like that was part of the rent. Now he was bored. Still, he wasn't so bored that he would make up a job like this one.

"No," he said. "It's not the leach lines. It's backing up into the house. It's between the house and the tank."

When we uncovered the pipes, we found them all cracked and crumbled. Which I was sort of glad of, because if they hadn't been, they would have been after I hit them by mistake with the pickax a few times. I must have been favoring my sore foot, because each time, I'd aim for a line parallel to the pipe and end up splat, dead center in it. The pipe would split open, and out would ooze raw sewage, toilet paper, and other things I tried not to look at.

You can only hold your breath so long, so after a while we walked around to the front to take a break. I looked back at the trench we were digging: my father's part was farther along than mine.

My grandmother brought us some coffee. My father watched me put the three spoons of sugar in mine.

"You want some coffee with your sugar?" he asked. He seemed in a better mood now that we were working. He didn't know any better than to think digging a hole was a nice way to spend a Sunday.

Actually, I didn't feel too bad about it. After all, you have to help your grandmother out if she needs help. It was true, too, that my father and I got along better when there was work that had to be done. I know that my father, even though he had decided it himself, at least partially blamed moving into the apartment for the fact that he hated me.

"Ma," he said to my grandmother, "you don't happen to be missing a hairbrush, do you?"

"Oh, no," my grandmother said.

"That's not the whole problem," my father said, "but it didn't help matters. Anyway, it's not so bad. A few feet of new pipe and you'll be back in business."

That took the rest of the day, but it worked. We just laid the new pipe next to the old pipe but at a slightly steeper pitch, then my father connected it up to the house while I filled in the ditch. When we were finished, my grandmother took me aside and slipped a ten-dollar bill into my hand.

"No, Gram, I don't want that," I said.

"It was so nice of you to help," she said. "A lot of boys wouldn't think of helping their grandmother. And such a dirty job. Take it."

I tried to give it back a couple times, but I took it. My father would kill me if he knew. He'd also yell at my grandmother.

"If you want to give him a present, go ahead," he would say, "but don't *pay* him, for God's sake. It's his duty, whether he wants to do it or not. Don't make him think he's doing you a favor."

Now, at least, I didn't have to ask him for money if I wanted go out this week. You can imagine what that was like.

On the way home he asked me, "How's your foot?" Nice time to ask. It was killing me.

"It's a little sore," I said.

"Well, when we get home, you can take a nice hot bath and soak it. I'll take the first shower and be out of your way quick."

Talk about pulling stuff. He gets the first shower, while I have to stand outside with the neighbor's cat sniffing me because my mother won't let me inside because I smell so bad, and he acts like it's a great sacrifice for him to get clean first.

8 On Monday, Coach Sisskind showed the game films. Before the lights went out, he said, "Watch Robbins." He didn't say another word during the whole film, even though there were a lot of great plays. Everybody gasped when we saw Joey Napolitano take that hit, and people started saying "Great play, Joey" to whoever got hit hard after that, but otherwise, we all watched Robbins.

"That was the greatest game I've seen you play," Coach said to Robbins afterwards. "Maybe the greatest game I've seen any lineman play."

"I was highly motivated," Robbins said, putting the emphasis on motivated.

"Well, if you can keep from getting too swelled a head, you might just motivate yourself into a pretty good athletic scholarship to college next year." Coach said motivate like Robbins had.

"Anyway," he continued, "you all played a great game. Nobody should be ashamed of not winning it. We played a hell of a team, and we proved that we're a hell of a team. That's all for today."

I went into the whirlpool for my foot. Robbins was in, too, for his whole body. Coach came up to us while we were soaking.

"That was a nice play at the end there," he said to me. "Thank Robbins for giving you the opportunity."

"Thank you," I said.

"Anytime," Robbins said.

· · ·

In French class on Tuesday, Madame Garnaud handed back our dicté. Mine didn't have a mark on it. Except at the bottom, in small letters, not like her usual comments at all, which went right over your paper like SOLD OUT over a concert announcement, "Please see me after class."

I walked up to her desk after class.

"Why did you write this?" she asked me.

"I don't know, Madame Garnaud," I said.

"I thought you liked French," she said.

"I do," I said.

"But this is . . . this is like making fun of it. It's like making fun of me."

"I'm sorry, Madame Garnaud. I guess I just thought it was funny."

"Well, perhaps it is. I suppose if that's all it is, we should forget about it. But students find it hard to be sympathetic to a different culture and to things that are a bit different from what they are accustomed to."

I had hurt her feelings. I can't stand it when I hurt someone's feelings. I'd rather die — I'd rather they died — than stand there trying to figure out how to make everything okay again. Madame Garnaud continued to look at me. I shifted from foot to foot. My foot still hurt from being injured, so I put my weight on it gingerly.

"What's wrong with your leg?" Madame Garnaud asked.

Everyone loves a dog with a hurt paw. But you have to do it right. You trot on by — in pain, obviously, but still going about your dog business, not asking for sympathy. You are friendly, as a dog often is to strangers, but you don't ask them to look at your paw. The one you finally allow to look at it, especially if there are other people around, will feel very proud. Even if he says, "Well, fella, I can't find anything wrong with it," just keep limping bravely when he lets go. Don't even look back.

I have no idea how I became that dog. All I know is Madame Garnaud couldn't find anything wrong with my foot, but seemed very pleased that I hadn't run away. And I am pretty sure she gave me a pat on the head before I limped out of the room to my next class.

Walking down the corridor, I was a boy. For an instant, though, I had been a dog. At least I felt I was a dog. And Madame Garnaud had acted as if I was a dog. Like those guys in the tunnel had acted as if I was a rat. Did Madame Garnaud *think* I was a dog? Did those guys that were going to mug me think I became a rat? Did they see a rat? Did Madame Garnaud see a dog? Did Madame Garnaud see a boy, then a dog, then a boy again? If so, what was she thinking now? Or did I only act so much *like* a dog that she had sympathy for me *like* she would for a dog?

Bizarre, I thought. Anyway, here's somebody who thinks I'm a monkey, I said to myself when I saw Karen Cleary down the hall. I started scratching under my armpit and walking like a monkey.

"Paul, why are you acting like a monkey?" Karen said. "You look stupid. Is it supposed to be funny?"

My face went red. "I guess so," I said. I guess I didn't turn into animals, after all. I didn't look back, but I could feel her still looking at me. I felt like such a jerk.

The Health Science teacher was Mr. Stahl. He would have liked us to call him Mr. Steel behind his back, but we preferred Mr. Stalin. He didn't seem to like teaching Health Science, though none of us knew why. It looked like a pretty easy job the way he did it. Mostly the class read a chapter from *Your Body* and answered the questions in the back, while he sat at his desk drawing x's and o's. His real job was being the backfield coach for football.

The Health Science class was where he waited for practice to begin.

Whenever Mr. Stahl did have to teach us something about Health Science, he would stand up behind his desk and look down for a long time, frowning. He would look just like your father about to explain sex to you. Even if he was going to talk about the Four Basic Food Groups he looked embarrassed.

That day, Tuesday, Mr. Stahl announced, with obvious distaste, that there was going to be some sort of contest run by the National Science Foundation. First there would be an oral quiz given to each class, like a spelling bee; then the class winners would be in a second elimination contest, until one person was left. That one person, the winner for the whole school, would then take a written test. So would kids from other schools, until there were regional winners, and so on. If you made it to the national level, there would be science scholarships or something.

Mr. Stahl was going to be running the quizzes. It didn't cut into practice time, but still, spending all those valuable class hours asking questions about science was going to just about kill him. So we all had to stand up around the room while Mr. Stahl asked questions out of the contest booklet and hoped everybody missed the first time around. He asked the questions with about the same amount of enthusiasm that the cafeteria lady has as she dumps the mashed potatoes on the plates.

"Nope," was all he said when somebody missed a question, or else, "You're gone." He didn't bother telling us the right answers until we all started yelling at him.

And of course the test was real fair. The first two kids would get questions like "Name the third planet out from the sun" and "What animal breathes through gills?"; then the third kid would get nailed with "In the electromagnetic spectrum, the range in radiation frequencies extends from what to what in cycles per second?" Mr. Stahl stumbled a couple times reading that one. Then a few more "Pasteurization is named after what French scientist?" and "What is the science of weather forecasting called?" then, suddenly, "What is the word used to describe a crystalline structure of three mutually perpendicular axes of different lengths?" Or else "What is the atomic number of osmium?"

That was one I got. First I said "Donny and Marie," then I guessed it right. Seventy-six. Actually, I started to guess a hundred seventy-six, but I said the hundred so softly Mr. Stahl didn't hear it. Later on, Andy Espada told me the chances of guessing right on that were 102 to 1. They were better than that, though, because I already knew hydrogen, helium, oxygen, carbon, and uranium — though as it turned out, I thought uranium was number 88, which it isn't.

Andy Espada himself went out trying to define pleiotropism — the control or determination of more than one characteristic or function by a single gene, as we found out later. The very next week we learned that, sort of, in biology. The question before, which I had answered correctly, was "In mammals, what organ controls the circulatory system?" (Answer: the heart.) It was a shame for Andy. He was the school chess champion, he had gotten two 800's on his SAT's, and he took a special theoretical math class at some college. He tutored one of the football players in physics, even though he, Andy, hadn't taken physics yet. Ever since fifth grade, he had always won some kind of prize for his grade in the science fair. But he didn't know what a pleiotropism was, so that was it for Andy.

Eventually, Jerry Raynor from his class, me from mine, and two other kids from different classes were the finalists. Mr. Stahl asked Jerry the scientific name for Java man. Without hesitating, Jerry answered "*Pithecanthropus.*"

"Sorry," said Mr. Stahl. "It's *Pithecanthropus erectus.*"

Jerry went immediately nuts. "They're all *erectus*, you moron!" he said. "*Pithecanthropus erectus, Sinanthropus erectus, Australopithecus erectus.* They were all smarter than you, you asshole!"

The whole room shook when he slammed the door. At least the glass didn't break. If he hadn't called Mr. Stahl an asshole, perhaps all four of us contestants together might have convinced Mr. Stahl that Jerry's answer was good enough — was, in fact, correct. Now there was such a bad taste about the thing that nobody wanted to win.

In the end, I did. Jerry didn't blame me, but I think Mr. Stahl did. Now he had to stay late after school on Friday to give me a written test to determine whether I would be a regional winner. If nobody had won, he wouldn't have had to stay late.

The whole time I was taking the test, he kept sighing. When I was done, he just grabbed it and beat me out the door. He never said "Good luck" or anything. I never heard my score, or who won, or anything else about it ever again. He probably threw the thing away. He was probably afraid that if by some fluke I won, they would make him do something else horrible — give me another test or oversee my science project or something.

I wasn't that good in science, anyway. Jerry should have won, or one of the nerds Andy Espada was always doing math problems with, or else Andy himself. He was the smartest without a doubt. Even in the eighth grade, when Three-Fingers Spaulding made the bomb that gave him his nickname, Andy knew what must have gone wrong.

"You can't put sulfuric acid in a polymer," he said

76

then. "It's not only corrosive, it creates an unstable bond."

We didn't know what he was talking about, and neither would Larry Spaulding have, had the two of them ever gotten together to discuss it. Larry just liked making big noises.

9

It was easy to ask Karen Cleary out. All the kids were talking about this concert they were going to on Saturday night. There was no way I was going, not at sixteen dollars a ticket. Then Karen said she never went to concerts.

"It's just noise," she said. "Noise and dope. Everybody acts like animals."

I perked up at the word animals. I asked her what she did Saturday nights. She said she always did something, then she said she didn't have any plans for this Sunday.

"Me either," I said.

"Well?" she said.

"Well, what?" I asked.

"Well, what do you want to do?" she asked me.

I was startled and said the first thing that came to mind.

"Want to go to the zoo?" I asked.

"Okay," she said.

Then I told her we'd have to take the bus because I didn't have my license, and she said that was okay, and suddenly I had made a date with Karen Cleary.

I walked over to Jerry's for our usual Friday night.

"I'd come and get you," Jerry said, "but there's something wrong with the carburetor. At least I think it's the carburetor. You'll pass it just before you turn onto my street."

"The carburetor?" I asked.

"The whole car."

When I got there, Jerry and his grandmother were sitting in the two armchairs watching the news. Jerry had a box of something in his hand. He offered his grandmother some.

"Here, Grandma," he said, looking at me. "They're called Bait-Bits. Like Cheez-Its. Try some. They're good."

Bait-Bits were rat poison. You sprinkled them out where you thought the rat would find them and waited for it to gobble them up. According to the box, the rat dies because rats can't throw up. Once the rat swallows the poison, he can't get rid of it. He's a goner. For humans and other animals, if they eat it by mistake, you're supposed to "induce vomiting." I didn't know that rats can't vomit. With all the crap they eat, you'd think they'd have a built-in mechanism for it. They must make mistakes all the time, where they end up eating a piece of glass or some wire or something.

Jerry's grandmother was looking very steadily at Jerry with narrowed eyes. She reached out her hand. Jerry held out the box in such a way that she could see the words Bait-Bits on it, but not the picture of the rat.

"Okay. I try one," she said and made a grab for the box.

Jerry snatched it away. "Oh, no, Grandma. I know you. You won't leave any for me. Just take a few. I'll hold the box."

"You eat Bit-Bites, too?" Jerry's grandmother asked me.

"Not that often," I said.

"How come?"

"They're not that good for you."

"Too much chemicals, huh?"

"I think so."

"That's what I'm thinking, too. Could probably kill a rat. You eat it, Jeddy."

We watched the news for a while, with Jerry's grandmother going "Ach" and "Oy" at the different things that happened. "Why do the bleck people live where there is so many fires?" she asked.

"I don't think they planned it that way, Grandma," Jerry answered.

When the news was over, we left Jerry's grandmother saying "What a world, what a world" to the TV set, like the witch in *The Wizard of Oz*, and went into the kitchen. Jerry put the Bait-Bits away.

"You got rats now?" I asked him.

"Mice. I think Grandma's hiding food in her room. In case there's another pogrom, you know what I mean?"

"Probably afraid you're trying to poison her."

"Yeah. I wanted to get a cat, but my father says no."

"How come?"

"No reason. Just doesn't want to. So when I ask him why, he says, 'Jews don't keep pets.'"

"That's not true."

"No kidding. Anytime he decides we can't have something, he gets up on his hind legs and says, 'Jews don't do that.' My mother wants to go on a picnic, he doesn't want to go: 'Jews don't go on picnics.' Last year for JV baseball, I wanted to try out for third base. 'Jews don't play third base,' he says. 'First base was good enough for Hank Greenburg, it's good enough for you.' Then, when you say something like, 'Okay, if Jews can't have a VCR, how come Ben Kaufman has one?' he goes like this" — Jerry lowered his eyes and shook his head back and forth slowly —" 'Not a good Jew.'"

"You ever mention to him that Jews don't in general whack their kids around?"

"I did, as a matter of fact, but in this case, he says, 'The Law makes exceptions.' Like be poor instead of rich, and park their vegetable truck in front of their house — like quit high school and join the army and get tattooed. Ever hear of a Jew doing those things?"

"Jeddy," his grandmother said. She had been standing in the doorway listening. "If you got no respect for your father, you shouldn't say nothing. Your friend don't want to hear you talk like that."

We went down cellar to play Ping-Pong.

"I want to get a pool table," Jerry said, "but Jews don't get pool tables. Until their father decides he wants to play."

"Do Jews usually have shitboxes for cars that they have to leave down the street?" I asked.

"Yeah, well, he's not too happy about that, either. Listen, I had a date with Sandra Clausen, you know her?"

"Real short, black hair?"

"Yeah. So I was going to drive her home from school. She takes one look and says, 'I'll ride, but I won't push.'"

"I think a lot of girls are like that," I said.

"What's the score?" Jerry asked.

"I don't know," I said. "I didn't know we were playing yet. You serve first."

"Karen Cleary, huh?" he said.

"Yup."

"The zoo."

"Yup."

"I suppose," he said.

We concentrated on Ping-Pong for a while. We played that everything was inbounds — off the cellar walls, the pipes, the water heater — as long as the ball hit the table after. Jerry beat me three games straight, and we quit.

We went upstairs to get something to eat before I went home.

"What are you watching, Grandma," Jerry called.

"I don't know," she yelled back. "Something. The girl shoots the guy, then walks around in a bathing suit, so the policeman is looking at the girls in the bathing suits. He don't know what she looks like except her tuchus in the bathing suit. Now he's at the beach, but somebody's sneaking around behind him. Same tuchus I think, but I don't know yet. What you eating?"

"Ice cream. You want some?"

"What kind?"

"Bacon-flavored. It's good."

"Ach," she said. "Bring me some. Unless it's strawberry."

"You're a regular now, aren't you?" Jerry asked as he walked outside with me.

"Pretty much," I said. "I played the whole last game on defense. You study for the biology test yet?"

"Nah. I know all that stuff already. The brain of the arthropod. Little more than nerves formed into a bundle. Brain's primary function — contrasting and inhibiting sense data that determine how animal will react to environment — often performed by sense receptor itself, such as eye, or organ of smell. Differentiation of brain and organs of perception relatively undeveloped. Brain of arthropod recurs as ganglial endings at base of our brain. The complexity of our brains developed from this ganglial core."

"Pretty good," I said. "Did you memorize it?"

"Sort of," Jerry said. "But I know what it means. I can explain it in my own words, too."

"What gets me is that the brain of the insect is the core of our brains."

"No. You keep saying stuff like that. The nerve connections that control sense perception and reaction to the outside world are the core of our brains. It's similar to the insect's brain, but entirely different."

"Different because we're not bugs. But the same because a part of us *is* like them. A part of our brain is like their brain. So inside us, there's a tiny part of our brain that is acting and reacting like an insect. Listen. If that part could act all by itself without interference from the rest of our brains for a minute, we would act just like giant bugs, right?"

"I wouldn't put it down on the test," Jerry said.

"Well, no," I said. "I don't mean really. I just mean there are real connections, even between us and bugs."

"Sure," Jerry said. "I'm cold. I'll see you Monday. Good luck on your big date."

 When I woke up Saturday morning, it was raining. My heart sank. If it kept raining through Sunday, we wouldn't be able to go to the zoo.

In the kitchen, my father was drinking coffee and reading the newspaper.

"Do you know if it's supposed to stop raining?" I asked.

"It always has," he said without looking up.

"I know that," I said. "Do you know the weather forecast?"

"Well aren't we grumpy today," my father said. "No, Mr. Grumpy, I do not know the weather forecast."

Unless the field was flooded, we'd play, rain or not. It wouldn't be fun, though. Maybe it looks like fun to play in the mud, but it isn't. The mud makes you grunt more while you're playing. In fact, anytime you have to do something in the mud — push a car that's stuck, dig a trench for the water to run off — you end up grunting a lot. It's hard to say whether it's the mud or the kind of thing you always seem to end up doing in the mud that makes you grunt so much. I think it's the mud, because the same activity, without the mud, can be done with much less grunting. In fact, I would go so far as to say that if pigs didn't have to spend so much time wallowing in the mud, they probably wouldn't make the sound they make. They would make an entirely different sound, perhaps like humans talking while they eat, or something like that.

I was thinking these things as I walked down the block on my way to the stadium. In fact, I was sort of daydreaming that I was saying them to my teammates in the locker room in preparation for the game. But I was stuck for a conclusion.

A very soft growl woke me from my silly speech. Ken had snuck up on me and had stuck his nose right between my legs. He was snuffling in there, growling, feeling around for the right place to clamp down. His eyes were looking up into mine. I didn't move, not even to shift my weight a little. Especially not to shift my weight a little.

"Ken," I said. "Let's have a talk. Dog to dog. Maybe we can get this thing straightened out."

Ken looked at me like I was crazy. Dogs can do that. Ken sat down. I squatted next to him. We didn't say much — dogs can't talk, of course — but we did clear up a few things. No, I didn't really hate him, but I did find him a hard dog to like. Eventually, I agreed not to throw stones at him anymore, and he agreed not to bite me in the crotch. I had a stick in my hand, which I was poking in the mud, and Ken, of course, was watching the stick.

"Never mind the stick," I said. "That's not important." I put down the stick. After a minute or so, Ken picked up the stick and started gnawing on it thoughtfully while we talked. We talked about the little kids and about Ken's barking, and Ken told me about a dog's having to protect his territory.

"But it doesn't apply," I said. "These aren't other dogs. They're little kids. Most dogs would protect the little kids, too. They'd consider the kids as part of their territory. They wouldn't harass them as if they were intruders. They're part of the neighborhood. Your neighborhood."

Ken had never thought of it that way. He had only thought of his own yard and all these brats racing around. The way they were so frightened of him made him mad.

"A mad dog, huh?" I said.

"That's not what I meant," said Ken. "You should never say that. It's not good to say that."

Anyway, if we didn't quite part friends, at least we left with a bit more understanding toward each other. Actually, we agreed that on Monday morning on the way to school, I would pat him on the head, and he would stand still without raising his hackles, and in this way we would try to show the grade-school kids that they didn't have to be afraid of him anymore.

About halfway to school, the oddity of what had just taken place struck me. Not so much the fact of my talking to Ken. People talk to dogs all the time. But Ken's talking to me . . . "One of us," I said to myself, "is crazy." As I realized what I had just said, I burst out laughing. People on the street turned to look at me. I shut up and hurried along, blushing a little. I thought, unless right at this moment Ken is laughing, too, it must be me.

Moose and I sat back-to-back on the floor of the locker room. It was Moose's way of thinking about the game and my way of trying not to. Most of the other players were stretching or pounding each other on the shoulder pads or whacking each other with forearms. At first I did that, too, but it didn't really get me up for the game, and people kept hurting me, so I didn't bother anymore. The floor in the corner with Moose was a good spot because we wouldn't have to move when Coach Sisskind sat us down for the pregame talk, and also, Tommy Hanes couldn't come up from behind and belt me between the shoulder blades as he did when I sat by my locker.

"Execution will win this game," Coach Sisskind told us. "Whoever makes the fewest mistakes will win. The ball's going to be slippery. So's the footing. Make sure of your handoffs. Don't fumble. Moose! What'd I just say?"

"Don't fumble," said Moose.

"Good. You're awake earlier than usual today. Defense! Anticipate the run. Be there first. Don't get caught chasing the ballcarrier. You won't catch him in the mud once he gets into the secondary. Be there first and make him slip and slide to get away from you. Let's go!"

Everybody gave a big clap and a yell, and we went out into the rain. Coach Fitzgibbons, the offensive-line coach, stood in the doorway as he always did and punched each player as we went through. He didn't like it if you flinched. He thought getting punched helped you get ready to play, so if you ducked, that meant you were fooling around and weren't mentally prepared for the game. "Get serious," he'd say, and push you with both hands hard, like he was starting a fight. Moose once stepped on Coach

85

Fitz's foot with his cleats just as Coach was about to punch him. From then on, Moose got a big slap on the shoulder pads instead of a punch.

It was a home game, so we trotted from the locker room out under the stands and into the stadium. After last week's game, it really felt like home: there were the nice stands, there were the nice people in them, there was the nice refreshment booth, the nice green field with the white lines. On the other hand, it didn't seem quite as normal, as perfectly natural as it always had. In fact, it seemed a little artificial, like a man-made pond stocked with trout.

It was a good place to be a trout. It was windy, and the gusts of wind made ripples across the wet field and sudden glasslike sheens on the surfaces of the deeper puddles.

It was raining in gusts, too. It was impossible to look up. Nino Cappellano was doing his punting warm-ups on the sidelines, and all the backs who were fielding them just let them bounce and then tried to catch them. They didn't really bounce. Then Nino kicked a boomer and went up in the air as if he had slipped on a banana peel and fell flat on his back in the mud. Coach Fitz ran over to see if he was all right. He took one look at Nino's uniform, got this horrified expression on his face, and started yelling to all the defensive backs. When he got us all together, he told us, "Watch out for the tackle eligible! Watch out for it!" He had been holding on to Nino the whole time, and now, like he was showing us some Horror Beyond the Imagination, he pointed at the back of Nino's uniform.

"You can't see the number!" he said. "They could send anybody down and you wouldn't know! It could be a tackle or a center or anybody!"

Nino continued to stand there patiently, like the person in first-aid class who's supposed to be the victim, while Coach Fitz pointed at him. I couldn't see what all the excitement was about. I wasn't that sophisticated a football player. Whoever came into my zone, I covered. Whoever it was, if he tried to block me, I tried not to let him. If he tried to catch a pass, I tried to stop him. If he had the ball, I tried to tackle him. So far, that's all I had learned.

Coach Sisskind came over. He raised his eyebrows, but then he said, "Watch the formations. If they line up funny, watch for something funny. If you see a big fat tackle all covered with mud running downfield, keep an eye on him."

Then he went back under the stands out of the rain. We weren't allowed to laugh at Coach Fitz. He was very serious about football. He was slightly less serious about Driver's Ed, and perhaps even a bit offhand about Civics. He himself had been good enough to play a year of pro ball in Canada. All the linemen said he really taught them how to block, how to use their hands, how to shift their balance without changing their stance — stuff like that he was excellent at.

But he was always telling the linemen, "Don't be a dumb lineman. Don't get fooled." He never said who was trying to fool you, or whether he meant in football or in life or something, but he was always coming up with things like these bizarre agility drills where you tried to block the other guy while hopping on one foot, or else the quick-energy drink he read about in *Pro Quarterback* magazine that gave the whole offensive line the runs during a game the year before.

It was funny, though, because in the matter of basics, of "just plain pushing and shoving," as he called it, he couldn't be beat. And he wouldn't let his players do anything fancy. If somebody tried to scoop up a fumble

87

with one hand, he'd make him practice falling on the ball the right way ten times. Still, as John Robbins put it, "Coach do get razzled by dazzle." He was afraid that other teams were smarter and would trick us.

It had stopped raining when we took the field. There were a lot of people in the stands, considering what a rotten day it was. My mother had said she'd come and bring Luke if it wasn't raining too hard. I wondered if Karen Cleary was there. I had no idea whether she went to any football games. I had actually only talked to her about four times in my life, all outside of English class. When you play sports, you think they are the center of everybody's life because they take up so much of yours, but it was possible that she didn't think about them at all. Last week's game had certainly reminded me that not everybody in the world cares about football. Although I didn't know it at the time, this was to be my last football game. And it was to be because of a tackle eligible pass.

I don't know whether I got the idea from Ken or from Coach Sisskind or from the condition of the field, but when the defense took the field, I immediately started marking out my territory. Coach was always saying if such and such happens, go help out the linebacker, or go help out the other safety, meaning leave your territory and help defend somebody else's territory.

Great Play Joey — that's what everybody called him now — called over, "Do you want to stay with the man if they cross?"

"No," I said, "territory."

"You mean zone," he said.

"Zone. Yell 'Cross' to let the other guy know, then defend your own territory. Your zone."

It seems that a lot of ideas that people have, animals

also have in their own way. Or what's more likely, a lot of ideas that people have are actually animal ideas that people dress up in human-sounding terms. Like territory and boundaries. Every animal has a territory it protects against invaders. Just like people with their fenced-in yards who don't care what happens two blocks away, an animal doesn't care what happens in the next patch of woods or field. But inside his territory, whether it's one square yard, like a penguin's, or twenty square miles, like a leopard's, he will fight. Even little songbirds will attack a hawk if it comes inside their territory. They'll drive him away, too. Outside his territory, though, the little birdie goes back to being what he usually is to the hawk: lunch. Somehow, he can't fight as well outside his own territory.

This idea possessed me. I was completely taken over by it. There were no boundaries on the field: both the sidelines and the yard markings had been obliterated by the mud. The line of scrimmage is the only actual boundary anyway; but I knew my range and patrolled it ferociously in all directions. I didn't pay any attention to what down it was, or what formation they were in, or anything that keys you in to what the offense might do. I just attacked anybody who came into my territory. My own teammates I bumped into as if they were rivals from the same pack — the others I drove out. After every battle, I gave a little roar of pride after them as they retreated to their huddle. All in all, I was acting like the dominant male of the species.

Of course, there are many species, from the lion whose roar reverberates for miles telling all other lions to stay clear and the great elk who stands on top of the highest hill he can find impressing the other elks with the size of his antlers, all the way down to the little thrushes and phoebes singing on their branch. We call it song, but the birds call it a contest, a fight for territory. Considering my size and general prowess out there on the football field, it probably sounded like I was going tweet-tweet-tweet to scare the other team away. Perhaps the bluebird thinks he's roaring, too.

The thing to have become during that game, had I had the choice to make, would have been a gorilla. Gorillas are very peaceful. The boundaries of their territories change a lot: they live in little bands, going from place to place eating leaves and picking berries, very helpful to each other, very nice. If they meet another gorilla band, they talk with them, share their food, and then move on. But if one band crosses the invisible boundary into the place the other band considers its own, then they beat their chests and roar until the other gorillas leave. If necessary — if there's really no other choice, that is — they fight and drive them out. That's probably what the two teams were most like. We were all totally covered with mud, except for our faces and hands, the same parts of the gorilla that, since they are so bare, make them look so human. We wandered up and down the field in two bands, not bothering each other until one band tried to cross into the other's territory. And our territory, even though the referee marked the line of scrimmage, seemed totally arbitrary. There were no boundaries, just an expanse of mud, like the gorilla's trackless forest. Certainly our defensive linemen, waiting for the other team to come to the line of scrimmage, looked like gorillas, nodding to each other with their big round helmeted heads, and their huge human hands dangling at their sides. I wouldn't have looked out of place rising up in the secondary to beat my chest.

My thoughts were much vaguer than that, though. I noticed how much we *looked* like gorillas, but I never thought we *were* gorillas. It wasn't like turning into a rat or talking to Ken. Still, in a general way, I had turned into an animal again. This time, a sort of universal male animal.

At the beginning of the second half, the defense took the field first. By now, the field was whatever we said it was. There were no markings of any kind. Still, I knew the boundaries of my territory. I began to have an almost uncontrollable urge to pee around its perimeters. I, the one Coach said would get to play because I was so intelligent out there, wanted to lift my leg to mark my territory. I restrained myself.

At the end of the third quarter, we led seven to nothing, the result of Moose plowing forty yards through the mud as if he had four-wheel drive while everybody else sank up to their hubcaps. Then, about the middle of the fourth quarter, they had the ball second and seven somewhere around our thirty. Maybe a surveyor could have told us exactly. I was rooting around out in the secondary, when I caught a whiff of something in the breeze. I stretched way up on my legs and started sniffing the air. They were upwind, and I caught the scent. I could smell a pass coming! I moved stealthily closer to the line, alert for the slightest movement in my direction. I kept stopping to put my nose in the air. The scent was much stronger near the line. I looked. The wide receiver didn't seem threatening: he was actually three or four yards behind the line of scrimmage. The tailback was in his stance, far away. The ball was snapped. Their left tackle lumbered by me like a bear on its hind legs. I kept watching the backfield, paying no mind to the bear. Bears are basically ruminants — they eat berries and roots, but they rarely bother other animals. In the same way, a tackle who wanders into the secondary is harmless. Then the bear caught the ball and started loping toward the end zone. I caught up with him at about the ten, nipping

91

at his heels and harassing him like a little dog chasing away a bear who's been eating the garbage. Of course, the bear didn't want to be there, either. It paid no attention to me, just kept running for the safety of the woods. The end zone, that is. Finally, the bear took a swipe at me with its paw and went down on all fours. Bears, after all, can't stand on their hind legs forever. We both went down, me underneath, and slid through the water all the way to the two. They never did score, we won seven to nothing, everybody was happy, and I, having been rolled on by a bear, had a cracked rib.

I didn't know that yet. I just knew that it hurt to take a deep breath.

But I wasn't thinking about that. I was thinking how drained I felt now that I didn't feel my territorial impulses. The feeling had lasted so long this time, but now it was gone altogether. I couldn't recapture it. I tried to think of defending my locker as my territory. It was ludicrous. Oh, well.

11

In the kitchen, my father was making pancakes. He did this often on Sunday morning — Dad Cooks a Special Breakfast for the Kids While Mom Gets to Sleep Late. It always took him about two hours, making the juice, then the bacon, setting the table, heating up the syrup in a pan, for some reason, and then cooking the pancakes two at a time. Long after everybody was full, he'd still be there asking who wanted more, trying to finish off the batter. He always made way too much. He also always made an incredible mess, which we kids were supposed to clean up, all in the spirit of some demented vision of Sunday morning with the family.

Luke and Jessica were sitting at the table waiting.

"Oh-oh," my father said when I came in, "Look who's here. It's Mr. Grumpy. Good morning, Mr. Grumpy."

I went over to the stove to see approximately how long it would be before there were any pancakes. There were two in the pan, with the uncooked side still up. There were none on anybody's plate. So, one for Luke, one for Jessica, then clear off the pan, start again. It was going to be a long wait.

"No, no, Mr. Grumpy," said my father. He was talking in a voice like someone on a kids' TV program. He brushed me away from the stove with the spatula he was waving.

"Kids," he said, "tell Mr. Grumpy to wait his turn. We all have to learn to take turns around here, even Mr. Grumpy. Isn't that right, kids?"

"That's right, Mr. Grumpy," said Luke.

I had to smile. Luke was so nice sometimes. He wasn't teasing me in a bad way, he thought it was funny to call me Mr. Grumpy. So of course did my father, but my father also liked poking me with the hot spatula while he said it.

So I sat down between Luke and Jessica and made a horrible face at my father's back so the kids would think it was all in fun.

"Daddy!" Luke screamed. "Look!"

"What?" asked my father.

I was looking at my plate, of course. When my father turned away, I did it again.

"Daddy! Quick! Mr. Grumpy's making faces at you."

"Oh he is, is he?" said my father. "Now listen here,

93

Mr. Grumpy, there'll be none of that. Not unless Mr. Grumpy wants pancakes with glass in them."

"Okay," I said. "Enough with the Mr. Grumpy."

"Mr. Grumpy said something!" my father yelled. "Mr. Grumpy can talk! I didn't know Mr. Grumpy could talk! Say something else, Mr. Grump. Say — I'm a little grump. Humpety-humpety-hump."

The kids were both laughing. My father was dancing in front of the stove. Some things you just have to wait out. So I sat there. I started to ask how long before the pancakes were ready, when suddenly, without really meaning to, I looked at Jessica and said with a straight face, "I'm a little grump. Humpety-humpety-hump." She laughed, and Luke yelled, "Daddy, Daddy! He said it. He said Humpety-humpety-hump!"

My father turned around and looked at me. He wasn't smiling. He was looking at me suspiciously. That I would actually participate had never crossed his mind.

"Well, Mr. Grumpy isn't grumpy anymore. Can I give him some pancakes, kids?"

They said yes, and he gave me the next batch of pancakes from the pan.

"It's clearing up," he said. "We're all going to Grandma's house for the afternoon. Are you coming?"

"I can't," I said. "I have a date."

"On a Sunday afternoon?" he said. He said it like he didn't believe me.

"Yes. On a Sunday afternoon. This Sunday afternoon, as a matter of fact."

"Where? If I may ask."

"We thought we might go to the zoo," I said.

He looked at me. "Good spot for you," he said.

So somehow I had managed to disappoint him again. So what else was new. I don't know why he wanted me to come. Four out of five times he would have told me to stay home. Suddenly he wants me to come.

"I haven't been to the zoo since I was a kid," Karen said as we got off the bus in front of the entrance. "What made you think of going?"

"I took my little brother here last year and he really liked it," I said.

"Little kids always like zoos," she said.

Right then we passed a little kid who was throwing a fit in front of the gate. "I hate the zoo!" he was screaming. His mother was kneeling in front of him saying how he would get to see Tigger the tiger and Little Roo and Kanga, and the kid's father was standing to the side looking like he wanted to belt him.

"Some kids love it more than others," Karen said.

On the bus ride over, we had talked mostly about how sorry Karen was that her older brother was home visiting from college when I came to pick her up.

"He acts like that whenever I have a date," she said. "He thinks he's funny."

In a book I read once, it said there are two ways to give a crusher handshake: a certain way if the other person is expecting it, another way if he's not. "Nice to beat you," he had said as he applied the grip.

"You know, he's not really that kind of person at all," she said. "He's actually a very thoughtful guy. But whenever I have a date, he thinks he has to humiliate me."

"Do you have a lot of dates?" I had blurted out stupidly.

The first thing we went to look at was the seals. The seals lived in a huge tank that was built into the side of a hill, so that when you were on the top of the hill you could see them lying on their rocks and swimming around in the water; and when you walked down the steps around the tank, you could look through a big window and see them underwater. One big one kept swimming in a large circle around the tank and stopping right in front of the underwater window to look out at us. He had a funny expression with his whiskers and everything. All the mothers and fathers kept putting their babies up next to the glass so they would be surprised when the seal suddenly appeared right in front of them. The seal seemed to like it, too. Some of the babies would be laughing, while some of them didn't seem to get the point.

There were two baby seals, and that was what everybody was concentrating on.

"Oh, look at the little baby ones," everybody kept saying. "Aren't they cute?" Of course, when they swam by, you could see they were already about seven feet long. They probably weighed three hundred pounds apiece.

The same thing happened with the giraffes. The mother and the baby giraffe were leaning their necks over the fence trying to get the popcorn people were holding out, and everybody was saying how cute the baby giraffe was. The thing must have been a good twelve feet tall, and I'm sure it would kick your head off if you got too close. Karen, too, had liked the baby seals and the baby giraffe, and she loved the baby rhinoceros trotting after its mother.

"How come girls like baby animals so much?" I asked her.

"Why do you think?" she said.

"Yeah, but a baby rhinoceros? I mean, I can see a baby lion or something — at least that looks like a kitty — but a baby rhinoceros weighs about half a ton, and it's as ugly as a grown-up rhinoceros."

"It's still a baby," she said.

"Well, I don't understand," I said. "Even a baby tiger or something, maybe it looks playful and cuddly, but you know it's going to grow up into a real tiger — you know that, even if you raised it yourself, as if it were your own baby, when it grows up it's going to eat you."

"But it hasn't grown up yet," Karen answered. "That's the whole point. It's the same with our own babies. We love them when they're helpless.

"Maybe," she said, "we love them *because* they're helpless. When people grow up, they can turn on you, too."

"That's kind of cynical," I said.

"You're just being cynical by pretending not to like baby animals," she said. "Come on. Admit it. Isn't the baby rhinoceros cute?"

"How about a baby snake?" I asked. "Or a baby mole? Did you ever see a baby mole? Very cute."

"What's your point?"

"Or a baby bat? There's an animal just waiting to be cuddled."

"I thought you liked animals."

"I do. I just think they're different from people, and you can't go around calling them cute."

"Some are," she said.

We started walking toward the Aviary.

"Anyway," she said, what do you think a rhinoceros would think looking at a human baby?"

"I don't know," I said. "I'm not a rhinoceros."

"Well, pretend you are for a minute."

She spread her arms wide and did a little pirouette in front of me.

"Here I am," she said, "a little human baby. Am I cute or repulsive?"

I hunched over and looked up at her nearsightedly. She was right in front of me, but I couldn't see her very clearly. I grunted and trotted up to get a closer look. She squealed and ran away a few paces. That made me mad. I lowered my head and charged. She moved out of the way, and I bumped into a bench. Then I stood up straight again.

"You're neither," I said. "A rhinoceros can't tell whether anything's cute. The reason he likes lady rhinoceroses is because they're the only things that don't run away when he gets close."

Karen was laughing. "You scared me," she said. "That was the best imitation of a rhinoceros I've ever seen. I mean you really looked like a rhinoceros. Wow. I mean for a minute I thought you were really going to ram me."

For a minute I was. Imitation of a rhinoceros? Huh! I grunted again like a rhinoceros. Karen giggled. I had been foolish to let that happen, though. There had been no reason to really turn into a rhinoceros. We were just pretending.

"You're probably right, though," Karen was saying, "about anthropomorphism."

"About what?"

"Anthropomorphism. That's when people give animals human characteristics. Like saying baby rhinoceroses are cute, or foxes are tricky, or weasels are cruel. They're not. They're just animals."

"The other way around is more like it," I said. "Animalmorphism. That would be giving people animal characteristics. Animals may not be like people, but people sure are like animals."

"Like who?" she asked.

"Like Nino Cappellano," I said. "He's like an animal."

"You're right," she said. "He's cute."

She laughed, and I grunted like a rhinoceros again, and we continued walking up the hill toward the Aviary, comparing kids we knew to different animals.

The Aviary was like a giant greenhouse, about three stories high, full of trees and tropical plants and waterfalls and little streams. It was hot and humid inside and smelled

98

like the jungle. It sounded like the jungle, too. All the birds could fly wherever they wanted. There were no cages or barriers, just a long, winding ramp bringing you up from the ground level, around and around through different levels, up to just under the roof. Wherever you went, you were looking into one part or another of the jungle. There, under all the foliage you'd see strutting around an Argus pheasant, then up in a tree you'd notice a bright red and blue parrot, then a little farther on among some low branches you'd suddenly spot a couple of greater birds of paradise, with their yellow heads and strange feathers. Then you would hear screeches from somewhere within the jungle, but you couldn't see the bird that was doing it. But when you went up the ramp a little bit, it would take a turn, and you could find whatever bird it had been from behind. When you reached the top, you were at the height of the highest trees, looking down into the jungle. There, you were on a level with storks and kites that live in the treetops.

It was a terrific place. Besides all the squawks and screeches, there were birds that sang songs that sounded as if they were being played on a flute.

We leaned on the railing, looking down over the jungle.

I said, "Did you know that when birds sing, and everybody says, like, the song of the thrush is so beautiful, all the birds are doing is staking out their territory? And when you hear two birds singing back and forth, we call it singing, but it's really just an argument, a fight over who owns what?"

"Of course," she said. "Everyone knows that. So what?"

"Well, it just goes to show you, that's all," I said.

"Goes to show you what?"

"I don't know. What we were talking about before. Something. I forget."

She laughed. I looked down at my feet. I was smiling, too. For some reason, I liked her laughing at me. Then she took my hand, and we walked outside again.

Next to the door to the outside, there was a plaque we stopped to read. It said:

THIS PLAQUE HAS BEEN PLACED HERE IN MEMORY OF A HORNBILL WHOSE NEEDLESS DEATH WAS CAUSED BY A VISITOR WHO CALLOUSLY FED IT A LIGHT BULB.

"That's horrible," Karen said.

"Yeah," I said.

Then we looked at a display they had made up of all the stuff that crazy people had fed to the animals — keys, rocks, razor blades, buttons, pieces of a record, pennies, lighted cigarettes, a fishing lure, some wood putty.

"They shouldn't do that," I said. "It only makes it worse."

"What do you mean?" Karen asked.

"They shouldn't show people this stuff. It gives them ideas. Like 'Oh, wow, I never thought of wood putty.' The more you tell people they should care for animals, the more you seem to make them want to hurt them. There are really a lot of crazy people around."

"Or else splenetic," she said.

"Or else what?"

"Splenetic. Full of spleen. Mean."

"Mean," I said. "Yeah, there are a lot of them, too. But mean isn't the same as crazy."

"But you can feel so mean, you do crazy things. Like for example all the beer cans and other crap you see by the side of the road, or that you find in the woods — or the bottles that people actually throw into the lake right where everybody swims. It seems the more beautiful the place, the more people have to mess it up."

"That's not spleenness," I said, "that's just stupidity."

"No, it isn't," she said. "Maybe a long time ago people did it without thinking, but now, with all the feelings about the environment and about littering and pollution, it has to be on purpose. It's out of spite — like a way of getting back at somebody."

"But who? Who could they be trying to get back at by destroying the woods or the lake? Especially when those are places these same people like to go back to themselves?"

"That's my point," she said. "They say no animal fouls its own nest, but we do."

"What do you mean fouls its own nest? Oh, I see. Is that true? No animal fouls its own nest?"

"Of course. What animal would?"

"Except us."

"That's right."

We left the Aviary and continued to talk about how bad people could be. Karen said she was thinking of becoming a vegetarian. I said I thought that was avoiding the problem, and that we should become man-eaters, instead.

"But wouldn't that make us worse than they are?" she asked.

"Not if we disposed of the bones properly," I said.

She really laughed, and I felt happy. I was having a lot of trouble breathing deeply, but I thought that was only natural, considering. I still didn't know my rib was cracked. We walked into the monkey house, still holding hands. My hand was all sweaty, but I wasn't worried about it. All the books about boys and girls I had ever read always talked about how embarrassed the kid feels about how sweaty his hand gets when he holds the girl's hand, so I knew it happened all the time. When she let go of my hand, I wiped it off on my pants and took hers again.

The orangoutang was trying to hide behind a pole. Every part of him but his face was visible.

"Oh, look," the people were saying, "he's hiding. Isn't that cute."

It kept peeking out from behind the pole and then putting its face in its hands to hide again. It looked totally miserable. Then it spat — a real lunger, too — and put its face in its hands again. The spit landed right on this one guy's sweater. "Oh, Christ," he said, really disgusted that he had monkey's spit all over him, and everybody walked away. At the same time, though, more people came in behind us and started pointing out the orangoutang to their kids, saying, "Oh, look. He thinks he's hiding. Isn't that cute." When there were a whole bunch of people watching it again, it spat a second time. This time it got three people, two girls and a kid, with a big spray. "Aagh," they all said, like the first time, and moved away. I wanted to wait and see if it could fool everybody a third time, but Karen pulled me away.

"Why don't they just let him alone?"

"He doesn't want that," I said. "He was playing a game. Like the people said — he's just pretending to hide. Then he spits at them. That's his game."

"Spitting isn't a game. Spitting is an aggressive act. It's done to humiliate another person."

"It isn't a nice game. But he's not mad. If he was mad, he'd smile at you and show his teeth. He's just trying to amuse himself."

"Well then, he's no better than a human."

"Actually, he's very similar," I said.

We were in front of the chimpanzees. They had a nice, big cage, with a steel jungle gym, some rocks, a stream, and a couple of wooden things vaguely like trees to climb

102

on. There were two families of them, with father, mother, and baby. One family was sitting all in a row, baby first, then mother, then father, with the mother picking lice from the baby while the father did the same for the mother.

The other family was up on the jungle gym. The baby was trying to walk from the mother to the father, then back to the mother again without falling off. It was just like a human family teaching a baby to walk. The parents had their hands out and were calling the baby to come to them. Once again, all the mothers and fathers were showing their kids the baby animals.

"Look at the baby monkey, Nathaniel, isn't he cute?"

"Look at Baby Nathaniel," I said to Karen, "isn't he cute?"

"He looks like a monkey," she said. "But look at the monkey, how scared he is learning to climb. You never think that baby monkeys have to learn to climb.

"But did you know," she continued, "that a two-year-old chimpanzee is developmentally more mature than a two-year-old human? Is really smarter, I mean?"

"Of course," I said. "It can do many more things. It can climb much better."

"No. I mean is smarter. A chimpanzee understands more words and can do more math. It can conceptualize better. It's only later that a human child catches up to a chimpanzee."

"Is that really true?" I asked.

"Yes," she said. "And some never do. But I won't mention any names."

"Nino. Where did you learn that, though?"

"In biology last year. I know a lot about animals. But so do you."

"Some," I said. "Mainly rats and ants. And dogs."

"Everybody knows about dogs," she said.

"I don't know about that," I said. "There's more to dogs than people think."

"Oh, you're wrong," she said. "There's less. People think their dogs are human. They treat them better than they do their own kids. In fact, a lot of people have dogs *instead* of having children. And they treat them like they *were* their children. They buy them presents, they take them out to eat, they even talk to them."

"Talk to them?" I said.

"Yeah. You should see my father when he comes home from work. 'Hiya, Herman, how's the boy? How was your day?' Not, 'Hiya, Karen, how was your day?' No, it's 'Gonna watch the Series tonight, Herm?' I love Herman. We've had him ever since I was little. I'd feel terrible if anything happened to him. But still, he's only a dog."

"Maybe your father thinks he'd feel terrible if anything happened to you, but still, you're only a girl. Do you ever talk to Herman?"

"Oh, come on."

"I'll bet you do."

"Well, what if I do. I'm just saying. Anyway, let's get out of here. All the monkeys in their cages is depressing. And it's a little creepy looking at the baby monkeys. I wonder why the other animals are all so cute and cuddly, and the ones most like us seem creepy."

"Maybe they're not most like us, but we're most like them."

We passed the gorilla's cage, but it was empty.

"He's escaped," I said.

"He put on a man-suit and walked away," Karen said. For a while, we tried to figure out which person was really a gorilla dressed up in a man-suit.

Outside the Primate House, the sun seemed twice as bright as it had been. We walked over to where they had the antelopes and zebras and other grass-eating animals.

104

On the way, we stopped to look at the hippopotamuses. Here, too, all the parents were showing their kids the baby.

"Look," one lady kept saying to her kid, "it's Happy Hippo. It's Happy Hippo. This is the zoo where Happy Hippo lives."

Happy Hippo's mother was eating a big pile of hay, and Happy was trying to get some, too, but his mother wouldn't let him. She kept turning in place, blocking him with her body. He would step back, let her swing by, then try to scoot up her other flank, but she'd just swing back the other way and knock him flying again. Whenever he got behind her, his mother would raise her hind leg and try to kick him.

"Poor Happy," the kid's mother said.

The wildebeests were all lying down in the shade too far away to see, but the kudus and springboks were wandering around in little troupes grazing. The springboks were so little that everybody liked them and tried to get them to come up to the fence to be patted. The people would try to feed them through the fence, too. Some people tossed the food through the fence, but most of them wanted the animal to eat it from their hands. The little springboks would put their lips out for the peanuts or whatever it was, but often their antlers would get in the way of the fence, and they couldn't reach the food. Then they would shake their heads to get clear of the fence, making a big racket against it with their antlers, and try again.

"I guess there's really no way to stop them," I said.

"You mean from feeding the animals," said Karen.

There were Please Do Not Feed the Animals signs all over the place, with lists of all the reasons why it was bad for them.

"It's kind of a natural instinct," she said, "especially wanting to feed the little ones."

"Yeah, but it's not good for them," I said.

"Well, I don't have anything to feed them anyway," she said.

"Peanuts!" I said. "I'm sorry. Would you like some peanuts? They're right over there." I felt embarrassed at not remembering to ask her if she wanted something to eat.

"Or would you rather have a hot dog? Or a Coke? Or a hot dog *and* some peanuts. You can have both if you want."

"Peanuts would be fine," said Karen.

"What about a balloon?" I asked her.

"Are you going to try to feed me a balloon?" Karen asked. "They'll have to put a plaque up for me if you feed me all that junk plus a balloon. Just peanuts is fine. I'll be right here looking at the gazelles."

I hoped she didn't think I was cheap. Usually if I go someplace, say with Jerry or some of the other guys, we all eat like horses. We can go to the beach for the whole day and never get out of sight of the refreshment stand. Every time one of us is finished eating, another one is hungry again. I hoped Karen wasn't real hungry and too shy to ask. I decided to get a hot dog and peanuts both, and then tell her to pick whichever one she wanted.

"Um, the peanuts," she said when I gave her the choice. "And maybe one little bite of the hot dog. How much do I owe for the peanuts?"

"Nothing," I said. "It's my treat."

"Oh. I'm sorry. Thanks." She could tell she had hurt my feelings.

"Anyway, look at those amazing horns on that one over there." She pointed to a greater kudu who had antlers that went up in a spiral about three feet over its head.

"Why do they have such amazing horns like that?" she asked.

"Protection," I said.

"I don't think so," she said. "Their protection is running. And the big ones, like elk and buffalo, their protection is their hooves."

"Why, then?" I asked her.

"I think it's to show off," she said. "All the male animals show off. Either their horns or their mane or their feathers or something. Boys are the same way." She smiled to show she was kidding me.

"Do you think I was showing off when I bought you the peanuts?" I said.

"Oh, come on. I said I was sorry. I didn't know it was your treat. You don't show off. That's why I like you."

"I haven't learned how yet," I said, looking down at my feet.

"Oh, yes you have," she said with a big grin. "What a cute little pout you can do."

When I looked up, she laughed at me.

"Wait a minute," I said. "The females have horns, too. Look at that one over there." There was a springbok with her baby. She did have antlers, too.

"That's right," said Karen. "I forgot. Deer don't have them, though. But cows do, don't they?"

"Yup," I said.

"Oh, well."

In the same area they had put some of those birds that don't fly, like ostriches and peacocks and pheasants. Actually, pheasants can fly. Maybe these had their wings clipped, or else maybe they don't usually leave a place if they don't have to.

Two secretary birds walked by. A mother was trying to get her little kid to look at the guinea fowls.

"Look, Aaron," she was saying, "it's pecking the other bird. What's it doing, Aaron?"

"Pecking."

"That's right. It's pecking the other bird."

Aaron had a brand new chocolate ice cream cone he was eating. When he looked up at the bird pecking the other bird, all the ice cream fell out of the cone. He looked at the ball of ice cream between his feet, then at the empty cone, then at the ice cream again. Then he looked up at his mother. She was still looking at the different birds. He didn't say anything. He put his foot in the ice cream and squished it. Then he stared through the fence for a minute.

"One, two, three . . . now," I said.

Aaron started to howl. His mother looked down at him, but couldn't find what was the matter. She looked around, didn't see anything, then started brushing at his head and back as if there might be a bee or something. He still had his foot on the ice cream. She knelt down in front of him and started smoothing back his hair and nuzzling him like the mother antelopes do. Then she saw the ice cream.

"Oh, Aaron, look what you stepped in," she said. "You've got it all over your sneakers." Then she realized it was his and got mad at him for a while before agreeing to buy him another one if he'd stop crying and be more careful.

"All these little kids screaming is beginning to get to me," Karen said.

"Hah!" I said. "And you with your baby animals!"

There were some real howlers, though, it's true. We seemed to be being followed from exhibit to exhibit by this one family with two kids who took turns bugging each other and then telling on the other one.

"Jordana hit me."

"No I didn't. You hit me first."

"She's imitating me."

"Jason's climbing on the bars."

"I am not. She's a liar."

"You blubberface."

"Go poke your eyeball out."

"Booger-snothead."

And the parents kept saying over and over: Stop it right now. Do you want to go home? If you don't cut it out, we're leaving right now. That's enough, both of you. If we have to go because of you, you'll both be in trouble. Once more and that's it. Leave her alone. We're never coming here again. One more thing and we go. Stay away from him. Don't answer her. Get down!

We sat down on a bench to let them get ahead.

"What was that crack about baby animals for?" Karen asked.

"I don't know," I said. "I didn't mean anything. I just mean you don't have any younger brothers and sisters. I'm used to it."

"Maybe we should go anyway," she said. "I'm tired from all this walking."

When we reached the gate, I remembered we hadn't seen the new Snake House.

"That's okay," Karen said.

12 On Monday my side hurt so bad I couldn't go to school. My mother took me to the doctor's, and they took X rays and told us I had a cracked rib. They said there was nothing to do about it except be careful until it healed. I asked the doctor if they could wrap it up with an Ace bandage or something to keep it from hurting so much when I moved around, but he said no, you weren't supposed to do that. If you wrap your chest up, he said, you don't breathe deeply enough, and your lungs don't get enough air. Then you're liable to get pneumonia. In fact, he told me to stop a number of times during the day and breathe deeply, even if it hurt, to make sure I got air all the way down into my lungs. He also said I wouldn't be able to play football again for the season.

We had to stop at the desk on the way out while my mother filled out all the forms so the school would pay since I was hurt playing athletics.

My mother left me off at school so I could talk to Coach Sisskind about it. Everybody was getting ready to watch the game films. I asked Coach if I could see him for a minute first.

"That's for sure, is it?" he asked. "They took X rays and everything?"

I said yes.

"But you can still move around. You could still practice without contact. You'll still be able to play Thanksgiving."

I said no, the doctor said I would be out for the year,

and he looked at me hard. That was another reason I wanted the bandage. Coach hated quitters. If he thought you were faking being hurt or were dogging it in practice, he would really punish you.

"If you quit in practice," he would tell us, "you'll quit in a game. Because you'll have gotten used to quitting. If you quit in practice, you're only quitting on yourself. But when you quit in a game, because you're too tired, or too discouraged, you'll be quitting on your teammates, too. And if you're a person who's willing to quit on your teammates . . ." Then he would look past us at the wall and not finish the sentence.

He also thought that if you went out for football, you should stick it out, even if it was hard, even if you never got above third string. If you got hurt or had difficulty with your grades or had to give up some other activity, that was the price you paid for sticking it out. You just weren't supposed to quit.

If you did quit, it had to be because something bad had happened in your family. Otherwise, Coach never spoke to you again. When it was your turn to do something in gym class, he would just point at you. When he was marking the attendance, instead of calling out your name, he'd look up from his sheet to find you, then mark you present without a word. When he did have to say your name, it was as if he was naming some food he didn't like.

Actually, though, what he hated the worst was a big kid who could have gone out for football but didn't. A really fat kid, one who couldn't help being fat, and who couldn't do sports at all, he was nice to. Not that he didn't pick on him in gym class. He certainly did. But also, he'd talk to him after gym, joke with him, encourage him to try. But if you were a big kid, maybe a little too heavy, but strong, say, and for some reason didn't like football, gym class was torture.

"Ferdinand the Bull" he would call the kid. "Well, Ferdinand, smell any pretty flowers today? Why don't you give me two laps around the bullring for forgetting your sneakers."

When he looked at the Stevenson brothers in gym class, he would stamp his foot and turn his back on the class until he got himself under control. Then he would look at them like they were two full grain silos and he was a poor cow left out in the snow.

"A pair of two-hundred-and-twenty-pound canaries!" he would say. Their mother wouldn't let them go out for football. They were in the Glee Club instead.

Once Barry Stevenson got tired of it and said, "We're not canaries."

"Fatty is as fatty does," Coach said. "You're two monster tweety birds."

All the kids, especially on the football team, said how fair he was, though, which was true in a way. He never asked you to do something he couldn't do. The only trouble was there was nothing he couldn't do. He was a real Mr. Meat. He could step in and do the blocking drills without pads. He could throw the pass on target every time while the receivers ran their pattern five times in a row. He could do eight wind sprints at full speed with the backs and then join the ends for eight more.

So I didn't want Coach Sisskind to think I was a quitter.

"Well, that's too bad," he said. "You were coming along pretty good. It looked like you were beginning to enjoy yourself out there. But if you can't play, you can't play. I want you to stay with the team, though, you're still part of it. And there's still next year."

I sat through the game films. All that mud made it

112

look like a film of a game that had taken place a long time ago. Already, it seemed that way, too.

At suppertime, my family didn't put all that much work into feeling sorry for me. Luke was disappointed because there was nothing to see, and Jessica, once she was sure I could still take my turn with the dishes, forgot about it.

"That's too bad," my father said. "Gets you out of football, though, doesn't it?"

Well, I suppose it did, but it was just like him to think of it like that. I didn't want to get out of football. Part of me did, or at least part of me was relieved about it, but the rest of me had tried very hard. But of course he would jump on that tiny part that was relieved it was over. I don't know how he could even know I felt that feeling. He could find the tiniest, most innocent feeling or thought that you had, something that hardly counted at all or was hardly even there, and turn it into your most secret guilty motive. It was a real talent he had, believe me.

While I was missing school that Monday, the teachers must have all gotten together in the teacher's room and said to one another, Let's hammer them this week, because the next day, every assignment was a monster.

First period was American History. We were all told to choose a topic in Westward Expansion and prepare an oral report to present in front of the class. Oral reports are supposed to be easier than papers, but I've never been sure of that. It was usually okay once I got going, but right when I started, I always blushed. I don't know why. I didn't blush because I was embarrassed, but I certainly got embarrassed once I was blushing. Then you have to keep on talking while the heat slowly goes away from your face. Offhand, I couldn't think of any topic. Even in the movies I thought wagon trains were boring.

In English, Mr. Wells gave us almost the same thing. From the poetry section we had just started reading, take two poems by different authors and compare and contrast them.

Then in French class, Madame Garnaud gave us one million irregular verbs to memorize by Friday. Just doing the review in class that day made my head feel like a kennel when a new dog arrives. All those words were just barking in my brain. Who knew which ones would get loose when we took the test.

In English class, Karen Cleary had paid no attention to me, and was gone before I finished getting up from my seat. In the cafeteria, she waved back when I waved to her, but she was sitting with a bunch of other girls, so I didn't go over. Then in study hall, she was studying her chemistry notes, so I studied, too. There wasn't anything to ask her, since I wasn't taking chemistry. In front of me, Jerry was studying *Scientific Blocking and Punching*, which he had sent away to *Ring* magazine for. Everything was very quiet. About the middle of the period, I thought I heard a sound like "moo," just once, so soft I wasn't even sure I had heard anything. When I looked over at Karen, she had her head down, studying very hard, but trying even harder to keep from smiling. Jerry turned around and gave Karen a look. That's all there was, but when the three of us turned back to our books, we could feel the eyes of Miss Moran on us. Ten seconds passed.

Then, from the front of the room came, "Mister Raynor. I have been trying to forget that you are here. You would do best not to remind me."

Jerry threw out his arms and turned his eyes up to heaven, like Kareem Abdul-Jabbar when he's called for a foul he didn't commit. Janey Boudreau turned and

114

smirked at him. Jerry leaned toward Janey as if he was going to bite her.

"I *love* you, Janey," he said in this ferocious whisper, "I *need* you."

Janey snapped her head back frontwards and gave Jerry a snort of contempt. It came out much louder than she must have meant, though — it sounded just like a horse snorting. She gasped and looked up at Miss Moran, who was looking at Janey with her eyes wide open in amazement. Miss Moran's mouth opened and closed. Janey was frozen solid. Very slowly, everybody — Janey, Miss Moran, Jerry, Karen, and I — looked back down at our desks.

When the bell rang, Jerry said to Janey, "One of these days you're going to get us all in trouble making those noises."

She looked at him like he had throw-up on his shirt. She went up to Miss Moran's desk to get her seat changed. Jerry followed her.

"Miss Moran," he said. "That was not me."

"Of course not," she said, "but who could it have been, do you think?"

"It was Janey," Jerry said, "but I would never squeal on her."

Janey Boudreau waited for Jerry to leave the room altogether before she talked to Miss Moran.

Jerry and I walked to biology together.

"I don't believe your girlfriend," he said.

"Karen?" I said. "Me either. Neither did Janey Boudreau. Or Miss Moran."

"Well is she or not?" he asked.

"What?"

"Your girlfriend?"

"I don't know," I said.

13

Mr. Fideles had decided to let us take the biology test at home.

"We have too much material to cover in class," he said. "We have to get on to the next unit. So it will be an open-book test, you can take all the time you need, and I expect everyone to do very well. You'll hand it in tomorrow."

Some people were relieved, but most of us groaned. We wanted to get it over with. Studying for a test is a little like filling a bucket with a hole in the bottom. If you don't use the water quick, it all leaks back out. By the time we got home, our heads would be empty, and instead of using the book as a sort of reserve supply to top off our answers, we'd just be pouring the water straight from the book onto our papers.

But Mr. Fideles wanted to talk about frogs.

"The frog, of course, represents a great advance over the animals we have just finished studying. Some of the differences between the frog and the flatworm, for instance, are enormous: the respiratory system, the digestive system, the reproductive system, the structure of the body — even the very existence of a central nervous system complex enough to be termed a brain. The frog, as a member of the class Amphibia, represents that great evolutionary leap into the phylum Chordata, and more particularly, the subphylum Vertebrata — animals with backbones. In a way, the leap from Anura, the frog, to the primates, that is, us, is less than the leap from arthropod or mollusk to chordate."

"Is that how the leapfrog got its name?" asked Jerry.

Mr. Fideles looked up from his notes.

"Yes," he said. "That's exactly right."

"And the hoppy-toad?" I asked.

"No," Mr. Fideles said. "Not you. One Raynor per class is enough. May I continue?"

He looked at his notes for a second. "And one remark per Raynor per class will also be enough," he said.

"Now. In spite of what I have just said, there is still a certain continuity to the development of the organs of perception. And here, though the frog's perceptive apparatus is much more complex than that of the insect or the mollusk, the same principles apply: the animal's most basic functionings within its environment are automatic responses to external stimuli; these responses being triggered by the central nervous system, depending upon whatever the specific sense receptors take in as data."

"What was that again?" somebody in the back said. Mr. Fideles looked up.

"Could you repeat that?" another voice said.

Mr. Fideles frowned.

"Is this movie in English?" I heard a whisper from behind me ask. "Where's the subtitles?"

"All right, then," Mr. Fideles said. "The function of the brain in all the lower orders is simply to collect and organize the data given it by the organism's sense receptors. The function of the brain is *not* to make choices, at least not among the lower animals. Often the most important choices are made by the sense receptors themselves.

"The frog doesn't choose to catch a fly; the frog's eye chooses whether or not to catch the fly. The frog's eye tells it whether a fly is there to be caught. The frog's brain is merely the neurological link between its eye and its tongue; the eye sees the fly, the tongue reaches for

117

it. The brain in this case does two things: it coordinates the discrete data being recorded by the various sense receptors — the two eyes, in other words — and combines them into a single coherent pattern: distance of fly, speed and direction of flight; and secondly, it triggers — I'm sorry, this is exactly what I'm trying not to say — it doesn't trigger — the very reception of the information into the brain triggers the response of the tongue. When all the connections are made, which is what takes place in the brain, the correct electrical impulse is triggered."

There was a sort of growing undercurrent of sound in the class. It was a little like when we put on *Julius Caesar* the year before, and everybody in the crowd scene had to go "Hungunga, umumuma" over and over while we were being mad at Marc Antony.

"Ssh," said Mr. Fideles.

"So. The main principle concerning the senses, and thus concerning the brain, at least in terms of sensory perception, is that of inhibition and contrast. And these processes do not take place in the brain; they take place in the nerve endings of the sense receptors themselves. The frog's eye decides — by the nature of its structure — what to inhibit or to let pass into the central nervous system as information."

By now, the class was beginning to sound like the mob outside the sheriff's office all going "hungunga, umumum" to each other until one guy finally yells out, "Let's lynch 'im!"

Mr. Fideles stopped.

"Am I going too fast?" he asked.

"Umuhung," we all said angrily.

"This is complicated, isn't it?"

"Nnnuh, hunn," we said, looking at each other.

"Perhaps we could slow down and take it a bit at a

time, until we all understand. I know you can understand it if I can explain it more clearly. Shall we try again?"

Everybody looked at each other and started nodding grudgingly like they were thinking hard about what the sheriff was saying about bringing law and order to the West.

Jerry was the first to go over to Mr. Fideles's side. "There's a good picture of it in the book," he said. "It shows what you're talking about."

"What page is that?" asked Mr. Fideles. He didn't even wonder whether Jerry was going to have us turn to the picture of human reproduction that everybody already knew was there; or maybe the chimpanzee with the briefcase walking out of the door that said Biology Dept.

"Two-eighty-one," Jerry said.

We turned to page 281. There was a picture of a frog sitting there. All around it hung dead flies suspended on strings or thread. Some were high, some low, some near, some farther away. The caption under the picture said that the frog would starve to death surrounded by all those flies because he was unable to recognize them as food.

"This is it, exactly," Mr. Fideles said. "The brain is not the only organ that decides what is important to the frog. The senses themselves decide. In the natural environment there are no dead insects suspended in front of it. This frog won't starve because it doesn't *like* dead flies, rather it will starve because it doesn't even *see* them. The eye itself inhibits the reception of certain stimuli before they can be judged by the brain. In other words, the senses decide what information to pass on to the brain — in some cases they don't bother to tell the brain what they have seen or smelled, or so on. So the frog sees only what it needs to see, hears only what it needs to hear. The rest isn't even noise: it doesn't even exist.

119

Now, does this picture help to clarify what I am trying to say?

"The functioning of our own brain, as vastly complex as it may be, begins with, and *depends* upon, this preliminary screening process.

"Okay?" he said, sort of pleadingly. I think he was a little winded.

Everybody was looking down at their desk, pretending to be still studying the picture of the frog. Nobody wanted to be the one whose eyes Mr. Fideles caught and looked into trying to see whether it really was okay.

"Okay, Raynor?" Mr. Fideles asked.

"Hurrump," croaked Jerry the bullfrog. "Hurrump, hurrump."

The bell rang and Jerry hopped out of the room before Mr. Fideles had even closed his mouth in order to open it again. Mr. Fideles shook his head at the rest of us and then began putting his stuff into his briefcase.

After school, I started down to the locker room as usual. I knew I wouldn't really have to show up and watch all the practices. I had no therapy to do, and I couldn't run around the practice field in my sweats the way other injured players did to recuperate while the rest of the team practiced. As an inactive member of the team, I could still hang around and be part of it, but unless I wanted to pass out the towels or something, there wasn't much for me to do. There were only three more games left, including Thanksgiving, which was the most important one. We had a good chance of being league champions. I would still go to the banquet after the season, of course. I had played in way more than half the games, so I would be part of a championship team. A part of a part, I guess, without those last three games.

Karen Cleary was getting her things from her locker

as I came down the corridor. She saw me coming and leaned against her locker waiting for me.

"Hi," she said.

I dove right in. "Would you like to do something Friday night?" I asked her.

"Oh, I'd like to," she said.

"Good," I said.

"But I already am."

"Oh," I said.

"I promised Nino Cappellano I'd do something with him."

"What?" I said.

"What do you mean 'what'?" she asked.

"What did you promise you'd do with Nino?"

"Go out someplace," she said. "What do you think?"

"You're going out with Nino?" I said.

"Is there some reason I shouldn't go out with Nino?" she asked.

"He has fleas," I said.

She laughed really hard. "I think you're jealous of him," she said.

"No, I'm not," I said.

"Listen, I made this date with Nino two weeks ago. I can't just tell him no now. Let's do something together on another night."

"Okay," I said.

"When?"

"When could you?" I asked.

"Anytime. You have to ask, though."

"How about next Friday night, then?"

"Fine. I'll plan on it."

"Okay," I said.

The whole thing was highly unsatisfactory. Was I jealous of Nino? Hah! I knew what I'd like to do to Nino, and his little dog Toto, too.

In the locker room, I went over to Moose.

"Well, you're gonna have to carry the load now, Moose," I said. "It looks like I'm gonna have to hang 'em up."

"That's tough," Moose said. That's all he said.

I stood next to him while he suited up. He finished lacing up his cleats, stood up, and looked at me. He shrugged his shoulders. I shrugged mine back. We went out the door together, then he started jogging toward the practice field.

Robbins and Williams jogged by. "Uh-oh," said Bennie, turning his head back to look at me. "Somebody's faking."

"Limp!" yelled Robbins. "At least limp!"

Most of the other players glanced back as they ran by but didn't say anything. Joey Napolitano pulled up next to me.

"What's up?" he said.

"Hurt," I said. "Broken rib."

"Is that right?" Joey said. "You out for good?"

"Afraid so," I said.

"Who do you think they'll put in?" Joey asked.

Nino passed. "Pick it up, Napolitano," he said.

Joey started running again.

Coach didn't say anything about my injury at practice. He just shuffled different players in and out for the drills as usual. For a while, I stood on the blocking sled for the linemen, but Coach Fitz kicked me off.

"I'll do it," he said. "You're not heavy enough."

It was cold just standing there. It was a real gray, chilly, autumn day, the kind where you think you saw a snowflake but you're not sure, the kind that tells you that winter really is going to come again. The team came back together for a short scrimmage before practice ended. I watched from the hill on the side toward school. The practice field had no stands or boundaries or field markings; it was just an empty, flat field, and the team seemed very small and far away in the middle of that big open space under that gray sky. The claps and yells as they broke from the huddle didn't carry at all. The thuds and grunts of the tackling and blocking seemed bare little sounds.

When they started their wind sprints, I started walking back to the locker room to get my books. Pretty soon the first of them began to trot by. Moose caught up with me and slowed to a walk. With the noise his cleats made on the sidewalk and the nodding of his head inside the helmet, it was like walking along with a tired horse.

Nino ran by. "Come on, Moose, pick it up," he said.

Moose looked at him as if he had said something in a foreign language — or as if a passerby had yelled something at a tired horse — and continued to walk with me to the locker room. Then I picked up my books and left.

When I got home, my mother said to me, "Your father's going to be late tonight, so we'll have supper early, just the four of us."

When we sat down, I asked Luke, "What did you learn in school today?"

"Nothing," he said.

"Nothing?" I said. "You must have learned something."

He thought for a minute. "Nope," he said.

"What did you do there all day, then?" I asked.

"Nothing," he said. "We learned about fish."

"What about them?" I asked.

"They live in the water," he said.

"Is that right?"

"And they look like this," he said, and made his eyes all goggly and sucked his cheeks in and out.

We all laughed.

"Do you know Robbie Loumine?" Jessica asked me.

"No," I said.

"Well, he goes to your school," she said.

"I still don't know him."

"He's in the tenth grade," she said.

"What about him?" my mother asked.

"He's a hunk," said Jessica.

"A hunk?" my mother said. "Do kids still say that? That's what we used to say."

"Was Dad a hunk?" Jessica asked.

"Was Dad a hunk?" my mother said. "Well, no, not exactly. Well, yes, I guess he was. Yes, your father was a hunk."

"Of what?" I asked.

"Of cheese," Luke said.

After supper, I started on the biology test. I found I knew the stuff pretty well, but I checked the book now and then to make sure I had the phyla and stuff spelled right. Then I looked at the chapter on fish. We had just skimmed over fish in class, even though fish come before frogs in evolution. According to the book, fish do live in water and look like that. But then it said some interesting things.

For example, all fish have something called a lateral line system. It is a system of canals with fluid in them running the length of their body that are sensitive to the pressure of the water pressing against the fish's body. This is how they detect other fish and objects in the water without seeing or smelling or hearing them.

That's why it is so difficult to catch a fish with your hands. Even if you go very slowly and manage to get your hands on both sides of the fish, as soon as you move them, the pressure of the water against the fish changes, and the fish responds. The fish reacts automatically — it doesn't have to think at all. That's why it's so frustrating trying to catch one: it seems like you've really snuck up on the fish, it doesn't seem to be paying any attention to you. And it isn't, because it doesn't have to.

The shark is actually a very primitive fish. By primitive, of course, they don't mean you can't reason with it. They mean it has cartilage instead of bones, and it can't see colors, only shades of black and white. Other fish have developed these things. It also can't float. It has to swim even while sleeping or it sinks to the bottom. So by primitive, they mean it didn't develop the kinds of things that eventually led to some fish becoming amphibians and getting out of the water. It didn't advance in that way. But a shark is the absolute master in the water, so why would it want to get out? And think of what would happen if they ever could. I wondered if Moose could float. Or Hanes. Or how about Madame Garnaud on water skis with a Great White Shark rising up behind her.

But, anyway, it's wrong to think primitive means dumb. A shark is more intelligent in the water than we are. It's like this thing my uncle once told me. He had some chickens, and one time he took me out to see them, and I said I didn't like chickens because they are so stupid.

"Chickens don't get paid for being smart," my uncle said. "They get paid for laying eggs. That's what's smart for a chicken to do. And you can't beat 'em at it."

Still, my uncle did admit that chickens are pretty stupid. In fact, he told me that chickens are so dumb that if it rains you should put them in their coop, because they will sometimes look up at the rain with their mouths open and drown.

Even so, a baby chick will run away from the shadow of a hawk. It just has to see that shadow come across and it takes right off. It doesn't have to be taught about

125

hawks, doesn't have to ever have seen one — which would probably be too late for it to learn from, anyway — it just knows. And it doesn't look up with its mouth open, it has a reflex action to hide, without thinking about it. It's when they try to think that chickens get into trouble.

I came across the picture of the frog that Jerry had pointed out in class. The frog sees only what it has to see, hears only what it has to hear. The rest isn't even noise, it doesn't exist. But what if we're like the frog surrounded by dead flies in the picture. What if all around us are different things, real things, that we don't see because our sense receptors have tuned them out before we can even think about them. What if God has strung all these beautiful dead flies in front of us, and we're starving to death because we don't see them.

14

The next night, I had three things to work on: the talk for American History, the report for English, and the irregular verbs for French. I was looking through the book for a topic for American History. I decided finally to do my report on the Cheyenne Indians. The book didn't say very much about them, except that they were the allies of the Sioux Indians against Custer, and that their best warriors were called the Dog Soldiers.

I worked for a little while on my English assignment, then I did what I had been avoiding for two days: I picked up my French book. Talk about filling a bucket with a hole in it. This was like trying to fill the bathtub without putting the plug in. Irregular verbs? Irregular socks was more like it. I might as well try to make them fit my feet as my head. I couldn't remember the last time I had flunked a test. Maybe never. Je flunk. Tu flunk. Il flunkie. Nous all flunkons.

I tried to memorize them, but I kept finding myself just staring at the whole page as if I was trying to memorize the way the page looked instead of the words on it. Outside, Ken was barking like crazy. Maybe he had treed a raccoon or a burglar or something. Maybe it was nothing at all. Who knows why dogs bark? I kept at it. I stared harder and harder. I stared right through the page to the next page, where there was more of the same. Every once in a while, my eyes would go by mistake to the subjunctive. Luckily, we didn't have to know the subjunctive, except for to have and to be and a couple others. *Aie, aie, aie* said the subjunctive, like the Mexican jumping-bean song.

It was ten-thirty. Ken had just barked for the four hundredth time. I decided to go out and see what was going on. My father was still up, waiting for the eleven o'clock news. I put on my jacket.

"I'm just going out for a short walk," I told him.

I went over to Ken's house. He was out in the front yard barking away.

"Ken," I said.

"Yeah," he said, looking down from the sky over to me.

"What's all the barking about?"

"The moon," he said.

"What about it?"

"It's full."

So what?"

He had been sitting on his haunches. He got up and walked over to me.

"I don't know," he said. "I always bark when the moon is full."

"You know how many times you've barked at it tonight? Do you?"

"No," he said. "I don't usually keep track."

"About four hundred," I said.

"Well, it's more a question of rhythm than any specific number," he said. "You get into a comfortable rhythm and you can just keep going. A lot of dogs'll bark one-two-three-four-one-two-three-rest. I like a three-count with a sort of syncopation in it between phrases. Like bark-bark-bark-breath-bark-bark-breath-bark-bark. Makes it more interesting."

"It's driving me crazy."

"What can I do?" he said. "I can't help that. They leave me out, you know. If I was inside, I wouldn't bark."

"Yeah, but still . . ." I said.

"Paul, you don't understand. The moon — it looks at me."

"That's crazy," I said. "The moon doesn't look at you."

"It does, too. It looks at whoever's out in the dark. It's looking at you right now."

I looked up at the moon. It was true. That great white eye was looking back down at me through the darkness. I could see his point.

"Even so," I said, "you don't expect me to sit and bark at it with you, do you?"

"Not at all," said Ken. "The thing to do is to go home and bark from there. I'll hear you, then I'll bark back. There's a dog two streets over who'll join in, too. Butch his name is. With the three of us, we can last all night. Then the moon will go down, and we can lie down and get some sleep."

"Ken, I can't stay up all night. I've got a test tomorrow."

"Well, if that's the way you feel about it, I'll have to do it myself. Butch will help if he's out. But they usually take him in after a while."

"Why don't they take you in," I asked.

"I chew the furniture," he said.

"Oh," I said. "Listen. I have to go home. Do me a favor, though. If you can't quit barking, could you at least stay in some regular pattern? It's the sudden quiet and not knowing when you're going to start up again that drives me crazy."

"Sure, Paul," he said. "Those are the clouds you're talking about. Whenever a cloud covers the moon, I rest.

"Ah, the hell with it," he added. "I guess I'll pack it in for tonight. I'll go under the porch where it can't see me. That way you'll get your rest."

"Wait a minute," I said. "Don't do it just for me. Bark if you have to bark. I'll live through it. I've lived through it enough times before."

"That's all right," Ken said. "I can skip one night. The moon will always be back next month."

"Well, do what you want," I said. "I didn't mean to disturb you."

When I reached my front walk, I looked up at the moon again. The full moon does funny things, evidently, both to dogs and to people. How otherwise could I have just discussed barking at it with Ken? But did it really make a dog talk? Or perhaps a boy had barked. Loony: it comes from the word for moon. Well? I let that one pass and went back in.

15 The next day was Thank God It's Friday, but it didn't go very well. And I had really thought it would, even the French test. I had studied hard for it.

First came English. Comparing and contrasting two poems isn't too hard, once you've figured out what each of them means. If they're assigned, you know they're going to be about the same thing, but even if they're not, the same method works. What you do is go back and forth from one poem to the other, line by line, saying on the one hand the first poem, on the other hand the second poem all the way down. You show how for the one poet, whatever it is he is thinking about keeps reminding him of something else, so he keeps using similes and metaphors, while the other poet concentrates just on the thing itself and describes it without any similes or metaphors. Then you show how, if it's the poem with the similes, they make you see the dawn or the flowers in the field or love or whatever it is in a new way, and then with the other poem how the sounds of the words and their rhythm, or the precision of the words builds up a perfect picture of how the dawn really does come up or what the flowers really do look like. Then you wrap it up by saying that the two poems are really about the same thing, but are two different ways of looking at it or feeling about it.

The one thing you are not allowed to do is say that the poet is wrong. That, for example, there's no way the flowers "smile today." It couldn't happen. You can say, if you're careful, that you don't like a poem, or even that you don't think the metaphors work very well to give you the mood.

"This poem here is wrong," I told the class.

"It's called poetic license," Mr. Wells said. "It's the freedom of the poet to ignore the strictures of daily experience in his or her search for higher realities."

"But it's not right," I said. "A hawk isn't like that. You can't say you are like a hawk shaking its head at a mouse because a hawk doesn't do that."

"You're missing the point," Mr. Wells said. "The truth of the poem is in its difference from — in its contradiction of — everyday reality. A real hawk may not — what? — shake its head at a mouse — but this hawk does. Because the writer isn't merely describing an ordinary hawk. He's making a momentary leap out of ordinary reality in order to bring a new light to everyday experience."

"I disagree," I said.

"All right, then," said Mr. Wells, "explain to the class exactly what you don't like."

"It's not exactly that I don't like it," I said. "I just think it's wrong. If he thinks that hawks shake their heads at their prey, he'd never get anywhere as a hawk."

"You're still missing the point. He has no intention of getting anywhere as a hawk. He is not trying to convince you that a hawk shakes its head at a mouse when in reality it does not. Is that true, by the way, what you're saying? Why couldn't a hawk shake its head at a mouse?"

"Because when a hawk dives, it stays absolutely still. It tucks its wings in and puts out its talons and then just plummets toward the mouse. Or else leaves its wings out and glides in. The mouse doesn't see anything, even if it looks up, because the hawk comes at it in a perfect line, just a dot that looms bigger and bigger. If it shook its head or flapped its wings, the mouse would see the movement. When a mouse runs away from a hawk, it's because he saw the hawk before it started its attack. That's when it might shake its head or flap."

"Well, it still doesn't seem important enough to harp on. Can someone else help me?" he asked the class. Nobody could. Nobody ever pays attention when somebody else is reading his paper.

Finally, Karen said, "I think I understand what Paul means. I think he means that if the metaphors in the poem aren't accurate, the whole poem suffers because the connections the poet is trying to make don't work."

"Well, that's a good point," Mr. Wells said. "A very good point. But if you'll look at the poem again, you'll see you've misread the emphasis of the metaphor. The poet says 'As if the hawk . . .' It's not a simile that depends on accuracy. It's a metaphor the poet is making up. He wants you to see things differently — wrongly, even — he wants to destroy the way things are for a moment, to cause a disruption in the way we see reality, so that by the end of the poem we'll see it in a new way. Does that help you at all?" he asked me.

I should have said yes, but I didn't feel like it.

"No," I said. "I think it's okay to say 'the flowers smile today' because everybody knows that's only the way the poet feels. But you can't say, 'as if a hawk shook its head at a mouse,' because it's not the way things are. Or the way they could ever be."

"Why do you persist?" Mr. Wells said. "I'll say one more time what I said when we began reading poetry. A poem is not the same as prose. A poem can say anything it wants. Here, for example, we have the real hawk, and the hawk of the poem. Now, if the poem works, our perception of the real hawk has been changed by the hawk of the poem. But without this suspension of our ties to the exact way things are, without the ability to imagine, we can't read poetry. Does that help you at all to see how the hawk functions in the poem?"

"I guess," I said. "But I still have to say that it wouldn't last a minute as a real hawk."

"It's lasted a hundred years as a poetic one!" Mr. Wells shouted. "I don't know whether you're trying to be facetious or what, but this has gone on long enough. Sit down."

That was English. Then came biology.

"The tests," Mr. Fideles said, "were not that good. Most of you got the names right, and the phyla and orders right, but your interpretations of the behavior of the various organisms showed, in many cases, a real lack of understanding of the way animals function in relation to their environment. Anthropomorphism, I believe it is called in literature, but it could have another name. Paul, do you remember?"

I said I didn't.

"In any case, you have confused, many of you, the two meanings of the word feel. We cannot say that an insect 'feels' hungry. Or even that it 'feels' pain. Insects — bees, for example — do not 'feel' cold or 'feel' hot. The bee's sense receptors trigger various degrees of electrical energy to its nerve center — its 'brain,' if one has to use that word — in other words, if the hive gets too hot for them, the bees automatically begin to beat their wings to lower the temperature of the hive, by creating a breeze within it, back to normal. But the bees don't do it because they feel hot. They do it because they *are* hot. There is no distinction between the reception of the stimulus and the response to it. There is only the time it takes for the electrical impulse to travel the neural path — which is almost instantaneous. So we can't say a bee 'feels' hot or cold. What we must say — and this

133

is *all* we can say — is that when the temperature deviates from the optimum temperature for bees, the bees react — *re*act, not act — automatically, without deviation, according to whatever information their sense receptors . . ."

"Their feelers," Jerry said.

"Nngh," said Mr. Fideles, "whatever information their sense receptors — what we call their feelers are only one of these — are given."

"Now, we had much the same problem with the mollusks. You simply cannot say that a clam feels hungry."

Everybody laughed at that.

"Don't laugh. Many of you did just that. This is especially disheartening since most of you correctly answered the question of the clam's passive ingestion of food. How can you write that a clam gets hungry when you can't even say that it 'eats'?"

I wasn't worried. This was very similar to the problem I had just had in English class with Mr. Wells. I had been trying to explain the same thing to him: you can't say things about animals that aren't true. That's why I was so surprised when Mr. Fideles handed back the papers. Yes, I had said clams eat. Yes, I had said insects feel hungry. Yes, I had put down, "when the insect feels threatened . . ." Every time a sentence like that occurred on my paper, it had a big red circle around it, and in the margin, HOW DO YOU KNOW?

There was HOW DO YOU KNOW AN INSECT FEELS THREATENED? HOW DO YOU KNOW A CATERPILLAR *DECIDES* TO SPIN A COCOON? HOW DO YOU KNOW THE MAYFLY *WANTS* TO MATE?

The mark was an 80, not terrible. I wasn't the only one who had done it. But when Mr. Fideles began talking, I had thought perhaps I was the only one who hadn't done it. Old Jerry got a 97.

"Look at this," he whispered. "I got crustacean wrong."

I wanted to ask Mr. Fideles if it was all right to say that we feel upset about our marks, or whether we should consider our feelings, too, as simply stimulus response. I was afraid, though, that Mr. Fideles would think it was a wise-guy question. You can never tell with teachers.

And finally, there was French. English and biology were still ringing in my ears, and all those French verbs were rubbing against my brain like sand in your shoe. Madame Garnaud passed out the test papers. Name, period, date. Conjugate the verb to be. Present tense. Big blank space. Imperfect. Big blank space. Subjunctive. Huge blank space. Why? The subjunctive wasn't bigger than the other tenses, was it? Madame Garnaud hadn't even given us the French word to start us off, just the English: to be able, to know, to fear, to please, to see, to want. I went down the paper filling in the easy ones first. I did all the conditionals. The conditional had been easy ever since Joshua Rudnik had translated the whole of How Much Wood Would a Woodchuck Chuck into French. Some of the vocabulary, though, I just forgot. It was like forgetting somebody's name when you go to introduce them. A lot of the words I knew, but it was as if they had gone somewhere else for a while, and they couldn't be there for me because they couldn't be two places at once. To feel . . . big blank space in my brain. The words must have been over in somebody else's brain.

When I finished all the ones I knew, my paper looked like one of those early maps of the known world, where Unknown covers most of South America and Africa. Vast rivers of pluperfects, huge mountain ranges of subjunctives remained uncharted. Whole populations of primitive French-speaking tribes — empires of them — remained undiscovered.

Then something began to happen. My head started making hissing and popping and sputtering noises. These are my brains, I thought, these are my very brains breaking down. These are the cords, the what-do-you-call-thems, the ganglia coming loose, spitting electricity from their busted connections. The wires are frayed. The cables have popped.

But it wasn't. It was French words, all tangled together and hissing in my head like a nestful of snakes. They writhed around, all entwined together, their tongues darting out. Then one got loose and began to crawl up the inside of my skull. I put my hand up to the side of my head and felt its flickering tongue just inside my ear. "*Sois*," it hissed. "*Sois, soit, soyons, soyez, soient.*" Then another uncoiled itself and wriggled free. It slithered up to just behind my eyes, its tongue flickering. "*Puisse, puisse,*" I could hear as it got closer and closer to my eyes. "*Puissions, puissiez . . .*"

Up from the deepest part of my brain — the reptilian brain — came the snakes. I was terrified. I wrote down what I heard. It was their sounds I transcribed onto the paper, without daring to move or to make any sound myself. I didn't dare close my eyes. I finished the test. I passed it up the row to the front, making only the slowest, most gradual movements, keeping my head as still as possible. The snakes seemed to calm down. The slithering subsided. Perhaps it had been the paper with the French on it that had aroused them. But I was really shaken. Talking dogs are one thing, people turning into buffalo is one thing, but pulling French-speaking snakes out your ears! When I saw Jerry at the end of school, I went la la la to myself before I spoke to him, to make sure what came out of me would be a human voice.

16

"How's school going this year?" my father asked at supper.

"Okay," I said. "Some of the teachers, though."

"You don't like your teachers?" my father asked.

"They're all right, I guess. Mr. Wells, though, what a jerk."

"Which one is he?"

"English," I said.

"That's usually your best subject," my father said.

"Not this year," I said.

"I remember Mrs. Dingham from last year," my mother said. "I thought she was a little flaky, but you did very well in her class."

"Well, give Mr. Wells time," my father said. "How's science this year? Biology is it?"

"Yeah. I don't know. It's interesting, but the teacher, Mr. Fideles, he's harder to understand than the biology book. It is interesting, though."

"Well, that's the main thing," my father said, "as long as you stay interested."

"And French?" my mother asked.

"Oh," I said.

"Is Madame Garnaud still there?"

"*Aie*," I said. "Is she."

"French was always my favorite subject," said my mother.

"Madame Garnaud would fix that," I said.

"What's the matter with *her*?" my father asked.

"I don't know. You should see her. She acts like French

is the greatest thing since they made the earth round. She makes you feel like a real toad if you don't get it."

"She's supposed to be a very good teacher," my mother said.

"It doesn't sound like you're getting along very well in school this year," my father said.

"I am," I said.

"See that you are," he said.

I headed over to Jerry's for another night of nothing to do. This was the night Karen was out with Nino. Jerry and his grandmother were still eating supper. There was a big bag of Kentucky Fried Chicken on the table between them.

"This is not good chicken," Jerry's grandmoher said.

"It's not chicken at all, Grandma," Jerry said. "You know that. It's a baby. A nice, plump Christian one. Eat up. She calls it chicken 'cause you're here," he said to me.

Jerry's grandmother gnawed on her chicken leg without answering him.

"Have some," Jerry said.

"I already ate," I said.

"Sit. Eat. It's not good," Jerry's grandmother said.

I sat down and picked up a leg.

"Good, huh?" Jerry asked.

"You like this?" his grandmother asked me.

"Grandma's mad because it's been baptized. In Poland she used to get them unbaptized. She thinks the baptized ones have more preservatives."

"Jeddy," she said. "You are not annoying me." She pointed her finger at his chest. "But be careful you don't annoy God."

"What do you want to do tonight?" Jerry asked after his grandmother had gone to watch the news.

"I don't know," I said. "What a day. Let's get drunk."

138

"Want to?" Jerry asked.

"Sure. Got any liquor or anything?"

"I'm sorry," Jerry said, "Jews don't drink."

"Thus spake Jerry's father," I said.

"It's true," Jerry said. "They don't. They 'entertain.' "

"Well, let's entertain ourselves, then," I said.

Jerry stood on a chair and opened the cabinet over the refrigerator. "It's way up here on the top shelf," he said. "My father must think I can't reach it. Or maybe I don't know how to use a chair to climb on."

"How did you learn?" I asked.

"I read about an experiment where a chimpanzee did it to get some bananas that were too high. How about vodka? We can mix it with orange juice. We'll be falling down in no time."

He closed the cabinet door and jumped down off the chair, then got two glasses from the sink and the orange juice from the refrigerator.

"What do you think?" he asked. "Is half-and-half about right?"

"I have no idea," I said.

He filled the glasses up to the top and sat down opposite me. He raised his glass in a toast. It was a Snoopy glass. I had Woodstock the bird.

"How's life?" Jerry asked.

"Hard to say," I said. It was, too. I wanted to tell Jerry, or at least tell him something, but I wasn't sure what. Never mind how. "I think I'm having an identity crisis."

"You mean like you don't know whether you're a boy or a girl?"

"No, like I don't know whether I'm a human or an animal. I mean like in evolution, all we are is the highest form of animal life. So what if that is all we are — a collection of animal parts? What if all the different animals we've evolved from are still inside us, and all a person is, is a big habitat? Bacteria live in the stomach, like in a swamp, and viruses live in the blood — that's the rivers — reptiles live in the deepest part of the brain . . . That's true, you know, they call that part of the brain the reptilian brain. And real snakes live there. I know it."

"What about the other way around?" Jerry said. "Maybe it's not that other animals are part of us, but we're all parts of some gigantic animal. Like the trees are his hair, and we live on his skin. We're just little skin bacteria crawling around."

"That's stupid," I said.

"All right, how about this: we live inside, and when the sun comes up, that's just him opening his mouth, but for us it's like it takes a whole day for him to open and close his mouth. See, all the natural phenomena we feel, like rain and snow, cold and hot, it's all stuff he's doing, like breathing, eating, brushing his teeth, et cetera. You know what an earthquake is? That's when he French-kisses somebody! Or maybe that's a UFO! Or an eclipse of the sun!"

He liked that idea a lot. "Or a tidal wave! See, the ocean's just his saliva anyway."

"How do you like this stuff?" he asked. "Finish it up."

He got the bottle down from the refrigerator and refilled our glasses. He leaned back in his chair to think some more.

"Yeah, but I'm serious," I said.

"Me, too," Jerry said. "God is everywhere, they say. We all live within God. Well? What if we do live in God, but just in His mouth? Going to hell happens when he swallows you. There you have your whole cycle of life, birth, death, reincarnation, everything. You go down the intestines, through hell, out the other end, lie in the

140

earth — His earth — for a while, but not as dust, as His shit, then get taken up into some plant. Like maybe before we're reborn we start out as rhizoids or nitrogen or something, then we're dormant for a while until He eats us again and we're back in the world inside his mouth. Like in the Catholic church, but we don't eat the Host, the Host eats us. What's your idea?"

"Oh, I don't know," I said. "It's almost as bizarre as yours."

"More?" he asked. He pulled the chair over to the refrigerator to get the bottle down again. The chair slipped as he climbed up.

"Oops," he said. "Little trouble with the chair, nothing I can't handle, though."

He poured vodka into the glasses again.

Well, I thought, here goes nothing!

"Listen," I said. "Here's what's happened to me."

"Oh, hi, Grandma," Jerry said.

She was standing in the doorway looking at him.

"You don't mind if we get drunk, do you?"

She stared at him without moving. Then she started to shake her head slowly back and forth.

"Wait a minute, Grandma," Jerry said.

"No," Jerry's grandmother said.

"Everything's okay," Jerry said.

"The end," Jerry's grandmother said.

"Look, Grandma, I'm putting it back," Jerry said.

"The disgrace," she said.

"I'm pouring it out, Grandma."

"The shame on your father's head. On this house."

"Grandma, we were only kidding."

"No," she said. "You will have to go. You will have to leave this place."

"Here, Grandma, you have some, too. It'll help calm you down."

"It will be cold. He will wander. No one will take him in, a young man who is a drunkard."

She stepped back into the other room. Jerry turned to me.

"We've got to stop Grandma before she gets going. She'll forget to inhale and she'll die."

He followed her into the other room.

"From village to village," she was saying, "driven by the devil of drunkenness."

"Grandma," Jerry said.

"The clothes torn, the hair dirty," she said.

"Grandma, can you hear me?"

"With lice," she said. "Through the streets, the children follow. They ridicule him." Didicule, she said.

"Grandma," he said. "We're here to help you. If you can hear me wave your arms. If you want to stop but can't, try to signal me somehow."

"A scholar he could have been," she was saying, "not a bum."

"A contender, Grandma. I could have been a contender instead of a bum, not a scholar."

"Stay away," she said, "your breath is the breath of a *shikker*."

"Grandma, stop. Come back into the kitchen. Paul and I just had one drink to see what it tastes like."

"Ach, Paul," she said. She came back into the kitchen. "And your father, if he knew this?" she asked me.

"He wouldn't like it," I said.

"I bet," she said.

"Now go outside. Walk, do something. Come home later."

We put on our jackets to go out.

"Here," Jerry's grandmother said. "Eat this so your fathers don't find out." She gave us each a raw onion she had peeled. "Let me see you eat first."

142

We did it, then walked outside.

"Are you drunk at all?" Jerry asked.

"Some," I said. "Maybe a little."

"Same here," he said. "That onion was just what we needed, though, wasn't it? Let's take the car out someplace. It's fixed."

"Maybe I should just go home."

"Oh, come on. Let's find some girls and breathe on them."

Jerry drove so slowly I was afraid we'd get stopped for it. "I could walk faster than this," I said.

"We're in no condition to walk," said Jerry. "We have to ride."

We went down to the mall and walked around for a while, then Jerry saw two girls he said he knew and dragged me over to talk to them.

"Hi," he said. "Remember me?"

"No," said the girl.

"Jerry," he said.

"So?" said the girl.

"So what's yours?" Jerry said.

"Forget it," she said.

"That can't be your real name," said Jerry. "Listen, this is my friend Paul."

"So?" the girl said and started to walk away. The other girl with her hadn't said anything.

"Which one of you is Lassie?" Jerry called after them. "Your owner wants you to come home."

The two of them spun around and the one who hadn't said anything gave Jerry the finger.

"And good-bye to the equally lovely E.T." Jerry called.

17

The game the next day was at home again. It was a little cold, but bright and sunny. All the trees were at the height of their fall colors, especially the maple trees, which were a brilliant red.

I stood by the end of the bench with my hands in my pockets watching the warm-ups before the game. I had on a sports jacket, but still felt cold.

"No tie?" Coach Fitz asked me.

"I didn't think you had to," I said. "Just the jacket."

"Tie next time, okay?" he said, then went out to lead the linemen in their drills.

I watched the game from the end of the bench. A real tall kid named Steinway was in my position. He was an end, usually. The only pass they threw in his direction was overthrown out of bounds.

We won pretty easily. By the end, Coach had all the subs in. I couldn't help thinking that, had I been healthy, I might have gotten a chance to play offense for once. The kid they put in for Moose scored a touchdown.

By the end of the game, it was a hot day. In fact, it turned out to be the first day of almost two weeks of Indian summer. It was as hot as real summer, sunny, bright, and sticky. All the insects were fooled into coming back out. It's amazing how quickly they appear if it suddenly turns warm. There were flies, hornets, wasps, and bees all over the place. They didn't come out in droves, though, like in summer. Each one seemed to be wandering around all by itself.

They took a long time to warm up. In the morning, you'd see a wasp or a bee just sitting there on top of a car waiting for the sun to give it enough energy to fly. They weren't as lively, or as nasty, as they are in the early fall when they seem to know that their time is almost up. The flies just hung there in the air and were easy to kill, and the bees seemed to bump into things a lot. Only in the afternoon did they really buzz around like they're supposed to. Otherwise, they were so sluggish you could actually hold a wasp by the wing if that was something you wanted to do.

It was a big mistake for them to come out, though. There was nothing for them to eat, and the temperature went back down to almost freezing at night, so a lot of them died each night from being caught outside. Probably all of them died when it turned really cold again. They had lost their little warm houses where they had been going to last out the winter. But I guess they couldn't help it, especially the ones like the flies that had probably been eggs. The warmth made them come alive, so they had to do what they did. The ones that had spent so much time preparing to last the winter must have thought they had done it, only to fly out into a bleak world of no flowers, no green buds, no mating, no eating, no laying eggs, no building hives or nests. Just a few short sunny days and then freezing cold.

In my room, the spiders had come alive, too. You can always find a spider or two in the house anytime. I think they can live all year-round; but it must be a long wait between meals sometimes.

I was trying to finish my talk for History when I noticed this spider that had caught a bug in a web underneath my windowsill. It was perched on the belly of some kind of beetle-looking thing, I don't know what it was exactly, that was much bigger than the spider was. The beetle, or whatever, was stunned but still alive, quivering. The spider was moving around very daintily on the tips of its legs — her legs, actually, since all spiders you see with webs are females — and placing them very tentatively on the body of the beetle, picking up a leg when the beetle quivered, moving all around and over the beetle, touching, probing, and then, as the beetle's jerking got weaker, more and more just an occasional vibration, it perched on its belly and lowered its mouth to a spot where there was a space in the carapace and began sucking out the juice.

Then nothing moved at all for a long time. I got bored watching. When I remembered to look again about an hour later, it looked like nothing had moved or changed. Except now the spider was perched on the beetle's head instead of its abdomen, with her mouth attached to the head, and the beetle's body had begun to shrivel up.

The next day was better. I was doing homework in the afternoon after school again when I thought of seeing whether there were any more spiders around. Right on the outside of the windowpane, where I could see perfectly, a small, tan-colored spider was wrapping up a bee. The bee was already all tangled up in the web but was still beating its wings strongly. The spider was hovering in close to its abdomen, biting it I would guess. In less than a minute, the bee was all curled up, still beating its wings some, but mostly just shaking. I could see its stinger vibrating in the air and its abdomen pulsating. I don't know whether the bee was trying to sting it or not, but the spider didn't pay any attention, even though the stinger was stabbing the air all around her. She started at the bottom, wrapping up the bee's abdomen first. Every once in a while she grabbed hold of the bee with her mouth or her legs, but mostly she just moved her back two legs really fast, like my mother wrapping the thread back on the spool after sewing. She was playing the thread out from her abdomen between those flying legs, and the bee, of course, was the spool.

After each few wrappings, she would move up slightly, pulling everything tighter, folding the bee in on itself. All this time, the bee was still struggling, but it couldn't move very much now. You could see the bee's mouth moving, too.

So the spider worked her way up the bee's body, tightening as she went, then moved up to the head, did a couple of quick wraps, and folded the bee right in the middle. You could still see the bee shaking and twitching, but if you hadn't known it was a bee, you couldn't tell now.

Meanwhile, one of those deerflies with the striped wings flew into another part of the web and got stuck. It was buzzing and twisting and shaking the whole web. Sometimes spiders run up to the far corner of the web when they feel it shake like that and wait to see what it is, or whether it's safe, or whether the insect is ripping the whole web apart or what, but this time the spider didn't even look up from the bee as far as I could tell. Maybe they can tell when a bug lands just right in the web by the feeling, like when a ball lands just right in the web of your glove. So in one corner, the spider is busy wrapping up the bee, and in another corner the deerfly is getting more and more tangled up and tired.

Pretty soon all you could see was this pulsating *thing* wrapped in gauze. The spider hooked a last thread around it, let out a little line, and pulled it up to the top of the web. She secured it there, then wrapped it up good, but this time as she spun out the thread with her back two legs and wrapped with them, she turned the bee-package over and over with her front legs.

The instant she was finished, she ran across the web

to grab the deerfly. She stopped, then gripped it by the wing. Whether she bit it on the wing or just grabbed onto it I don't know, but that was pretty much the end of the deerfly. The spider didn't bother wrapping it up; she just hauled it across the web and stuck it next to the bee. Then she let go of the deerfly and moved off to the side. There they were, three yucky things sitting in the corner of a spider's web. The bee was totally unrecognizable. It looked like it had been there a month.

Nothing happened for a long time, and I got tired of it. The next day, though, I remembered to look. Just the top corner of the web remained. No spider, no deerfly, no bee. I wonder if something else came along and ate everybody. Or else it was just the cold at night and then the heavy dew that wrecked the web.

The first time my mother reminded me to knock down the spiderwebs that were inside in my room, and I told her I wanted to leave them, she laughed. But when they were still there when she came in to put some of my socks away a couple days later, she got mad.

"It's cute when you're about five and you like frogs and toads and snakes, but it's not cute at sixteen. Take the broom and get rid of them. You don't want spiders in your room."

"I do," I said. "I like spiders. Nice juicy spiders."

"Why don't I help you," she said. "I'll teach you how to clean your room. You know, when you go to college, you'll have to do everything for yourself. If you don't know how to keep your room clean, you'll end up with bugs. And not just a few spiders. Bedbugs, lice, roaches."

"But Mom," I said, "I like bugs. They make handy snacks. And they're nutritious, too."

"That's fine, now you start on your clothes. Everything that's dirty put in the laundry. Everything else hang up."

She left and came back with the broom, the dustpan, a sponge, a pan of water, the Ajax, the Windex, and the Lysol. She had trouble getting everything through the door without whacking the handles against the opening.

She was very fussy about not wanting to touch anything on my desk, or even looking at it.

"Whatever you have that's private or you don't want me to see, you put away. You pick up and I'll clean."

"But you could come in anytime and look through my room when I wasn't here if you wanted," I said.

She was running the sponge across the top of a windowsill. The water on the sponge turned the dust into mud and left a streak on the wall.

"Listen," she said. "I would never come in and spy on you. I respect your privacy. You can tell I do, because I would never have allowed your room to get this filthy."

She finished the windowsills and the top of my bookcase while I picked up the clothes and magazines and junk.

"All the glasses and cups go out in the kitchen," she said. We gathered up about five of them, plus a Coke bottle with a drowned fly inside. She showed one of the cups to me.

"Juicy Juice," I said.

"I haven't bought Juicy Juice in months," she said.

"I've been saving it," I said.

"Juicy Juice isn't green," she said.

"It is if you save it long enough," I said.

"Well, drink up," she said, "and I'll buy you some more.

"Move the bed for me," she said. "I think I can take it."

I moved the bed out from the wall.

"What's that!" she screamed.

"It's a sock," I said.

"Why is it covered with fur?"

"That's just dust," I said. "I'll get it."

"Here, poke it with the broom to make sure." She was laughing. I laughed, too, even though I was beginning to get embarrassed about my room.

"All right, no stopping now," she said.

She grabbed the broom and started sweeping out the corners, hard. She'd sweep a big ball of dust out into the middle of the room, and then we'd see a couple of the dust pieces keep right on going after the rest of the dust had stopped. They were spiders.

"Ma," I said. "You're heartless. Spiders got to live, too, you know."

She was really into it now, stabbing the broom into the corners, sweeping with power.

"Do you remember when we moved here?" she asked. "And the reason your father wouldn't let you have a dog? Because dogs are outside animals. It's the same with spiders and ants and whatever other little pets you keep in here. Now strip the bed."

"Oh, Mom, the bed's okay."

"Strip it!" she said. "Look at this." She pointed to the pile she had made. It was a pretty good size.

"Get a garbage bag," she said. "Or do you think we should get a permit to burn it all right here?"

"Oh, Ma," I said.

She started pulling things out of the pile: another sock, a pair of underpants, an eraser.

"Here's that nice belt your grandmother gave you last Christmas," she said. She was reaching right into the pile, not squeamish at all. I wouldn't have stuck my hand in there for anything, even if it was my own stuff.

"What's this?" she asked, holding up a little green thing between two fingers.

"Oh, boy," I said. "It's my old Kermit D. Frog. I lost him when I was about eleven."

"Eleven," she said. "That was when we were back in the old house. It must not be the same one."

"It is," I said. "It's still got the red marker from when Luke drew on it."

"Do you think it actually followed us here?" she asked.

"Stranger things have happened," I said.

"In this very room," she said. She picked up another hair-covered sock. "These things breed faster than you can kill them," she said. She thought that was funny.

"Listen," she said. "I know the proper pet for you, since you like animals so much. Do you know what a ferret is?"

"Yes," I said.

"I think a ferret would thrive here in your room, don't you?"

"No." Sometimes when she was having a good time, she tended to get a little like my father.

"Also," she continued, "if you are so interested in learning the facts of life, you can ask me or your father. We'll explain them to you. There's no need to set up your own barnyard."

She looked to see if she had shocked me. I didn't deign to reply.

Finally we were done. I have to admit the whole thing made quite an impression on me. It was a little like one of those shows "Life on the Forest Floor," where everything starts off quiet, and you don't see any life at all, just rocks and leaves, and then the more you look, the more alive the place becomes, until what you see is a whole miniature world full of creatures living, dying, mating, killing, raising their young, and so on. That was what my room had been like.

"Why, I was lucky to have found you still alive," my

mother said. She was still keeping it up. Then she said she was going to have a cup of coffee, and why didn't I sit with her in the kitchen and have some milk.

I knew what was coming, but there was nothing I could do about it. My mother was going to have a talk with me. When I was little we used to sit and have talks sometimes, about whether other kids swore or used dirty words and what I thought of that, or about how school was and what I was learning, or about if some of the kids didn't like a certain kid and how I thought we could make that kid feel better. But this one was going to be about me.

"When do marks come out?" my mother began when we were sitting at the table.

"Right after Thanksgiving," I said.

"Are you keeping up? I know football took a lot of time."

"Oh, sure. There's an awful lot of work this year, but it's okay. I like studying."

"Well, I know. And you do very well in school. But your father and I were a little disturbed at the way you've been talking about your teachers."

"They're all right," I said. "I don't have to love them to learn from them."

"No, of course not," my mother said. "That's a good thing to keep in mind. You may not always like them — in fact, sometimes you may get one who isn't a very good teacher, even — but you do have to remember that you still don't know everything yet, and that even a not very good teacher still has something to teach you."

"I do, Mom, of course. But sometimes I have my own ideas to express, too. I don't always have to agree with what the teachers say."

"You don't argue with them, though," my mother said.

"No," I said.

"You just complain at home," she said.

"Yeah."

"Because I don't see how you could argue in biology class, for example, where everything is factual. It's all very straightforward. Right?"

"True," I said.

"You can disagree with a teacher," she said, "but it's all in how you do it. Just like at home, you and your father can disagree about something. If you approach it in one way, it's a fight, but if you approach it in the right way, it can be a constructive discussion. Right?"

Here's what all this has been leading to, I thought — a discussion of Fart Face and why I can't get along with him. But I was wrong.

"Have you been under a lot of stress lately?" she asked.

"I don't know," I said. "What do you mean?"

"Well, more stress than usual. Is anything bothering you? Has anything happened?"

"Like what?" I asked. I had been resting my chin in my hand. Now I put my thumb up to my mouth and slid the thumbnail between my teeth. I felt it with my teeth, played with it, bit down gently without quite tearing it. I hadn't bitten my nails for over three months. They were big and juicy. It was like a pet dog that's got hold of a chicken. It's only playing, but if it shakes its head too hard or bites down a little too much, it will taste blood, and from then on it's a chicken killer. If I bit down too hard on my thumbnail, I'd ravage all of them.

"I don't know," my mother said. "This girl you're going out with, is she a nice girl?"

"No, Ma," I said, "she's a real slut."

"I don't mean that. I mean do you like her."

"I only went out with her once."

"Does she like you?"

153

"She thinks I'm wonderful," I said.

"Well, so do I," my mother said, "and I'm your mother."

We both relaxed a little. She hadn't said anything like "Your father and I are a little concerned about the hair growing on your palms" or "Your father wants to chain you up when the moon is full, but I said we should give you one more chance."

"By the way, how did your talk go in American History?" she asked. "That's the one you called a bonehead?"

"A bonghead," I said. "It's like a bonehead, but all cartilage. It's what happens to you when the doctor does knee surgery on your head. The presentation went pretty well."

I told my mother how the Cheyenne Indians had tried to stay out of the Indian Wars against the white people for years, but that they were attacked so often by soldiers who couldn't tell them apart from the Indians they were supposed to be fighting, or else who didn't care, that some of them decided that war was inevitable and joined with others, especially the Sioux, to fight. They called themselves the Dog Soldiers. That was the first thing that had attracted me to them, and a lot of my report was concerned with explaining the Indians' relationship to animals.

Now their names seem funny to us: Little Wolf, Spotted Wolf, White Weasel Bear, White Antelope, Walking Coyote. But the Indians didn't see some animals as good and some as bad, like we do — a rabbit is good and a weasel is bad, for example. They saw the cunning of the weasel as a good thing — especially for a weasel. The Indians took their animal names because they thought that a certain part of that animal's spirit was a key part of their own character and spirit. So that if a white man went around calling Indians "you stinking coyote" or "you lying weasel," that wouldn't make sense to the Indians, especially to the one whose name was Walking Coyote or White Weasel Bear.

The white man's attitude toward animals was different. Wherever they went, they killed all the animals they could; they thought the animals were thieves in the way people are thieves. They called all animals, no matter what kind, "varmints," which really comes from the word vermin and means parasite. They killed off the buffalo, as everybody knows, and they also tried to kill off all the wolves, the coyotes, the eagles, and hawks. They especially hated the predators, which of course is what they themselves were.

My mother listened with real interest, as had the class and the teacher. But then I started to get in trouble when I tried to explain the white man's racism and his wanting to exterminate all the Indians in relation to his attitude toward animals, like Colonel Chivington, the man who started the Cheyenne Wars when he said you should kill all Indians, including the children, because, he said, "nits make lice." The white men called the children of an Indian and a white person who had married, a "half-breed." A breed is what you have in dogs and horses, where a thoroughbred or a purebred is a good thing and a mongrel isn't. The Indians accepted white people who married into their tribe, and especially accepted the children. They didn't call them half-breeds.

"Wait a minute, now," Mr. Molitor, the history teacher, had said. "There is no question that the Indians were victims of a great injustice. The Indian Wars you are talking about are a truly black spot in our history. But it's equally possible to take the image of the Indian as Noble Savage too far. There are plenty of instances of Indians turning on white settlers — and half-breeds — who had lived peacefully among them for years."

"I disagree," I had said. "Time after time they were promised peace and then betrayed and massacred."

"Absolutely true," Mr. Molitor had said. "We're arguing two different questions. No one could say the Indians weren't betrayed. The war against the Indians was close to a campaign of genocide. There is nothing to be said in favor of the white society's conduct. It's your portrait of the Indian as Noble Savage that I take issue with. The Indian as living in perfect harmony with nature, somehow understanding the spirits of the animals, and so on. It's condescending — that's a kind of racism, too. The Indians were quite capable of brutality, too. It was they who started the practice of scalping people, you know."

"But that's a good example," I had said. "Some people — not the Indians, though, I know that — eat the hearts or livers of their enemies after they kill them, in order to gain their strength or their courage, especially if the enemy was brave or a good warrior. It shows respect for the enemy's spirit."

Here everybody in the class who had been listening went "Ugh."

"And with the Indians, scalping was like that. It was a token of your bravery, and maybe of your enemy's bravery. But for the white man it meant nothing. It was more savage for them to do it than for the Indians. What I'm saying is that for the Indians it was spiritual, but for the white man it was just bloody."

"And what I'm saying," Mr. Molitor had said, "is that the Indians' spirituality could be just as bloody as the white man's lack of it."

My mother agreed with Mr. Molitor.

"But you really think that the whole difference between the Indians and the white settlers was in their relationship to animals?"

"Well, to nature as a whole," I said, which is what I had said in class.

"Yes," Mr. Molitor had said again, "but what about the fact that, even though, as you say, the Indians had a more harmonic relationship with nature, that the average life span of an Indian was about thirty-five. Doesn't that say something for the white man's approach?"

"No," I had said. "Their life span went down when they came into contact with white people. In fact, white people tried to kill them off by giving them diseases on purpose. They used to give the Indians blankets with smallpox infections. This is just before the white man's medicine learned how to kill germs by using other germs, like in vaccines, but they used the same method on the Indians. They treated them like viruses or vermin — they vaccinated themselves against the Indians by using real diseases to kill them off."

My mother grimaced at that, just as Mr. Molitor had.

"So what was the result of your talk finally?" she asked. "Did you get a good mark?"

"I don't know the mark. He just said it was all very interesting, but some of it was beside the point and some of it was overly romanticizing to the Indians."

"So forget it," she said. "I thought it was very interesting. And you did your best. I'm sure the teacher knows that."

"Yeah, but did he do his best?" I said.

"That's where you're going to get yourself in trouble," my mother said. "Don't be like that."

When I went to wash up for supper later, I noticed that all my fingernails were bitten. All that work trying to grow them back and in ten minutes I had wiped out the whole crop. I had harvested them.

157

18

Karen and I had fun on our date. Jerry asked if I wanted him and his grandmother to double with us just for the company, but I declined. We went to the movies, where I could never quite decide whether to hold Karen's hand or not, just like movies themselves show kids not able to decide whether to hold hands when they go to the movies. It's funnier there, though. Then we walked around the mall for a while, then decided to walk the whole way back to her house. We almost got killed crossing the highway and ended up stuck on the median strip for about ten minutes before we dared to make our final dash to the other side.

Actually, it was pretty exciting. When a truck went by, the ground would shake, then there would be about a three-second pause, then a terrific gust of wind would hit us right in the face and push us backwards a few steps, almost knocking us over. It was dark, but very noisy, with the wind in our ears and then the extra noise like long sighs as each car passed. The sound was a little like whipping a long stick back and forth through the air in front of your face.

The headlights from the cars in the left lane were the only ones that touched us. We could watch the path of the light reaching out, then it struck us, then it was past. Some of those drivers must have seen us for just that instant, because the cars would swerve then swerve back into the lane. I'll bet they turned to each other afterwards and asked if we had been real.

When a bunch of cars had passed and there were no more coming, it would be suddenly dark and quiet, and the wind would stop. That kept happening behind us. The whole highway on the side we had already crossed would become peaceful for maybe half a minute, and we would step out into that left lane, as if we were on an abandoned road. About a mile back in that direction was a traffic light, which is probably what produced the emptiness. Then the light must have changed, because all three lanes would become full of accelerating cars. The cars coming the other way, though, where we still had to get across, kept on coming. You almost wanted to put your hand out into their path to see if the light would pass right through it. Later Karen said they looked to her like flaming arrows whizzing by, and that if you stepped out, you'd get one right in the heart.

Anyway, for the longest time we couldn't get across. We made a lot of false starts. We didn't know whether to hold hands here, either. The worst false start was when we thought we could make it right after this one car in the left lane had passed us and before a whole bunch in the other lanes had caught up. The driver of the first car must have glimpsed us in his headlights, because he suddenly slowed down. We almost stepped out right into him. We twisted our bodies and hung there on the curb as he brushed by us, like the pictures you see of bullfighters as the bull goes by. We stumbled out into the lane, then leapt back onto the median strip. Then the other cars roared by about a foot away.

After that I had a bad moment. All those lights seemed to lose their definition and become blurs. I wanted to just hurry across, away from all this light and noise. In fact, I felt I had to get across quickly, back to the safety of cover in the woods. I almost bolted. I would have ended up just another furry thing on the side of the road. Luckily I was still holding Karen's hand.

We did finally make it, of course.

"I thought they were going to have to call the fire department to rescue us, like when a cat gets stranded on the highway," Karen said after.

"Now I know what a raccoon feels like," I said.

"I felt more like a dog," she said. "You know how sometimes in the daytime you see a dog halfway across, and you don't know whether to try to stop or not? Like if you stop, maybe some other car will smash into you or else the dog will run out to you and get hit. But the dog knows what he's doing. He knows those things are cars, he's just not sure he can make it, just like we were. I'm not sure a raccoon knows what's going on, just all those lights. A raccoon probably doesn't think or feel anything about it."

"No," I said. "It has no idea what's happening to it."

We talked most of the way home about all the things that get squashed by cars. Raccoons, first. Squirrels. Skunks. Porcupines, mice, chipmunks, rabbits, snakes, frogs, toads, bugs of all kinds, the occasional bird, deer, moose, elks, opposums. In other places armadillos, lizards, probably even an elephant at least once. Each of us remembered trying to scrape up a flattened, dried-out toad we had found ironed onto the road. Dogs and cats, of course, who know what cars are but sometimes misjudge them, little kids who run out into the street, bicyclists and pedestrians, people fixing tires by the side of the road, people who get thrown out of their own cars when they get into an accident and then get run over by another car while they're lying on the street injured.

"They're like sharks," Karen said. "They attack anything that moves. Even each other. When one gets injured, or sick or old, the others turn on it."

Then we discussed porcupines and skunks, the only animals that have enough courage to stand up to them.

"I wonder if they don't win sometimes," Karen said. "You see a lot of dead skunks and porcupines on the side of the road, but you see a lot of dead cars, too, and sometimes they've been dragged way off in a field far from any road, with their bones picked clean."

"And bugs," she went on, "think of how many millions of insects they eat a year. So in some ways maybe they're beneficial after all."

"They're part of the ecology," I said. "But maybe they should have a hunting season, like for deer, to keep their numbers down."

We went on like that until we reached her house. She invited me inside, but everyone was asleep, and the place was so quiet and empty-seeming that even after we turned on a light, we kept whispering. I felt uncomfortable, so we just stood in the hall for a while, then she kissed me good night, and I walked home.

19

The day before Thanksgiving was only a half day at school. All I had in school was Health Science and gym. I couldn't participate in gym, so Coach Sisskind had me referee the gym class rugby game we played sometimes.

When we went into the Health Science classroom, a big note on the blackboard told us to read Chapter 9, "Individuation and Identity." Mr. Stahl was sitting at his desk, but he took no notice of us as we came in. He was busy, and he expected us to sit quietly and look busy,

too. We did, and except for a few whispers when somebody pointed out the assignment on the board to another
kid who hadn't seen it, it was quiet. Mr. Stahl looked
up whenever there was whispering, like somebody being
disturbed in the library.

According to the book, it was normal, at the age of
between sixteen and twenty, to have an identity crisis.
An identity crisis wasn't when you didn't know who you
were. That's amnesia, and even the book would have
said you were in trouble if you had that. An identity
crisis was when you weren't sure exactly *what* you were:
what kind of a person, that is. Whether you were kind
or not, or sincere or not, or intelligent, or happy, or
loving. It could go as far as making you wonder whether
you were really a boy or a girl or some of each. It was a
crisis that took place inside of you, and everything that
up until then had seemed natural: your relation to your
family, your religious beliefs, how your teachers treated
you and how you got along in school, what you felt about
girls or boys, even about your own body, like whether
you were tall or short or fat or skinny — suddenly you
weren't sure of anything. According to the book it could
be very severe. It sprang up from deep inside you, a kind
of anxiety about what *was* deep inside you. Wondering
about yourself, you could lose all sense of yourself, to the
point of wondering whether there was any self at all.
According to the book, it was normal to have these
feelings: the identity crisis was a particularly difficult
period, but it was still a normal part of growing up.

Of course, according to the book, everything was normal, as long as you ended up normal. In other words, as
long as everything was just a stage you were going through,
it was okay as long as you got over it. When you were
three years old, you had a separation anxiety, but you
got over it. The book said it was normal when you were

162

ten or eleven to have a crush on an older teacher: you got over it. It was normal to be confused about your sexual feelings: as you grew up, you would get over it. (I read that part over to make sure it was just the confusion you got over. I liked the feelings.) An identity crisis was normal, too. You would get over it.

Mr. Stahl was having his own identity crisis. He didn't know whether he was an X or an O. The Thanksgiving game was tomorrow. Win that and we were undisputed League Champions. It was certainly too late to add any plays now. I couldn't imagine what he was doing, but he had a whole sheaf of papers spread out on his desk, different alignments, different blocking assignments, what could they be? The game plan for tomorrow had to already be set. But there he was, making little marks, scratching them out, comparing one piece of paper with another. He stretched out in his chair and reached down into his pants pocket. He got a bunch of change and scattered it on the desk. He looked up at me in the second row.

"Got any pennies?" he whispered.

I stood by his desk for a minute after I gave them to him. I had never seen him quite so concentrated. He always looked handsome and tall and at ease, like a great quarterback, which is what he had been in college. Even on the field he didn't always act like an assistant coach. He acted as if he was only helping out, advising us, showing us a few moves, the way the pros do in their summer camps for kids. Up in the college ranks they don't make the coaches teach Health Science. From what you read, they don't even make the players take it.

Anyway, he took my pennies and his nickels and quarters and made two teams out of them. Then he began moving them around. He kept consulting one of the pieces of paper. Over his shoulder I could see what it

163

was: a summary of the 1967 Nebraska-Alabama game. He was replaying it with coins for football players. He looked up at me and said, "Nebraska should have won. They were beat by superior mobility in the trenches. Things haven't changed." With his head, he motioned me back to my seat.

So there was Coach Stahl, the handsome quarterback with the beautiful girlfriend who came sometimes when he chaperoned a school dance, sitting there replaying old football games with toy football players. He should have been wearing a Napoleon hat or a toy football helmet with a plume sticking out. Maybe in his basement he had a model football field, with stands and everything, and toy football players that were perfect replicas, and at night he went down there and replayed some of the great games from history. Maybe he won some that had been lost. Maybe from other games he was finding out a strategy for tomorrow's game. I don't know, though. He looked pretty foolish to me.

School was over at noon. Some of the kids who had biology on Wednesday morning were standing by my locker, which was near Mr. Fideles's room, all looking through a field guide to the birds, which one of them had brought to class because we were about to start studying birds.

They all thought birds with the word tit in their names were funny. They were reading the names of the wrentit, the tufted titmouse, and the plain titmouse and giggling. John Robbins reached one side of the group just as I reached the other.

"Lemme see that book," Robbins said. He got the book with the page still open to the tits.

"You think you're something, don't you?" he said.

"Trying to find tits on a bird." He looked through the book.

"Wait a minute," he said. "Wait just a minute. Looks like bird-watching ain't just for white folks. We black folks got some of our own birds. With tits, too, man."

He read from the book. "We got the bushtit. We got the black-eared bushtit. We even got the black-crested titmouse. We got you white folks all beat for titbirds, no contest."

He started leafing through the book. Everybody waited. "We got lots of other birds, too. See, you white folks think you the only ones that appreciate birds. You think all we got is the blackbird and the crow. Racism is ignorance, man. We got birds you never heard of, secret birds. We got the rufus-sided towhee. We got the rufus-crowned sparrow. We got the rufus-winged sparrow. We got all the rufus-birds."

He turned some more pages. Nobody spoke. "We also got the olivaceous flycatcher. Treemendjous bird. Catch any fly alive.

"And you think you got tits," he said. "We got the brown booby, man! You ain't got no brown boobies. You ain't allowed."

He turned some more pages. "Course you got the red-faced warbler. Hee, hee. And here's Lincoln's sparrow. He's the one thinks he freed all the little brown sparrows. You tell that to the cat next time he brings one home in his mouth. You also got your common loon. I see them every day. But the frigate bird here, a black man discovered that one for sure. The end of a hard day out in the fields naming birds for the white man, he just up and says, That's a frigate bird, man, I quits."

Robbins looked up from the book. "Ain't that right, brother?" he said to Bennie Williams. Bennie nodded back. There were about four black kids there and about six or seven white kids. The black kids said "Whooee" or "That's right" after each bird John named, and the white kids laughed their heads off. Nobody could enter into it, though, because nobody else had any good bird names. John had the book.

"Now then," he said. "The red-whiskered bulbul. That's a bird that lives in Miami."

Everybody laughed again.

"That's a real bird, man. I'm not making this stuff up. It's right here in the book. The red-whiskered bulbul. Habitat and range: Miami, Florida. You can look it up.

"You got your cuckoos, of course, they come in all races, but the goatsuckers . . . Man, you know *we* ain't got no goatsuckers at home. You can have Woody Woodpecker, too. We got the kingfisher, of course. He's kind of old, but we love him."

He flipped some more pages. "Now the slate-colored junco. That's a tragedy, man, a real tragedy. Only thing worse is the slate-colored wino . . . On the other hand, you whiteys got your loon, like I said, and along with that," John made his voice very upper-class and snooty, "you got your coot, your American widgeon, your marbled godwit, and your ruddy duck. That's a whole flock of right-winged prejudice birds right there. No wonder we got slate-colored winos. Them American widgeons are nasty! I forgot the bufflehead, he lives there, too. A poor black duck can't even go swimming. He ain't allowed in the club."

"What are you?" a voice asked.

"A black vulture," somebody else yelled. Robbins looked hurt.

"No, man. I'm no black vulture. I'm just a hummingbird. A little ruby-throated hummingbird."

There were a lot of hoots at that.

"See that?" Robbins said. "Listen to that squawking.

All you gallinaceous birds," he read from the book, "you just cluck away. I got to fly."

He gave the book back and started to walk away.

"You know what that is?" he called back to us. "Gallinaceous birds? That's turkeys, man. Turkeys!"

20

We lost the Thanksgiving game. I had to stand there while the cheerleaders cried in each other's arms, and Robbins sat on the bench alone for about half an hour with his helmet in his hands, and the stupid band played bravely on through their tears until the stands were empty. I was a little surprised I didn't care more, but I didn't.

It was just over, that's all. Everybody had tried their best, the other team had, too, it had been a good game, and we got beat. Now instead of league champions, we were league runners-up. It was cold and windy. Thanksgiving really meant the end of fall and the beginning of winter. That was really what they were crying about: the end of the football season, which marked the end of fall. The last game is always the big game because it's the last game. A good season is a little like a good harvest used to be — it carries you through the winter until baseball, which is what people do nowadays in the fields instead of plant, in the spring.

When I got home, my grandmother was already there, and the apartment was full of the smell of the turkey cooking. My grandmother was working in the kitchen, while my mother kept walking back and forth between the kitchen and the living room, where my father was sitting watching the Thanksgiving Day parade on TV. She kept giving my father looks, but he kept his eyes on the TV. Then she'd go back into the kitchen and try to elbow my grandmother out of the way of the stove.

My grandmother had brought two pies that she had baked ahead of time, and plates full of deviled eggs and nuts and other stuff to eat before dinner. But she still wanted to help out. She kept opening and closing cabinet doors and asking my mother where she kept this or that, and my mother kept saying, Let me get it, or I'll do that, you sit down, but she wouldn't.

Somehow, I don't know why, when you clean up the house for a holiday, especially for Thanksgiving or Christmas, it's always harder to move around in. Maybe it's because the furniture is all where it's supposed to be. When I sat down to watch the pregame show on TV, I found I wasn't facing the TV, I was looking directly at my father on the couch. When I turned my chair sideways, the way it usually was, so I could see, he said, "Don't mess up this room. Your mother worked hard to make it nice."

While we watched part of the game, I asked my father about Driver's Ed. I could take it after school — they even gave one credit for it — it wouldn't cost anything, and then I could get my license.

"Who's going to pay the extra insurance on the car?" my father said.

I said I guessed I would.

"Do you know how much that costs?" he asked. "Double. It costs double to insure a car for an under-twenty-five driver. Particularly a male one."

"I'd be a good driver," I said.

"That's not the point," he said. "The insurance com-

168

pany goes by statistics. And the statistics show that male drivers under twenty-five get in more accidents."

We watched the game for a while.

"I'll let you get your license," he said, "on one condition. That you pay for the extra insurance; that you also pay for all your gas and oil; and that you contribute to the upkeep of the car. I think that's fair, don't you?"

I said yes, but I didn't know how I could do it.

He smiled at me. "It means you might have to get a job," he said, "after school. Or on Saturdays. I wouldn't want it to cut into your schoolwork, but something that gave you a little spending money of your own, something you could say you earned yourself. I think it would do you good to work. Don't you?"

I did not. All my after-school time? All my Saturdays? My father had this antiquated notion of what jobs there were for kids after school. He seemed to think you went down to the corner grocery store and friendly old Mr. Hooper gave you a job sweeping up and waiting on Big Bird. The waiting list for baggers and stockers at the Stop and Shop was years long. If you wanted to be a bagger at the Stop and Shop, your parents should have signed you up at birth, like for Eton in England. At that, it didn't pay much, and it was a stupid job to boot.

Yet he would happily have had me do that. Or anything else, for that matter, that he could give the name Work to. He would have had me get a paper route and compete with all the ten-year-olds on bicycles.

My father really thought that every boy should work. Even if he didn't have to, he should work just to show that he knew how to, or that he was ambitious, or something. His father had worked. He worked. I should work. He was more like an ant than I had realized when I first called him one. A decapitated ant will survive — and keep on working — for twenty days. Enlarge that to hu-

169

man scale. Instead of the usual picture of a person-sized ant carrying an automobile on its back, you get people working their whole lives without their heads.

"Dinner's ready," my mother said.

"Five minutes more for the gravy," my grandmother yelled from the kitchen.

"I'll get Jessica," my mother said. "You find Luke."

"Luke!" I yelled from my chair.

"Get up and find him," my father said.

He was down the street with some other little kids. When I found him, he asked if he could eat over his friend's house. The friend was having ham, which Luke liked better than turkey.

My mother brought the turkey out on a big platter. My father was right behind her carrying the carving knife and a giant fork.

Jessica stared at the turkey.

"Looks good, huh?" my father said to everybody.

"It looks like a poor dead bird," Jessica said.

"It is," my father said.

"No, it isn't," Luke said. "It's a poor dead turkey."

My grandmother came in with the gravy.

"It's poor Tom Turkey," she said. She stopped and recited. "Poor Tom Turkey that never did nobody harm, just lived in the dooryard and ate and grew fat. Now we've killed him and cooked him, plucked him and stuffed him, then something and something, dadledee, dadledee, I forget." She put the gravy down on the table.

My father started cutting the meat.

"Which do you like, Jess," he asked, "white meat or dark? The leg or the breast?"

"Neither," she said. "I don't know how anybody can eat a poor bird that was alive and breathing and could feel the sun and rain and everything. A turkey is a living animal just like us."

"Look," my father said, pointing to the slices of meat. "It doesn't look like a bird now."

"Before it was cooked it did. You could feel the skin and everything. And its neck had a hole and no head."

"They chop the head off," I said. "That's how they kill them."

"They pluck it off," my grandmother said. "My mother used to just grab them with one hand and twist their necks with the other, then pull the head right off."

"Oh my God," Jessica said.

"I think that was only with chickens, though," my grandmother said. "Turkeys are quite strong."

Now Luke was looking at the turkey, too. One side was all sliced, and you could see into the empty cavity with a ring of white meat around where its insides had been. The other side my father hadn't started on. The leg was still sticking up in the air like a dead stump and the wing lay there, with the skin all brown and crisp, ready to be yanked apart.

"And you know what?" I said to Jessica. "After you cut their heads off, they still run around with no head for another minute, with the blood pouring out of their necks and their heads on the ground with their beaks still opening and closing . . ."

"Shut up," Jessica said.

"That's enough," my mother said.

"I suppose you know all about how animals feel," Jessica went on.

"Some," I said.

"I suppose you know what a turkey feels like when they chop its head off. I suppose you know what the turkey feels like when it gets eaten."

"I know what an animal feels like when it eats the turkey," I said and speared a piece of white meat with my fork.

"You jerk," Jessica said.

My father laughed. "No eating until we take a minute to say thanks."

"Thanks, Turkey," I said.

"You insensitive moron," Jessica said.

"How did we become so sensitive suddenly about turkeys?" my father asked Jessica.

"Ham comes from pigs and we eat that," Luke said.

"So what," said Jessica.

Everyone sat down and started passing the food around. There were about ten different kinds of vegetables. There was all kinds of stuff we never had except on Thanksgiving — turnips and cauliflower and cranberry sauce. Some of it, like turnips, none of us would eat, usually, but with gravy and everything, it tasted good on Thanksgiving. That didn't apply to Luke, of course, but he still had to get a spoonful of each thing on his plate, even if he didn't eat it, and he wasn't allowed to complain about it or claim that just the presence, say, of the turnips contaminated the rest of the food on his plate.

"Look at all those good vegetables," my grandmother said. Luke looked at them like Jessica had looked at the turkey.

"Lettuce turnip and pea," my father said.

Luke looked blank. "Get it?" my father asked him. "Lettuce turnip and pea."

"I don't see lettuce," Luke said.

"Never mind," my father said.

Jessica ate her turkey along with the rest of us. She poked at it a few times with her fork, but when it didn't move, she put it in her mouth. One time, just as she started to cut a piece, I went "gobble gobble," but she just gave me a disgusted look and finished her bite. After a while, she forgot her problem with eating turkeys, whatever it was.

172

She had a point, though. I felt it a little bit, too, even if I did make fun of her. It didn't bother me to eat meat, but I didn't really like to think about how it got there. How they lead the live cows up the ramp and then blast them in the head and start cutting them up in pieces with big chain saws, just hacking away while the blood's pouring out all over them and the big cow's head gets booted across the floor. That is, after they cut out its tongue. Which is itself as big as a person's hand. Think of being the guy in the meat factory whose job it is to take the severed cow's head and open its mouth and pull out the tongue and cut it off. Still warm. Then he throws the tongue in a barrel full of bleeding tongues. A cow's tongue really is as big and thick as your hand. Once Jerry's grandmother tried to feed me a tongue sandwich. I couldn't eat it. I couldn't even look as she sliced it.

Or else how they hang the pigs upside down and when they cut their throat the blood spurts out like a fountain, and then they slit right down the belly and all the intestines and organs and guts and stuff all pour out and drop into a big bucket. Think of being the one who has to carry the bucket around from pig to pig. Or the one who does the cutting and then yanks all the guts out and rips them away from the tissue that holds them in place inside the animal. And then they all fall on his head.

Still, roast beef and bacon are probably the two best-tasting foods in the world, as long as you don't think too much about how they got there.

We don't get to eat much bacon, though, because my mother is afraid of the nitrites in it and afraid my father gets too much cholesterol. We get a lot of chicken, though, and even though a chicken is not as large or sensitive or intelligent an animal as a cow or a pig, it's when you're eating chicken that you realize exactly what

173

you're eating. Ham and steak don't look like a pig or a cow.

But a chicken still looks like a chicken even on the plate. And when you eat it, you get to pull its wings off and rip each leg from its socket. You get to tear the meat from the rib cage and you get to look at the carcass when you're done. After supper, a pile of chicken carcasses all picked clean is really something to look at. When you scrape the plates to put in the garbage, the bones all knock together. Jerry's grandmother used to make chicken soup with the head and the claws still in it. Jerry said he used to find them in his bowl sometimes. He'd be stirring the soup and a chicken's claw would suddenly rise up to the surface and then sink down again.

So I knew what Jessica was talking about. Sometimes chicken made me feel squeamish, too, especially if I bit down on a little bone.

Even so, after saying grace and piling our plates full, we all stopped worrying about the turkey and ate it. At the end, we sat there with the remains of the turkey in the middle of the table like a family of lions lying around the carcass of an antelope they've just devoured. We were all sleepy and stuffed.

21

Suddenly it was Christmas, just like that. The weeks between Thanksgiving and Christmas hardly existed. The time seemed to drag, but then there were only three days left to go. Christmas was on a Friday, so we had half a day of school on Wednesday, then a week and a half of vacation. After they announced the special class schedule for the morning over the loudspeaker, Kurt Herter got on and gave the weather conditions for Santa Claus's flight. Then Mr. Feininger got on and told us that the holidays were a happy but dangerous time and that holiday tragedies occurred when high school students drank and drove. Also that kids often got new skates for Christmas and went out before the ice was safe and drowned. Then he wanted to wish a special Merry Christmas to the teachers, the secretarial staff, the librarians, the custodial staff who do such a fine job, the bus drivers who get us to school safely every day, the fire and police officials, and to us and our parents a happy and safe holiday season and he'd see us all next year. The PA switched off, and you could hear yelling and cheering from all the different homerooms throughout the building.

I had American History, French, and biology. In both History and French, we didn't have regular classes. Mr. Molitor told us about the different ways Christmas had been celebrated in America in the past. In colonial times it hadn't been celebrated at all. The Puritans, in fact, were against it. They considered it a pagan ritual, something that no God-fearing Christian should have anything to do with. Their idea of celebrating a holiday was that you fasted and prayed, then you stopped fasting and kept praying. Giving presents and singing Christmas carols seemed too frivolous to them.

In fact, Christmas wasn't really celebrated, except as a day you had to go to church, until the middle of the eighteen hundreds. By then, other groups had come to America, like the Germans and the Italians and the Irish, who did celebrate Christmas as a time for feasting and rejoicing. In New England, Christmas wasn't made a legal holiday until about 1850, I think he said, and there was a lot of opposition to making it one. He reminded us that Scrooge, in England, had been mad at having to give Bob Cratchit the day off. Mr. Molitor said that "humbug" really means fraud or fake, and that when Scrooge said, "Bah, humbug," he was saying Christmas was a fake holiday.

And it was ironical, he said, that the one day when all commerce is supposed to be put aside, which is what made Scrooge so angry, has become the day that is more commercial than any other day in the year.

He told us not to watch the 1938 version, with Reginald Owen, which wasn't that good, but that the one to watch was the one with somebody else I never heard of as Scrooge, made in 1951.

Madame Garnaud told us about Christmas in France. It seems that Christmas in France is a lot like a vocabulary lesson in the United States. *Neige* means snow. *Cadeaux* is presents. *Père Noel* is Father Christmas, who is the same as Santa Claus but not exactly. An *arbre de Noël* is a Christmas tree. You decorate the *arbre de Noël* with *jouets* and *friands*, which I think means meat, but I can't believe even the French would decorate their Christmas trees with meat, so I guess I don't know what it means. Also, *bougies* and *chandelles* play a big part in Christmas in France, though I don't know what part, not having any idea what they are. Yes, I do. One means candles and the other is spark plugs. Their Christmas trees must be very beautiful all decorated with meat and spark plugs.

But finally, Madame Garnaud wished us all *Joyeux Noël* and *bonne vacance*, and we were out of there, with Joshua Rudnik leading us in Grrodolf zee Grred-nossed Grreindeer as we left.

Christmas among the animals, though, in biology, was like any other day: eat, reproduce, adapt, reproduce some more, adapt some more, mutate a little, develop hollow bones, grow some feathers and become birds. Meanwhile, a hundred and forty million uncelebrated Christmases pass. Mr. Fideles was having none of this last-day-before-vacation crap. This was *biology*. I don't think anybody paid any attention at all. It was all about the structure of the wing. It had evolved, ever since Thanksgiving, from primitive reptilian forelegs into a thin, handlike structure held together by a webbed membrane, which the tree-climbing reptiles had spread to help them glide farther as they leapt from branch to branch. Meanwhile, their tail, which had been used as a rudder to help them steer, had shrunk, and was replaced by a tail made of feathers, which could control their flights much better. Feathers had grown over the wings, too, completely covering the claws. In fact, the feathers had formed out of the same material the claws had been made of, keratin.

The bones had become much lighter, the shoulder and chest muscles that connected the wings to the body much stronger, and what had been long glides became flight.

All this we already knew. What Mr. Fideles was interested in today was how they fly. Hollow bones, two-chambered heart, special air sacs in the lungs, oil glands to lubricate the feathers, fifteen minutes to go. Would they finally learn to fly, or would we get out of there first?

They never did. They were still contemplating all the advantages they would gain by flying — all the bugs they would eat, all the enemies they would escape, all the migrating they could do — when the bell rang. Mr. Fideles wished us a good holiday. School was over.

As Jerry and I walked out the door to go to our lockers, another kid in the class, Dan Welch, came up behind us.

"Do you believe in that stuff?" he asked us to our backs. We turned around.

"What?" we asked.

177

"Evolution," he said.

"What do you mean believe in it?" Jerry said. "What do you mean *believe* in it?"

"I mean it's just a theory," Welch said. "The theory of evolution. A theory is only one possible explanation for something."

"Evolution is the explanation of how we got here," I said.

"Not necessarily," he said. "Have you ever seen evolution? Have you ever seen anything 'evolve'?"

"Come on," I said.

"Come off it," Jerry said.

"No, seriously," Welch said. "A theory is a kind of story, right? It's made up to explain things you don't understand. Like when you were a little kid, you didn't understand TV, so you probably made up a theory that there were little people inside the TV set."

"What do you mean there aren't little people in there?" I said.

"You know what?" Jerry said. "When I was a little kid, I thought the bad guys really were dead when they got killed. I thought they took real bad guys, like murderers, who were going to be killed anyway, like electrocuted, and told them they could die on TV if they wanted, if they would play the bad guys and let themselves get shot."

"That's a good theory," I said.

"That's what I mean," Dan Welch said. "Evolution's just like that. It's a story made up to explain how we got here. But it doesn't really explain it at all."

"It explains how *I* got here," Jerry said. "But how did *you* get here?"

"God made me. God created us all," Welch said.

"That's another one I believed when I was little," Jerry said.

"It's not true, that's all," said Welch. "It seems logical, but it's not. If evolution is true, why aren't we birds? Explain that to me."

"Birds?" Jerry and I both said. "Why would we be birds?"

"Well, birds would be the highest form of life, right? They can fly. We can't. If we really evolved from lower animals, how come we can't fly?"

Jerry looked at me.

"I don't know," he said. "How come we can't fly?" he asked me.

"Speak for yourself," I said.

"Listen," I said. "Who says flying is the highest form of life?"

"Of physical life," Welch corrected. "It just is. Or would be. It's obvious."

"Well then, why can't birds talk?" I said, "and don't say parrot because that's not really talking. Or think? Or build houses or cities? Or write books or invent computers or grow their own food or make clothes? How come there isn't a great bird civilization?"

"Exactly," he said. "That's what I'm trying to say." He pointed at a pamphlet he had clipped to his notebook, then started to read from it.

"Behold the fowls of the air; for they sow not, neither do they reap, nor gather into barns; yet your heavenly Father feedeth them. Are ye not much better than they?"

"What's that?" Jerry asked.

"It's from the Gospel."

"Uh-oh," said Jerry. "This is where I came in."

"Do you know the Gospel, Raynor?"

"It's not exactly required reading at temple," Jerry said.

"Oh, that's right," Welch said, "you're Jewish, aren't you?"

"A Christ-killer all the way," Jerry said. "Now there's

a guy who thought birds were the highest form of life. Jesus, I mean, didn't he say his father was one?"

"It's easy to mock," said Welch.

"It certainly is," Jerry said.

"Well, I know that both of you are very attracted to science," Dan Welch said. "It is very appealing. It's just that it doesn't have all the answers we're looking for."

"But you do," Jerry said.

"No, I probably don't," Welch said, "but I have faith. I feel sorry for you. I really do."

"What!" Jerry yelled. "Sorry! You feel sorry for me! You little twerp. You cretin. You turd. You air lock."

Welch turned red in the face, but he just shook his head. "I don't mean for just you, Raynor. I mean for all people who don't know Christ. Not just Jews. Paul, too, if he's not a Christian. But listen. Don't you feel left out on Christmas?"

"Hah," Jerry said.

"Not presents. That's not important. I mean when the whole world is full of His spirit, and the feeling of peace and rejoicing because you know your Savior is come, and that you will be redeemed. Don't you wish you could be a part of that?"

"Nope," Jerry said. "Anyway, I am a part of it. Jews celebrate Christmas, too, you know, but in our own way."

"Really?" Welch said. "How?"

"We go out and kill all the male children we can find under two years old. It's much better than a stupid Christmas tree."

"I don't believe you said that," Welch said.

"Yeah, well I can't fly, so I guess I'm not the highest form of life," Jerry said.

There was a long silence as they looked at each other.

"Listen," Jerry said. He flapped his arms. "I gotta fly."

180

He started flapping down the corridor. "Here I am," he was saying, "made in God's image, flying . . ."

I caught up with him.

"Don't leave me here with him," I said. "I don't know why we're not birds, either."

I was about to go with Jerry when Karen suddenly appeared at my locker.

"I didn't know whether I'd see you before Christmas," she said, "so I thought I'd give you this now."

It was a Christmas present, a little box all wrapped up with a ribbon around it.

"Oh, boy," I said, "it's just what I've always wanted."

"You don't know what it is yet," she said.

"Yes I do," I said. "It's a box all wrapped up with a ribbon around it." That was pretty weak, but I was a little embarrassed. I hadn't even thought about Christmas presents yet — not only not for her, but not for my mother or sister, or my mother and father or anybody. Actually, I had thought about getting Karen a present, but I hadn't known whether I should or not. I hadn't gone shopping or anything.

"Thanks," I said. "I haven't gotten yours yet."

"That's okay," she said. "You don't have to get me anything. This is just a little thing I saw and thought you'd like."

"Well, thanks," I said.

I did my shopping on Christmas Eve. I didn't have any idea of what I wanted to get for presents. I thought I'd just go to the mall and look through the stores until I saw something I liked. Because of the traffic, my mother dropped me off at the turnaround about a mile from the mall and left me to walk the rest of the way.

The cars were backed up on the highway all the way to the turnaround, trying to get into the mall, so that as I walked along the side of the road, the same cars would come up beside me and get a little ahead, then I'd walk up ahead of them, then they'd crawl by me again. The same people kept staring out the window at me, especially the little kids in the back seats.

The parking lot was gigantic. You walked and walked. My feet were freezing, too. They don't plow next to the highway, so I had to slog through all the slush from the cars and climb up and down across the snowbanks left by the plows. The mall looked like a distant city you were trying to reach.

In the parking lot just outside one of the mall entrances, they had Santa's reindeer in a big pen. They had them every year, but each year I was surprised at how little they were. Even the biggest males, antlers and all, only came up to your chest. They had some young ones, too, with just nubs for antlers, with still a little bit of fur covering them. The little kids would put their hands through the fence, and the reindeer would touch them with their noses.

Inside was like I had thought it would be. There were about five million people, all packed in against each other, all with their coats and hats and winter boots on, all moving around in and out of stores, getting backed up around the entrances, squeezing through each other, everybody loaded down, and every once in a while some poor man with a giant box, with a stereo or something in it, trying to carry it out over his head and whacking into people who weren't looking up.

I like Christmas shopping. Everybody gets mad when they get whacked by the box, but only for a second, then they all smile and try to help the guy get through. Actually, they're happy he bought a stereo for somebody, and they hope they can buy something nice, too. Everybody always says how frantic people get at Christmas, but they always smile and say sorry or excuse me or I'll never do this again, or something, so you know they enjoy it. I wouldn't want to be a cashier, though. By the time they get to the checkout, some people really have lost their Christmas spirit.

There were Christmas lights strung up all around the fountain, so that the water cascaded down in all different colors, and all the big windows in the shops were sprayed with frost. On one side of the fountain was the North Pole, where little kids could get their picture taken with Santa, and on the other side was a new Buick that you could win in the Lions Club raffle. People, mostly old ladies, were sitting on the stone benches looking at the manger and trying to hear the Christmas music while thousands of people hurried by in all directions. Some of the people sitting looked pretty numbed out.

All along the arcade part of the mall were little booths with people selling candles or silver jewelry or T-shirts or wooden signs engraved with your name. I thought Luke might like one of those to put up on his wall. I saw one with LUKE on it, but decided to keep it in reserve in case I couldn't find anything else. There was a T-shirt that said Best Chest in the West I could get for Jessica. She'd hate me forever if I did that. She was just getting little ones. I could picture her opening it Christmas morning, turning red, crying. She'd never forgive me. Neither would my father or mother.

Jessica was hard to get something for. My mother suggested clothes. The year before, I hadn't been able to think of anything, so I put five dollars in a card and put that under the tree. My father had a fit and said I was thoughtless and lazy and selfish and didn't know the meaning of Christmas spirit. Niggling, he called me. Then Jessica didn't know what to do. She tried to give it back. The next day my mother took her shopping, and they bought a Trapper-Keeper notebook, a perfectly nice present I hadn't even thought of. But they brought it back and showed it to my father and me, and said, Thanks, this is what we bought with the money you gave me. I think my mother felt bad for me. I know I did.

I must have walked through each store ten times. I almost bought a monogrammed pin for Karen, but then it seemed kind of tacky, so I put it back. Finally, after a long time, by a sort of sedimental accression, which is the way swamps turn into dry land, I had my presents. I kept what had adhered to me. I had a combination salt and pepper shaker that you turned upside down for my grandmother, some special soap and talcum powder for my mother, a wallet for my father (my mother had told me he needed one), a sweater for Jessica, and a magnet for Luke. For Karen, I had finally bought a cashmere scarf.

It was night when I left the mall. I had gotten there just before lunchtime. When I walked through the doors and got hit by the cold and the dark and the silence, it suddenly struck me that I had been in there for about six hours, just walking and walking. I was starving. By the time I fnally got home, supper had been over for an hour. Luke was bouncing off the walls and Jessica was barely managing not to.

They both came into my room and helped me wrap my presents, except for the ones to them. When I got to the scarf for Karen, they both looked at it as if it was some strange thing they had never seen before, like there was some sort of light coming from it, a glow or something.

"It's beautiful," Jessica said. She and Luke both touched it.

Then they had to get silly about it. Jessica put it on and started walking around the room with her arms out and her eyes closed and her mouth open, saying, Oh, thank you, darling, it's what I've always wanted, and for some reason Luke thought that was a signal for him to start jumping up and down on my bed, so I had to snatch it away and kick them out of my room.

Before bed, we all had to hang up our stockings next to the tree. Luke and Jessica both wanted one of my skating socks because they were the biggest, so they got those, and I put up one that had a hole in it for a joke.

Everybody got good stuff. Luke got an incredible amount of junk — a remote-control car that only went left unless you kicked it, special crayons that you baked the picture you made with them afterwards, a radio-operated inflatable robot that walked all around the house. Jessica got skates and clothes, and a new backpack, and I got a lot of clothes, mostly. My mother said I was the hardest to buy for. I also got some other stuff — shin pads and a new hockey stick, and a beautiful book with pictures on the endangered species of North America.

"Check and see," my father said, "you're probably in it."

Karen's present, when I opened it, turned out to be a real fisherman's knit wool cap, black. It was a real tight knit, not the fluffy kind. It made my head itch a little, but it looked tough. I needed one, too.

My father made pancakes for Christmas breakfast, and we all tried on our stuff and waded around in the wrapping paper for the rest of the morning.

In the afternoon I walked over to Karen's to give her her present. I should have called first, but I wanted to get out, anyway. She wasn't there. Only her brother from college was there, so I left it with him.

"Who shall I say it's from?" he asked.

"Just tell her Paul came by," I said.

"Paul who?" he asked.

"She'll know," I said.

"I'll put it in with all the other ones that were left," he said when he took the present. "It's awful little, isn't it?" He shook the box. "Anything in here?

"Okay, I'll tell her," he said. "Nick came by and left this teeny present. Right, Nick?" He closed the door.

What a winner. I'd hate to be his younger sister.

When I passed Ken's house on the way home, I noticed him up on his front porch sleeping. I decided to stare at him until he woke up. You can wake a dog up just by staring at it. Soon enough he began to get restless. He moved around a couple of times, then opened his eyes. When he discovered me staring at him, he tensed up and didn't move at all. Then he saw it was me and got up and came down the stairs with his head down and his tail wagging, but curled under him.

"What's wrong?" he asked.

"Nothing," I said. I put out my hand to rub his ear, but he cringed a little before he relaxed enough to let me do it.

"You were staring at me," he said.

"I just wanted to see if you would wake up," I said.

He shook himself out and lifted his paws up, one at a time, putting each one back down after giving it a little shake. He looked at the woods behind the Mullholland's house.

"You were staring at me," he said. "Of course I woke up."

"What do you mean?" I asked.

"You were just fooling around, I guess, but if I stare, I'm about to attack. That's what staring means. I couldn't stare at you just in play. Not for long, anyway. It would make me too tense. I'd have to bark or something to break the tension, or else I might attack in spite of myself."

"I know," I said, "I've read about that." I had to admit, though I didn't say anything to Ken, that I had felt the tension in me growing as I stared at him.

"Sorry," I said.

In the Mowgli book I had read to Luke, no animal could withstand Mowgli's stare. They all had to turn away. It was that as much as his ability to use fire, or the other human things, that set him apart from the other animals and made him the lord of the jungle. No other animal could stare, unless it was about to kill, or willing to die.

I had also read, earlier that day in fact, in my new book about endangered species, more about the way predators stare before attacking their prey. About how their whole body becomes still while their eyes focus with more and more concentration, and how their whole body seems to reach out to the prey through the eyes, until it is as if they were connected to it by an invisible string. Maybe one muscle in the tail twitches, but otherwise they are completely still. When they attack, and when the prey tries to escape, each move the prey makes pulls them closer. Sometimes, as I had tried to explain in English class a long time ago, they attack so perfectly along the sight line that they don't seem to move at all — just strike, like lightning. That is especially the way it is with birds of prey.

I knew that much about staring, but a few days later I learned a lot more.

22

One day during vacation, Jerry, Karen, and I were all at my house sitting around the kitchen table. My mother had left us stuff to make lunch and had gone somewhere with Luke. I don't know where Jessica was. We were just sitting and talking, and listening, though we didn't want to, to the Garveys. The Garveys didn't live in our building, but our kitchen looked down right onto their back porch. There were three kids and a mother and father, and all they did was scream at each other. The mother was constantly screaming at the oldest one, Michelle, who was Jessica's age, who was constantly screaming at Brandy, who was eight, who was constantly screaming at Shane, who was three. When the father came home he screamed at the mother. They didn't have a dog, which was too bad for Shane, but lucky for the dog. They did have a cat, but it's useless to scream at a cat, so Shane would corner it and whack it with his toy truck.

It was like the cartoon you see about the food chain, where the little fish is about to get eaten by a bigger fish, which is itself about to get eaten by a bigger fish, which is itself about to get eaten by a huge fish, except here all the fish had their mouths open just to holler. Then all the fish turn around and do it in the other direction, the littlest one screaming at the next littlest, that one hollering at the next bigger one, and so on. Sometimes they would choose hollerees at random.

The thing they screamed most at each other was "Shut up!" but none of them ever did.

It didn't actually go on all the time, or at least we couldn't always hear it, but once it did start, or once you started to hear it, there was no way to shut it out.

I really couldn't take it. Summer was the worst because the windows would be open, and also, they would sit outside on their porch and scream back and forth with whoever was inside.

One time I saw them put Shane outside just like people put out a dog when the dog doesn't want to go. Michelle just opened the door and gave him a shove with her foot, then started to close the door, but before it was shut Shane was halfway back in. She closed it on him, anyway. He was howling already, so you couldn't tell if it hurt or not, but it didn't matter. She pinned him with the door, then put her knee against him and shoved him out. He resisted, but she was twelve and he was three — his feet just slid across the threshold and back outside and she got the door shut with him still pushing against it.

He stood there quiet for a minute, then started howling again. The door was shut and nobody was going to open it, and Shane just squatted against it howling and howling. After a while, Shane stopped howling and began walking around the porch just poking here and there through the junk. Evidently, once he could tell he wasn't getting back in, he forgot about it. He investigated different stuff here and there, went down the steps and back up again, investigated some more, then settled himself at last in front of the door. He had picked up something, I don't know what, and sort of gnawed on it while he crouched up against the door right where anybody who came out would trip over him. It was winter, too, and cold. It was just like a dog, that's all.

This time their back door was wide open, even though

it was winter now, too. After about ten minutes of humongous screaming, there was a break. I was embarrassed having Karen, who had never been to my house before, have to hear this. It wasn't like it was my own family, but it was still pretty bad to have to put up with.

Then we heard, "Here's your lunch, Shane," clear as day, not mad, just in a loud voice. Then, a minute later, "Shane, eat your lunch." Still not real screaming, but enough to interrupt our conversation. Then, as we started to talk again, "SHANE, EAT YOUR FUCKING LUNCH!"

The three of us looked at each other.

"Holy shit," Jerry said. "We better eat our lunch."

"Every day," I said. "I can't stand it. I can't stand it."

I really couldn't. It felt like I couldn't breathe. I stared out the window at their door. I started pacing back and forth in front of the window, my eyes fixed on the door. I was breathing in little gasps. The blood was beating in my head. Then I saw a movement as one of them came up to the door from inside and slammed it.

Then it was quiet. They were in there, though. I could feel them in there. I could feel their movements, their scurrying around, their gnawing on their food behind that wall. I took off out of the apartment, down the stairs, leapt up onto their porch, and burst open that door. They were all there in their little burrow blinking at the sudden light and at me — the weasel who had ripped open the tunnel to expose the little nest of terrified field mice.

I stared at them. The mother was standing near the stove, the three kids were clustered together deeper in the hall, and the father was sitting at the kitchen table with his hand on a can of beer, his mouth open about to yell at someone. I hadn't heard him all morning. I

190

didn't know he was even there. It didn't matter. He made a noise in his throat. I just stared.

This was the stare before the attack. Here the predator gauges the prey's distance, its possible escape routes, and its state of alertness, and by staring, fixes all these into one picture as his concentration tightens. Growling and yelling are threatening gestures, as much defensive as offensive. Staring is not a threat. It is not a gesture of any kind. It is the coiling of the spring whose release is the attack. Staring at them, I could feel that the slightest movement would trigger me. I'd race through their little den snapping the necks of each one of them.

But until they moved, neither could I. They stayed absolutely still, the father panting a little. I don't think I breathed at all. Finally, the feeling began to ebb away. The back of my neck still tingled, but I dropped my eyes. As soon as I had done that, it was gone. I left quickly, not knowing whether still as an animal or in human form, and crossed the yard back to the apartment building.

"What happened?" Karen asked.

"What'd you do?" asked Jerry.

"I asked them to stop making so much noise," I said.

Karen looked at me. "What got into you before you left?" she asked. "Something happened to you. I never saw anybody move around like that."

"I don't know," I said. "I had had enough, that's all."

"You didn't threaten those people or anything, did you? You could get in a lot of trouble for that."

"I didn't do anything. I don't know what I did. I didn't touch them. I just made them shut up."

From the window we could see Shane standing in the middle of the doorway looking out. He wasn't making any noise. After about a minute, someone pulled him back inside from the still-open door and closed it very softly. Karen seemed relieved when she saw them. Jerry gave me a strange look.

"Well, let's eat lunch," Karen said.

"Eat your fucking lunch," Jerry said as he put my plate down on the table, and backed away from me, whether kidding or not I couldn't tell.

I was starving. I was so hungry I couldn't talk. I just bent my head down close to my plate and gobbled the food off it. Then I felt better.

Later on, Jerry drove off, and I walked Karen home.

"Do you lose your temper like that very often?" she asked me.

"No, never," I said. "I don't know what got into me." I did want to try to explain what had happened, but I had no idea how. I didn't want her to think I was crazy.

"I hope not," she said. "That wasn't pleasant to see. I didn't enjoy being part of that at all."

We walked along silently. Just those few words, and the way she said them, put her so far away from me that I couldn't speak. I was afraid of what was coming next. What if she was going to tell me she liked me a lot, but only as a friend, but that she wasn't really attracted to me? What if what I had done gave her the creeps, even if she didn't put it that way? I walked on, numb, unable to stop it from happening.

"I didn't mean to hurt your feelings," she said after some time, "but I had to tell you. When you like someone you have to tell them. Because someone with a temper like that, that just snaps suddenly and is out of control, is someone you can't trust. And I want to trust you because I really like you. I mean I really like you."

We stopped walking. We were looking at each other, and she seemed to be about to say something, but she kept hesitating.

"Really," she said. "Do you know what I want to say?"

192

She put her arms around me and we stood still and hugged each other for a long time. My face was pressed tight against hers. My heart was beating so hard, I'm not exaggerating, my coat only muffled the sound. If we had been in an airport, they would have thought I was a terrorist with a bomb. We walked all the way to her house with our arms around each other, and that's hard to do.

Karen had told me she loved me.

When I got home, I expected to be in trouble because of what I did to the Garveys. I wasn't sure, though. If they had seen the thing I thought I was, they wouldn't do anything. They couldn't. They would have no idea what to do, except maybe call the SPCA or the zoo or something. When nothing happened that whole night, even after my father got home, I began to wonder.

That night when I went to sleep, I discovered I could fly. Karen and I were birds, flying high over the land, soaring on the updrafts, drifting above the peak of mountain after mountain, then dropping low into the valleys to skim the treetops. We flew together, then apart, then together again.

Nothing is as perfect as when you dream you're flying, but the moment always comes when you feel yourself starting to fall, or stumble in the air. Sometimes you wake up suddenly, but sometimes the sensations seem to sort of evaporate slowly — you put a foot down to the ground, push yourself back into the air for a second, and you glide, but can't quite get off the ground again. There is a moment while you are waking up when you can feel you are losing your power, when you know you are waking up, and you stretch to keep it, but your very effort to hold on to it makes you wake up. I lay there still feeling the little bits of that dream. The effort to keep dreaming makes you wake up. The effort to keep flying makes you fall. Perhaps it is the effort that destroys the ability to do it. If you could just keep from trying, maybe you really could fly.

I knew better, though. Birds don't fly by not trying. They fly by flapping their wings real hard. Still, the difference between jumping and flying can get pretty tenuous. Among animals, there are many who almost fly. Flying squirrels, for example — they just miss actual flight. Flying fish — all they do is leap out of the water, but so far that couldn't that almost be called flying? There's also a kind of a desert mouse, the jerboa, that has two huge hind legs and can jump more than twenty times its own length. It moves not so much by jumping as by skimming across the ground like a skipped stone. It has whiskers as long as its body, which brush along the ground as it goes, telling it the contours of the ground it is passing over and what kind of surface it is going to touch down on when it lands. It can even change course in the air by using its tail as a rudder.

I know this isn't quite flying, but lying there thinking about it, how do you distinguish between what is flying and what is just taking great leaps and coming back down? If you could leap up and just not come back down, maybe you wouldn't exactly be flying, but it would still be a lot better than putting one foot in front of the other and plodding along like that forever.

I had certainly taken a few what they call "flying leaps," that's for sure. Turning into a rat. Feeling like a rhinoceros. Getting confused by the headlights and wanting to run for the woods. Turning into a dog with Madame Garnaud. Talking to a dog. I didn't like to think about that too much. The other things were momentary, almost like flashes, things that happened and went away, but talking to Ken was a real thing, it wasn't like a flash that was soon over. We stopped and talked together, then said good-bye and went our own way. It took place, there was no question in my mind. We talked out loud, Ken didn't just stand there while I made the whole thing up in my head.

But somehow to fly without trying. Not exactly to fly. That was for dreaming and daydreaming about, like pitching a no-hitter and hitting a grand slam in the same game, or beating up seven punks who had attacked your girlfriend. But the other, the turning into animals — it seemed in a way like a gift. Like some people are born able to play chess or do math or sing or understand physics. They are gifted in some special way that allows them to see the world and understand the way it works differently from the way the rest of us can.

I couldn't do any of those things. I wasn't gifted. But maybe this was like that. Or maybe it could be. Everything, even something you are gifted with, has to be developed. Even Einstein had to study and Mozart had to practice. Maybe I could practice my gift, too.

23

January was awful cold. Seasonably cold tomorrow, the weatherman would say one night, unseasonably cold tomorrow, he'd say the next. Bitter cold he'd say the third.

Every night he showed us the satellite pictures of this huge high pressure area of intense cold being pushed down from Canada by this second huge mass of arctic air, while behind that still a third huge polar air mass was forming and getting ready to push southward, although it was still too early to tell whether it would veer off to the north on account of this little tiny warm air system way down in the Gulf of Mexico where it's 85 degrees and raining.

"Maybe it's warmer on the other station," I would say, but my mother liked that channel's news, so I couldn't switch it.

It just got colder and colder. All those waves of arctic air masses was like in history, with the barbarian invasions. First you get invaded by the Visigoths, who rape and plunder and pillage, and you think, This is terrible, but then, just when you start getting used to being slaughtered by Visigoths, the Huns arrive, and they're worse, and they beat on you for a while, and hack you up and trample you with their horses, and when they're finally through with you, you look up and here come the Mongols.

The first two days back to school Jerry picked me up, but the third morning he called.

"You'll have to make it on your own," he said, "the car's dead."

Halfway to school I met Jerry coming from the other direction. His eyes were all watery and his nose was bright red. There was a bright red spot on each of his cheeks. He kept taking one hand and then the other out of his pockets and blowing on them.

"I'm going to kill my grandmother," he said. "Whoever heard of washing gloves?"

We walked along into the wind. In fact, even when we turned a corner, we were walking into the wind. According to the weatherman, the windchill factor was minus twenty.

"Then she hangs them outside to dry," Jerry said. "They look like Attack of the Severed Hands."

196

"How do animals make it in the cold?" I asked. "Even dogs. I passed a dog this morning, it was just sitting there on the porch like nothing. You know?"

"They have fur," Jerry said. "And fat. They don't have exposed parts like we do."

"Mine fell off a ways back," I said.

"Or they hibernate. Like my car."

"But there must be some way we could learn from them," I said. "They really do adapt better than we do. There must be some way to take what they've learned about staying warm and apply it to ourselves. Don't you think?"

"Sure," he said. "Wear them."

"Besides that."

"You know what you do in the arctic when you're getting frostbite out on the tundra and you're going to freeze to death?"

I didn't.

"You kill one of your sled dogs and slit open his belly and put your hands and feet in. Warms them right up."

"Nice," I said. "I'll have to tell that to Ken."

"Ken who?"

"A dog that lives near me."

"Yeah, tell him," Jerry said. "I'm sure he'll appreciate it."

Later on in the cafeteria I spotted Jerry eating lunch with Andy Espada and Eugene Franklin, a big, fat kid who took computer science with Andy. It was right after biology, and since biology was in the west wing of the school and the cafeteria was in the north wing, I had gone outside and walked around the wings to avoid the crowd in the corridor. In the one minute I was outside, my fingers lost all feeling. As soon as I got back in, my nose started running. Somehow Jerry, who hadn't wanted to take the shortcut outside with me, had beaten me to the cafeteria and had already been through the lunch line and was sitting down. He must have run the whole way.

In biology that day, we had started mammals.

"Well," Mr. Fideles had begun, "we're almost to primates."

"Some of us are already there," Jerry had said.

"I said primate, not primitive," Mr. Fideles had said. He had looked very pleased after saying that.

After I got my lunch and sat down with them, we talked about how cold it was.

"You're insulated," Jerry said to Eugene, "but us ectomorphs really suffer."

"How do Eskimos survive?" I asked.

"They don't always do as well as people think," Andy said. "I just read something about them that was sort of unbelievable. Do you want to hear the story?"

Andy was a nice kid, but his stories tended to be pretty boring. He liked puns a lot, and jokes about chemistry.

"I've got one for you, Andy," Jerry said. "In what way are Captain Kirk and toilet paper the same?"

Andy thought for a minute and shook his head.

"They both keep the Klingons off Uranus," Jerry said.

Andy laughed and blushed at the same time. That was the kind of joke he liked, even though it was a little risqué for him. Eugene laughed like a hyena, and I laughed pretty hard, too.

"But anyway," Andy said, "my brother is an anthropologist, and among his books are some on Eskimos. I was reading in one book about a small village of Eskimos who had a famine one winter. There were four or five families, all related, and they were starving to death."

"Not freezing," Jerry said.

"No, but wait. One day all the people went out to the ice to hunt seals. They left one of their babies with one of the older men. While they were gone, the old man, who was starving, ate the baby."

"You could dig that, couldn't you, Eugene?" Jerry asked, but Eugene just said, "Oh, God" and waited for Andy to continue.

"But when the other Eskimos returned, they didn't do anything to him. The way they live, everybody depends on everybody else. And the old man continued to live in the village as if nothing had happened. But the people didn't forget. They waited a whole year. The next winter they went out on the ice, seal hunting again. They were a few miles from their igloos. The old man who had eaten the baby was with them this time. It was minus fifty degrees out. All of a sudden, they all turned on him — they had never even mentioned the baby incident since it happened — and they stripped him naked. So you know what happened?"

"So he froze to death."

"No," Andy said. "He began running naked across the ice, calling for his wife. He ran in the minus fifty degree temperature all the way back to his igloo, but when he bent over to crawl through the door, his spine snapped. It had frozen straight while he ran. He lay paralyzed and quivering at the entrance to his igloo and *then* he froze to death."

Eugene pushed his lunch tray away and sat there.

"Nice story," Jerry said. "Congratulations."

Andy beamed back at Jerry. Then he tried to tell us about enzymatic changes in the chemical makeup of fat molecules that allow certain animals to adapt to the cold. Caribou, for example, can stand all day in the snow because they have different kinds of fat in their legs. One kind located at the foot end has a lower freezing temperature than normal body fat, so the fat remains pliable even buried in the snow. He had read that in one of the appendixes in the biology book, where the print is so small it looks like grains of sand, and where they don't even try to make sense for the student. This was interesting until Andy started diagramming fat molecules on the table, but it couldn't beat having your spine freeze solid and snap in half when you bent over.

24

January can be pretty exciting with the cold and snow, but by the middle of February you've had enough. Supposedly the days are growing longer again, but except for the fact that February seems to last forever, you can't tell. There are fifty-three seconds more light every day as the earth tilts back toward the north, according to Andy Espada. But school goes on, winter goes on, you feel like an old experimental rat they keep putting in the same maze over and over. By now you've got it memorized, the cheese at the end sucks anyway, but you've got nothing else to do so you keep going through it all over again, day after day.

When report cards came out, my father read mine over, then came into my room with it.

"I signed your report card," he said. "It's pretty good in general. Math is going well, I see."

"I like math," I said. "It's easy."

"Effort and attitude are a little low," he went on. "Two in effort," he read, "another two in effort, a three in attitude."

One was highest, five lowest.

"What's a three in attitude for?"

"I don't know," I said. "My attitude's okay."

"It's not like it is at home, is it?" he asked.

Nice way to put it. No, Dad, it isn't that bad. How could it be? Or else, Yes, Dad, it is. I'm just as bad in school, just as sullen, as discourteous, as impolite, as unhelpful, and as ungrateful. The teachers are just as nice as you are, Dad, and that's why I was lucky enough to even get a three.

"I'm trying," I said to him.

"You certainly are," he said. He said it again as he left the room. He always got extra flavor out of his remarks by chewing them twice.

After my father left, I went into the kitchen and called Karen. Being on the phone with Karen was like having two heavy breathers call each other up. Most nights I would wait until fairly late, when I thought people would have stopped coming in and out of the kitchen, to call her. Sometimes she would call me earlier than that. We would talk for a minute about English class or something that happened in school, and then just sit on the phone, sometimes for a long time, without saying anything. Being the last family on earth with only one phone made it impossible to have any privacy. If my mother came in, she would wave her hand at me and say, just mouthing the words "One minute" and slip back out of the kitchen with whatever she had come to get. My father would come in sometimes and just stare at me for a while. I would say Uh-huh into the phone even if Karen hadn't been saying anything, just to keep active until my father left. He'd always make some gesture, like nodding or shaking his head for no apparent reason, then turn on his heel and walk out.

He never wanted to use the phone himself, he just wanted me off it. It was funny, though, that for him, nodding his head and shaking it meant the same thing.

For most animals, including people, they mean the opposite. Most animals don't nod, except for birds, but almost all animals have a gesture where they shake their heads. Dogs do it — in fact Ken started shaking his head from side to side after I stared at him. Gorillas in the wild do it. For both it means the same thing: no, I don't want any trouble. It is the opposite of staring, and happens not when confronted by a predator, but when faced with another aggressive animal, usually of your own kind. People's "no" probably comes from the same thing. You shake your head with your eyes averted to show you mean no harm, and say no. You're supposed to be able to do that in the wild, too, to show an animal you've surprised that you mean no harm. You lower your eyes and shake your head back and forth slowly. On the "National Geographic Special" they did that to show the gorillas they were friendly.

But my father still hadn't gotten it right. And he had lived in contact with humans all his life. Ever since he was found by my grandparents in the woods behind their house, as a baby — a baby what, who knows — and raised by them as a human child. He grew up thinking he was one of the family. But as he grew to maturity the old traits began to reappear. Dropping back down to run on all fours. The restless prowling at night. Now the irritability at being confined in the apartment. It was time, I thought, to tell him the truth and to let him go. We should drive way out in the country, all of us, and turn him loose. He'd lope off into the woods, free again to roam with his own kind — the Great Ants. All sixes he'd run off on. We'd miss him, too, but he'd be better off. A full-grown wild ant is not a good pet.

Karen and I had this signal whenever he came into the kitchen when we were on the phone. I would mention the name of some animal and she would know he was there.

It was hard to hang up once we had been on the phone for a while. We would say what we had to say about school and wait. Sometimes Karen would tell me something else that had happened, like she told me about her friend Roberta, who went to put conditioner on her hair in the shower and grabbed a bottle of calamine lotion instead. She couldn't understand why her hair didn't squeak to show how clean it was, until she looked at her hands. I didn't like it when Karen started talking to me as if I was just anybody she was chatting with. I was never sure exactly what I wanted her to say, especially on the phone where I couldn't say anything, but stuff like that wasn't it. I never wanted to be the one to hang up first, but I didn't want her to hang up first, either. Sometimes I would say my father was waiting for a call. I never said my father told me to get off. He never actually did. He would come in and point at the phone with one of his semihuman gestures, and I would say, "Yes, Dad, that's a phone," and then I would have to get off fast because he would start walking toward me.

I liked the idea of my father as a stray, or an orphaned wild animal that my grandparents had taken in and raised. In this book I had about great zoos of the world, it said that whenever animals live together with people in conditions of intimacy, like a dog and its master, or a tiger and its trainer, the difference between the species tends to disappear — the trainer is regarded by the tigers as another tiger, the dog owner as a dog, and the dog as a fellow human. So my father considered us as fellow whatevers, and we thought of him as a fellow human being.

I liked it even better, though, when I reversed the idea and thought of myself that way. A sort of reverse

Mowgli, or a reverse Wild Child — a wolf foundling raised by humans and accepted by humans as one of them. Able to live in cities and towns, able to get his food in grocery stores and restaurants as well as any human, able to communicate in their language, knowing the Law of the Humans, but really all that time a wolf — a wild creature of the jungle.

25

On Sundays the Fine Arts Museum was free, so one Sunday Karen and I went there. I didn't know whether Karen knew more about art than I did, but it wouldn't have been hard, so I figured she was in charge. I figured she could lead me around to the different pictures and point out certain highlights, and I would stand back and be appreciative, and nod my head occasionally, like a visitor from another city knowledgeably comparing these pictures to those he's seen in other museums, for example the one in Paris.

It's hard not to laugh, though, looking at some paintings. Especially when you really don't know what's going on. I mean like the ones that look like the guy hung up the dropcloth and cleaned up with the painting. I started saying stuff like that and stuff like "too bad it got rained on," but Karen started to get annoyed, so I went back to appreciating them for a while.

Picasso is a great painter, though. Even if you had never seen a certain painting before, you would know it was by him. The museum had a whole room just of Picassos. I had been there plenty of times before, but when you visit a museum, sometimes you remember the feeling of the room rather than the paintings in it. This time, with Karen, I tried to really look at them.

"It really is a different way of seeing things," Karen said.

"For them, too," I said, pointing at the people in the painting. "You'd see differently if both your eyes were on the same side of your nose."

She gave me a look. I was playing the rube and hoping to say something smart. So far, no go.

"Flounders are like that," I said. "Flounders have both eyes on the same side of their face. They start off normal, but then one eye actually moves over next to the other one."

"So?" she said. It's hard to stop once you've started to annoy someone. I kept it up even though I, too, was beginning to wish I would stop.

Not only that, but in the very next room, in a nineteenth-century French painting, was a picture of a flounder on a plate. It was very realistic, especially the scales.

"See?" I said. "That's a flounder."

She didn't answer. When we passed another modern painting and I said "He had hiccups of the eyeballs when he painted this," she said "You have hiccups of the brain."

I did want to stop being like that, in fact, I wanted it to be like I had thought it would be, walking around, holding hands, looking at the paintings, being in love. But her being angry at me seemed to make me keep it up. She would say something about a painting and I would go, "Yes, exactly, the composition of the faces," repeating whatever she had said.

"Now you've got echolalia," she said.

"Echolalia?" I said.

"It's when all you can do is repeat what somebody else says."

"You repeat what somebody else says?"

"Not everything. Just the last few words."

"The last few words?"

"That's right."

"Right."

"Okay," she said. "That's enough."

"Enough," I said.

"Enough!" she said.

"Now you've got it," I said.

Things were not going well.

We walked through a couple of rooms with mostly furniture in them without looking or saying anything. When we came to the Greek statues, it felt like a great relief. The statues were of people, with an occasional animal thrown in. Their bodies and their heads, especially their necks, were perfect. Both the women and the men — you could look at them forever and keep saying to yourself, This is what a man really is like, or This is what a woman really is. Looking at a statue of the goddess of love, for instance, the way her back curved in and then back out, and the way her shoulders and neck were shaped, and the marble or whatever as smooth as skin — it didn't exactly make you excited, but in some way it did. I felt a kind of longing and wonder mixed together looking at it.

I don't know why all I could think of to say was, "If you put all these things together, you could make a statue that had all its parts. You know, like Mr. Potato Head."

Karen walked away to look at the statues alone. I followed her around the room one statue behind, and when she let me catch up with her, I said, "They really are beautiful. They show you how beautiful the human body really is."

"Both male and female," Karen said.

"Yes," I said.

"But you know," she said, "some of the beauty we see in them comes from the purity of their whiteness, the simplicity of just the perfect form made into a statue. I wonder what we would think of them if we saw them the way they were originally. You know originally they were all colored."

"No," I said. "That was the Egyptians. The Greeks were white people."

Then I had to walk behind her again. She didn't seem as much mad as unhappy. It wasn't the Greeks that were colored, it was the statues that were painted. Why I continued to act like that was beyond me.

We went to the museum café to have coffee.

"What's the matter?" Karen asked me.

"What do you mean?" I asked.

"The way you're acting," she said.

"Nothing," I said.

We went to see some more paintings, but without either one of us saying much. Karen tried to make up by talking about the paintings again, but now my feelings were hurt. I guess I sulked. Finally she stopped and turned to me.

"You know I could be here with Nino," she said. "He asked me out again."

What a mean thing to say.

If you were a rabbit and had just managed to knock out a fox with your carrot, you would not want to let him get up again. That's the way I felt about Nino. I wanted to make things better fast. I thought of just apologizing. That's hard to do, though. I thought of a lot more witty things to say about the paintings to try and bring back our mood, but none of them seemed right. My mind was racing toward Karen, but without any idea of what to do when it reached her.

Sometimes, though, it's possible to say something so

dumb, so overwhelmingly stupid, that it sort of cancels out everything that has gone on before. You can't do it on purpose, that way it always comes out calculated and off the mark. But it can rise up in you, something you didn't even know was in there, maybe from when you were a baby and believed stuff like no one could see you when you covered your face with your hands, or when you were just barely a little kid and came across some garbage that maggots had gotten into and thought you had found live spaghetti. That had happened to me. I don't know when I stopped believing spaghetti could be alive. I think it was gradual.

We were in front of a painting by a Flemish artist.

"Where's Flemland?" I asked. "A lot of really good artists came from there."

I didn't mean it as a joke, either. I was as serious as a little kid who has everything all wrong. Karen looked at me, then explained, then when I blushed at having been so ignorant, laughed and put her arm in mine.

In the painting, there were two people standing, a man and a woman, in a room with a big table and a cupboard full of china dishes. It was a portrait of these two people. To the side of them, though, and behind them, through the window of their house, you could see hills and a river, and far off in the distance, the sea. The more you looked, the more different scenes you noticed — little tiny ships sailing far away on the ocean, and way in the distance, in the back corner of the painting, not important at all, a whole war was going on, with microscopic cannons and smoke, and bodies all over the place, and a dog eating a corpse, but they're all so tiny, they don't seem important at all compared to the giant faces in the front of the picture.

Karen pointed all that out to me. She said, "Look. This is what we think we are — the people in the center of the picture. But what if this was our life — our life and death — just in the background of someone else's portrait?"

"You would have been mad if I said that," I said.

"No," she said. "I didn't know what you were doing. You seemed to be mocking me or something. Have I been acting like a jerk in the museum or something? Like a snob?"

I told her not at all.

"That's what I thought must be it," she said. "That you didn't like me and were just making fun of the whole idea of coming here."

"No," I said. "I just got in a bad mood for some reason."

Then we walked around the rest of the museum saying anything we wanted about the paintings and it was all right. Karen had a lot of interesting things to say, and believe I did, too. In fact, we started talking about everything, not just paintings.

We looked at a lot of medieval paintings of the Baby Jesus and his mother. They looked like she was feeding him from some place out of her neck, that's where her breast grew.

"That's not the way I'm built," Karen said. She said it sort of shyly, but she did say it.

"I'm glad," I said. I hadn't been worried, but on the other hand, I certainly didn't know yet.

After all the religious pictures, we talked about God for a while. Neither one of us really believed in God, but we didn't want to say it too loud in case He was listening. We agreed that all you could do was live the best life you could. We hoped He agreed, too.

"But what if you died," I said, "and you got there, and God sent you to hell anyway, for something you couldn't even remember. Like God says, 'All your life you killed ants. For no reason. You just squashed them. Why?' And none of your other sins mattered."

"I can't relate to that," Karen said. "If that's what's going to happen, it doesn't make any difference what you do.

"Sometimes I wonder if we're not just little white mice in God's laboratory," she added, "and all the things we do are just part of some experiment He's doing. We could be just rats in God's maze."

"That's just what I've been feeling about my life lately."

It seemed more than a coincidence that we had both thought of the same way of putting things.

Waiting for the train home, I told her about the dream I had had about people with animals for heads. It was in school. All the kids were like usual, except that for heads they had different animals on top of their bodies. It wasn't animal heads instead of human heads — it was the whole animal, feet and tail and all, like a pig or a duck on top of a person's neck. Sometimes the person would bend over and his animal head would start walking and the rest of his body would sail along behind.

She wanted to know who had what kind of animal for a head, like whether Tommy Hanes had a rhinoceros for a head, or Andy Espada had an appropriate head, but I couldn't remember. They didn't seem inappropriate, that's all.

Then on the train, sitting close together, I told her my secret. The telling didn't come out very well. The words made it seem more like a dream or a wish. I was trying not to exaggerate it. It didn't happen often and it didn't last long. But trying to describe it made it seem like less than it was. She really did want to know about it and understand it, and kept asking me questions when I gave up explaining, but the questions didn't really help, either. She kept asking if I really believed it or did I just feel in some way the way an animal would feel.

"No, it really happens," I said.

"A lot?"

"No, not a lot. Very rarely, in fact."

"But do you really believe you change into an animal?"

"Enough to act *exactly* like one."

"Yeah, but do you believe it now, when you're not?"

"That's when I'm not sure. But yes, I believe it."

"Is it like a spell or being high or something? Like a seizure? It sounds a little like a seizure."

"Not like any of those things. Not like a trance, either. Things don't slow down or speed up or anything. My perception changes, and I change."

"Do you hear voices?" she asked.

"I can hear yours," I said.

Telling her about the times it had happened when she was with me helped. She had noticed the change all three times, but hadn't been able to put what she'd seen into words. I don't know how much she actually believed me, but she did believe me. I mean she believed I was serious and really believed it myself, but she was skeptical about whether it really happened.

I hadn't planned to tell her about it, and afterwards I wondered why I did. If she had taken it differently, she could have thought I was just loony, or else making up stuff to be overly dramatic to impress her. But even though she kept looking skeptical and amused, I felt good about telling her. It made me feel less timid about my animals, and somehow more receptive to them. It was as if my telling somebody else that the animals existed was their way of telling me that it was okay that they did.

26

The day Jerry got thrown out of biology, we were learning about the various systems that are common to all mammals. The circulatory system, the respiratory system, the lymphatic system, the reproductive system, and the nervous system. Each of them has variations according to the different species, but they are essentially the same throughout all mammaldom.

The first fly of spring was buzzing around the room. I was watching it, thinking of the different reactions various animals would have to it. A horse would flick its tail at it if it came too close. A dog would ignore it, then snap at it, then ignore it again. A cat would catch it and look at it. When it landed on my desk, I watched it work its feet around the way they do. I reached out and it flew away. Then it came back and landed on the exact same spot as before. I swiped at it and it took off again. I had to open my hand to make sure I hadn't gotten it.

If I were a frog, my reaction would have been instantaneous. I wouldn't have tried to catch it. It would have appeared, my tongue would have flicked out, and the fly would have been eaten. I hadn't done anything out of the ordinary like that since I had told Karen, though. It was like when you've got a sore throat and you go to show the doctor that you can't even swallow, and as soon as you get there, you can swallow just fine.

Trying to turn into an animal when I wanted to hadn't worked. When we had our physical fitness tests in gym, I decided to try to be a chimpanzee and do a hundred pull-ups, but I didn't feel like a chimpanzee after the fifth chin-up. I did fourteen, but probably lost at least one by running up to the bar and swinging on it before I started. Another time, while we were still having the cold spell, I curled up outside by the wall of the school in the sun and tried to let my rete mirabile keep my internal body temperature high while my extremities got as cold as they liked. In animals that are adapted to the cold, the rete mirabile is a network of arteries and veins located where the main body and the extremities connect. They are connected in such a way that the outgoing blood, which is warm from the body, heats the blood coming in from the foot or the flipper or whatever, while the incoming blood that is now very cold, cools the outgoing blood. That way, the blood can feed the extremities without draining the body's heat and the extremities can stay cold, but still continue to function. Sea gulls have a rete mirabile for their feet, and seals have one for their flippers. They can stay for days in freezing water without freezing.

Evidently, I didn't have one. Where the sun had been shining on the brick wall felt warm on my back, but the rest of me, especially my ass in the snow, was freezing. Then this girl from my homeroom came by and asked if I was on drugs, so I had to get up and look where I had been sitting and say, No, are you sure you left them here? and that was the end of that.

Of course I only did those things in a halfhearted manner. I didn't really expect them to work. To tell you the truth, I was just fooling around when I did them. Still, none of the real times had happened again for so long that I began to wonder if they had happened at all. It even occurred to me that the whole thing was just stuff I had picked up from biology. Maybe learning that stuff had suggested things to me. That would be kind of disappointing, but at least it would explain things.

Except for Ken. Ken met me on the way home from school one day and asked me if I wanted to rob his house.

"I won't even bark if I see you sneaking around the place. Take anything you want."

"Ken!" I said. I was really shocked.

"Never mind," he said. "I take it back. I'd bark."

"But you know," he continued, "they've started to feed me that dry stuff. It's bad. A dog needs meat."

But now I started to think myself into a frog. Then I thought, Wait a minute. I don't want to eat a fly. I just want to play with it . . . the way a cat might play with it. As the fly kept circling, I watched it closer and closer, then flicked out my hand and picked it out of the air. I let it go. Flies are great things to play with. They react, that is, they dodge whatever is coming after them, but they don't learn. They keep coming back. I picked it out of the air and let it go again.

People with quick reflexes can sometimes catch a fly, especially if it has landed, by scooping their hand through its path of movement. But this wasn't like that. I was concentrating on catching the fly, but I wasn't chasing it, either with my eyes or with my hand. I was passive — I was letting the fly trigger my reflexes. What a game. I did it again and again, not once rough enough to hurt the fly.

Jerry had been watching the whole time, he told me afterwards, and he couldn't believe it. He said I had him totally hypnotized. Finally, he couldn't take it anymore.

"Either eat it or don't," he said.

"Raynor," Mr. Fideles said, "did you say something?"

"No," Jerry said. "Did you?"

"Aw, Jerry," I said. I had lost my concentration, and the fly, when Jerry spoke, so I heard Mr. Fideles say what he said, and was aware of biology class again before Jerry was.

"Out," Mr. Fideles said. He raised his finger and pointed to the door. Jerry looked at his finger, the way a dog looks at your finger when you try to point something out to it. Mr. Fideles kept his hand pointed at the door, and Jerry kept looking at his finger for a clue as to what Mr. Fideles meant. He still wasn't sure when he left exactly what he had done wrong.

When class was over, Jerry was waiting for me.

"What the hell did you just do in there?" he asked. "It was just like a cat. You were playing just like a cat for a minute. I thought you *were* a cat, for Christsake."

I was still shaking off being a cat.

"I was," I said.

"I believe it," he said. "Now I've got to talk Mr. Fidoodoo into letting me back in. I was watching you with the fly so much I didn't even hear him. Now I have to tell him I was dreaming you were a cat."

He turned to go into Mr. Fideles's room.

"You weren't," I said. "I was."

I know he heard me. He didn't have time to talk about it anymore, though. He had to get to Mr. Fideles quick. The thing about Jerry was that he couldn't apologize if he thought about it too long. And he would have to do it right, because Mr. Fideles had been waiting all year for his chance to throw Jerry out, so if he didn't get himself right back in, Mr. Fideles would make it permanent and he'd flunk biology. Even if he was the best student in the class.

I was pretty pleased about the fly, though. It had been easy.

27 One of the extracurricular activities you could participate in at school was the Community Farm. It was an old farm, I guess, that somebody had given to the school instead of selling the land for houses. There was a big barn, a couple of big open fields, some pens and small buildings for different animals, and a long solar greenhouse attached to the barn. They had chickens and ducks, geese, sheep, a couple cows, some pigs, and a lot of cats. They had turkeys you could reserve while they were still alive for Thanksgiving. In the spring they plowed up one of the fields and let people divide it up into little vegetable gardens.

The whole place was run by high school kids, almost all of them from the trades division. Kids from building trades had built the solar greenhouse and fixed the barn and the other buildings. Other kids took care of the animals and worked in the greenhouse. They grew vegetables in the greenhouse and later in their big garden outside. In the spring, you could buy seeds and plants from them, and in the summer they had a stand where they sold the vegetables they had grown.

It was pretty near Luke's school, so he went on field trips there all the time. He had already been there about six times just in kindergarten and first grade. At first, he thought it was neat, but now he thought it was just okay.

I had never been there until I had Luke take me there one day after I picked him up at school and he told me about their field trip that day. I knew about it, of course.

It was always one of the things you could sign up for. You could even get credit for it if it fitted in with your classes. But it's funny how those things work. I didn't know anybody who did it, either for extracurricular or regular credit. The kids who did, I guess, were all from trades. The honors division, which I was in, was the highest, of course, but there were still things you could miss out on that might be fun, or educational, that the other divisions had. I would never have thought of participating in the farm myself, but seeing it with Luke, I felt like it might be nice working with the animals or growing things in the greenhouse. When we lived in the house, my mother planted flowers, but we had never had a garden. And I always hated mowing the lawn. But growing up on a real farm might be different. Then you'd know things that other people didn't, you'd know real things about how things lived and how they grow.

Anyway, by now Jerry had his car going again and wanted me to come with him to the Community Farm to pick up a trunkload of manure for his grandmother.

"I'm not eating over your house anymore," I said.

"Didn't you come with me last year?" he asked. "When we had the two plastic bags full of manure and took the bus home?"

"It wasn't me," I said.

"Who was it?" he said. "It must have been you. The bottom of one of the bags was ripped and we left a big pile of it on the seat. It was right next to the window in the sun and it started steaming."

"It wasn't me," I said again.

"The bags weighed a ton and we ended up dragging them up the aisle of the bus. That's how the one ripped. And how they didn't smell at first because the whole place smelled, but when we got them on the bus they really stank? Don't you remember that?"

"I would if I had been there. But I wasn't."

"You were," he said.

"Jerry," I said. "I have never lugged a garbage bag full of shit anyplace in my life. I'm sure I would remember if I had."

"You know who it was?" he said. "It was Dennis Holden, that's who it was. Why'd you keep saying it was you when you knew it wasn't?"

"Why couldn't your father drive over and get it on Saturday?"

"Because," Jerry said.

"Weren't you embarrassed?" I asked.

"Are you kidding?" he said. "But she kept bugging me for it, so I just did it. You want to feel humiliated, by the way, try carrying a bag of cowshit onto a city bus some time. I'm glad I had Dennis with me, though."

We were in the greenhouse looking for somebody to give us permission to take the manure when I saw a strange sign on the wall. It said:

PLANTING AND TRAINING OF DWARFS
1. Expose graft
2. Cut off head of leader
3. Pull down side branches

"Jerry," I said. "Look at this. What do you think this is about?"

"Oh, my God," he said. "It's communists. Expose graft. That's always the first step. Cut off head of leader. That must be the president! It must be a plot to take over the country with dwarfs. Already you see them everywhere. You ever wonder about that? They're in the grocery store, on TV — I'll bet about half of the teachers are dwarfs, too. They're taking over. Pull down side branches. That's

218

the Congress. Or maybe our institutions of local government."

We were very serious and kept looking around to make sure nobody heard us.

"Look over here." He was pointing to another sign on the wall, this one with a lot of writing on it. It said Eradication of Pests.

"Don't laugh," he said. I couldn't help it. "That could be us.

"Paul, I think you've stumbled on something very important. We've got to tell somebody. Maybe the Pentagon."

Just then one of the kids who worked there came toward us.

"Act normal," Jerry said. "Pretend nothing's wrong."

As we walked along, Jerry pointed out the kids working. They were kneeling behind the beds of plants.

"See?" he'd say. "Another one. They're all two feet high. See that one?" he asked when a kid carrying a tray of plants went by. "See his shoes? Fake! He's walking on stilts with fake shoes."

The kid stumbled on the stairs on his way out, then crossed the yard, trying to keep his tray from spilling.

"Did you see him trip?" Jerry asked. "He can't walk right yet. Still in training. One slipup like that outside and the whole plot would be exposed. You can bet he'll be punished by the head dwarf tonight."

At first we were doing it on purpose and not laughing at all. But soon we couldn't stop ourselves. Suddenly everything about the place seemed to have to do with communist dwarfs. We couldn't stop laughing.

"What's the matter with good old American-size fruit trees?" he asked. "They can't reach them, that's what. So they're going to bring us all down to their level, which is three feet high."

When the kid showed us where to get the manure, Jerry asked him how big the cows were that produced it. The kid didn't understand, of course, and couldn't figure out whether Jerry was making fun of him or what. He couldn't see what was funny. They had a little tractor, and Jerry pointed that out to me. It went on and on, we just couldn't stop. Every time we saw anything small, like the pig's house, or the hoe with the cutoff handle for working in the greenhouse, we'd start again. We were laughing so much I felt sick.

When we were done with the manure, we leaned against Jerry's car and rested. For me it was over. But Jerry would stand there, then start giggling again, then catch his breath. He wanted it to keep going. He walked away from the car toward something he had spotted in the field. It was about waist-high with little drawers in it.

"See," he called back to me, "a bureau for a dwarf." He reached out and pulled one of the drawers open.

It was a bee's house. Jerry took off like a madman, waving his arms and running straight for me. I could hear the noise of the bees. A bee went by my head. I made a big snort through my nose and bolted. I galloped across the field to where some trees were and stood under them.

The bees hadn't chased me. I looked back and there was Jerry in the car with the windows rolled up. He waved at me to come back. When I got there, there were a few bees buzzing around the car. I jumped in and slammed the door quickly.

"Did they get you?" I asked.

"Look," he said. There were about five welts on the side of his face, just below his ear. His face was all swollen.

"You're all right till the first one gets you. Then they all zero in on the same spot. Fucking pheromones."

He started the car and we took off.

"You got out of there pretty good, though," he said on the way home. "When I finally spotted you from the car, I thought you were a horse out there. Then I saw it was you. How'd you get all the way over there?"

"I was a horse," I said. "That's how I got there."

"What?" he said.

"What do you mean 'what'?" I said.

"I mean what do you mean you were a horse? What kind of a horse?"

"Brown, I think. Was I brown?"

Jerry thought it was a joke, of course.

"Jerry, listen," I said. "This isn't the first time." And I told him about it.

"You don't have to believe me," I said.

"That's a load off," he said. "I'd be screwed if I had to believe you."

After a long pause, he asked, "Can you do this whenever you want?"

"Not yet," I said. "I'm working on it, though."

So now two people knew.

28

Track season had started, and Jerry had a good chance to run the 400 meters. Baseball practice had started, too, but I didn't go out. I didn't know why. It had always been my best sport. But I still wasn't a sure thing to make it, and somehow it seemed too hard. Jerry was surprised, and my father was surprised. They both tried to talk me back into going out. I didn't though. My father in particular couldn't understand it, and we ended up having a fight about it.

After school Karen and I would go to the library and do our homework, and sometimes she would skip the bus and we'd walk all the way to her house and then I'd walk all the way home.

On a nice day when you walked out of school all the kids would be out on the grass or over under the trees on the other side of the gym field, in couples with their arms around each other or holding hands, or just standing together in the middle of the field, looking like horses do in a field, the way they put their necks across each other and sleep standing up.

Karen was with me when I chased the squirrel up the tree. We had been standing under this tree across the field from school, and this one squirrel kept squawking at us from a branch over our heads. I guess he thought it was his tree. I started squawking back at him and we had a pretty good argument going. It was just noise, but Karen was laughing.

Then the squirrel started dropping stuff on us — little twigs, bark off the tree. I gave him a warning bark, but he kept it up. So up we went in a spiral around the tree as fast as we could. I chased him out to the end of a high branch, which started wobbling under our weight, but he jumped back to the next lowest branch, beneath me. He reached the ground first and zipped over to the next tree and went up that one. I was out of breath when I hit the ground. The squirrel was looking at me from behind the trunk he was clinging to. He was ready for more.

"You show-off," Karen said. "What if you fell and broke your neck from one of those tiny branches?"

"Almost never happens," I said. I could feel the big grin on my face, but I couldn't get it off.

"There are no branches for the first ten feet," she said, looking at the tree.

"I know it," I said.

"You went right up the trunk."

"I know," I said. "And back down again."

"No," she said. "You jumped back down." She shook her head. "My goodness," she said. She looked right into my eyes. "Oh my goodness."

I think that's when she realized that something was really up.

29

It was getting easier and easier. I still couldn't just lie back and think of what I wanted to be and then be it, but more and more, I could feel it coming on inside me and then be somewhat prepared for what was going to happen. I couldn't cause it, but I could let it happen. Actually, I had never tried to stop it. So I couldn't either cause it or prevent it, but still, it was me doing it, it was me seeing the relationships hidden beneath the surface, me feeling the inner parts of me responding, me relaxing into myself and waiting for the right combination of elements to transform me. What confidence I had.

One day Karen and I were out behind the school sitting with our backs against a tree. We were just looking up through the branches at the sky. The buds were just beginning to open up into little leaves.

A big hawk glided right above the tree and across the field. Its wings were absolutely still and its tail was spread in a fan. It circled the field without once flapping its wings and wheeled back to pass overhead again. It was snow-white underneath, with a little bit of red across its chest and a reddish tail. We both saw it and held our breath. It circled higher and higher, never moving its wings except ever so slightly to adjust its balance on the wind. It didn't fly — it let the wind carry it up and up, higher and higher into the sky, until it was just a dot, a possible wisp of cloud, nothing at all. From up there, somewhere, it was searching for a mouse.

Seeing things clearly. That's what it's all about. Concentrating, balancing, seeing. What did the hawk see from up there? Light and shadow? Sudden movement? Just the right size and shape? Or did it see everything, all the trees and lakes and houses and schools, all the people, the animals, the cars, all the stuff that we're in the middle of, did it see the pattern more clearly? So high up and able to spot a mouse. Did it ever get distracted by everything it saw? Spread your wings and you fly right up into the sky. Close them and you drop like God into the middle of all the little living things.

"Why so pensive?" Karen said suddenly.

"What?" I said.

"Why so pensive?"

"What?" I said.

"What are you thinking about?" she yelled.

"Watching the hawk," I said. "You weren't saying anything, either."

"No," she said, "but is everything all right? You seem a little off your feed today. Oops. Is it all right to say things like that? I didn't hurt your feelings, did I?"

"No, of course not," I said. Then I looked at her. Was she teasing me?

"I mean with blind people, you feel funny saying, See you tomorrow. It's okay if they say it."

"Wait a minute," I said. "You think I'm handicapped?"

"No, no," she said. "Just wondering if you were a little sensitive about it. You are."

"No I'm not."

"Okay," she said. "We don't have to talk about it."

"We can talk about it," I said. "Do you think there's something wrong with me?"

"No I don't," Karen said. She took my hand with hers. "But I think it's the strangest thing I have ever heard of in my life. It's very exciting — it's very exciting being with you. I don't know if there's something wrong with you or not. This other part of you does scare me a little, though."

"Do you believe me?" I asked.

"Sort of," she said. "I believe what I've seen. I'm just not sure what that is."

I relaxed. "Karen, tell me," I asked, "do I really look like the animal? Last time, did I really appear to be a squirrel?"

"I don't know," she said. "It's almost like it doesn't matter. I know it's you, but it's a squirrel — but it's still you."

"I don't disappear, then, like Clark Kent and come back as Superman?"

"First of all, sweetie pie, without hurting your feelings, you are not Superman. And second, Clark Kent doesn't really disappear, does he?

"I don't know," she said after a minute. "It's confusing. I like being in love with you, but I think to myself, what if this other stuff seems real just because of that? Like a folie à deux, you know?"

I didn't. When she explained, it didn't make me feel better.

"It's not a delusion," I said. "You know the hawk we just saw? I was thinking about how the hawk sees things."

"No, no," she said. "Don't even think about hawks.

225

What if you ever got up there and couldn't get back down?"

By now she was kissing me while she talked, and I was kissing her back, so we let the whole discussion drift off.

30

Mr. Fideles didn't let Jerry back into biology without a fight. He made Jerry sit down and have a long talk about what he thought Mr. Fideles should do with him. He asked Jerry if he thought *he* should teach the class. He asked him whether he thought that he, Mr. Fideles, had something personal against him. He asked him what he, Jerry, would do if he were the teacher and Mr. Fideles was a student who was always making wisecracks. He asked him if he thought biology was a joke. If he thought school was a joke. If he thought anybody else thought he was funny. He asked him if he acted like that at home. He asked him if he thought he was so smart he didn't have to listen. He asked him whether he thought Mr. Fideles stood up there just for the fun of it. He asked him whether he thought he had the right, even if he didn't care about learning himself, to disrupt the class and keep the other students from learning. He asked Jerry if he thought he could go through all of life with that attitude.

Once Mr. Fideles got going, Jerry didn't have much to do. He had to look down at the floor sometimes, and he had to look at Mr. Fideles sometimes. He had to answer No, whenever Mr. Fideles added a Well, do you? to one of his questions.

Eventually, Mr. Fideles began to tire a little, so he and Jerry switched from No to Maybe. Did Jerry think it would help to change his seat away from me? Did he think it would help if Mr. Fideles put him right up front with nobody to talk to? Would it help if he gave Jerry his own special assignments to do and report to the class sometimes?

Finally, Mr. Fideles and Jerry began the long climb back into class again. Yes, said Jerry, he was actually quite interested in biology. And he really did try hard in it. In fact, if he could stop fooling around, he could get a lot out of it. His tests showed he was capable of A work. He could probably even do extra-credit work, which might keep him more interested. That would be better than more demerits, which Jerry already had plenty of. So after Jerry said Yes to all those things, Mr. Fideles let him back into class. He said he'd make up some extra assignments for him, and if he did those well, they'd forget about his previous actions in class.

We were on the nervous system now, starting to study the brain. Mr. Fideles cleared his throat.

"So," he said, "the evolution of the brain. Once cephalization has begun — cephalization being the attribute of having a distinct head — what's funny about that? — the brain, once cephalization has begun, is basically an increasing enlargement of the end of the neural tube. Our brainstem merges with the top of the spinal column. The medulla oblongata grows out of the ganglia at the end of the neural pathway."

Every once in a while, Mr. Fideles would look over at Jerry. Jerry would look at Mr. Fideles eagerly, waiting for him to ask a question. Telling Jerry not to make wisecracks in class was a lot like telling a dog to sit. For a long time the dog sits, but then he wants to do something else. Sometimes he forgets he's supposed to keep sitting and just gets up and walks away. Sometimes he tries very hard to stay sitting, but his bottom just starts rising up all by itself. He's as surprised as you are, but there's nothing he can do about it. If it's a game, he can sit for a long time, though, waiting for you to call him.

Each time Mr. Fideles looked at Jerry, Jerry would have his mouth closed tightly and his eyes would be looking expectantly at Mr. Fideles. Sometimes he would clear his throat or say just one word, the way a dog sometimes barks as part of the sitting game.

"Do you remember what we said the primary function of the brain was, back in the fall?" Mr. Fideles asked.

"Inhibition and contrast," Jerry barked.

"Good boy," Mr. Fideles said. "Inhibition — the suppression of certain of the sensory data that the sense receptors are constantly feeding it.

"When we get to such human brain traits as memory, speech, and abstract thought, we will find the same mechanism at work — suppression of extraneous or unimportant material. And we'll see, in the disturbed mind, what happens when the brain is unable to suppress some of the impulses — impulses in both senses of the word — with which it is constantly bombarded."

We reviewed what we already knew about the nervous system and the neural pathways. We went over dendrites, axons, and synapses.

"You remember," Mr. Fideles went on, "that the frog's legs jump — the muscles respond — when an electric current passes through them. It is the nervous system's *own* electric current that triggers the frog's actions when it's alive. So. This same reflex action is our nervous system's most basic response to external stimuli."

He explained how a reflex works. Then he paused.

"There's a lot to cover," he said. "It's the human brain

that separates us most from other animals, yet it's in the evolution of the brain that we can best trace the course of our development from other animals. Our brains are much more highly developed, but the brain's structure, and its functioning, are remarkably similar. In its most basic functions, it harks back all the way to the most primitive and simplest brain.

"It wouldn't be wrong to consider the most complex parts of our brain — the cerebral cortex and all that that encompasses — as a sort of 'afterthought' to the basic nervous system control box that the brain originally was."

He waited to see what we thought of his joke. Then he stepped away from the board where he had been writing down the important words and sat on the edge of his desk.

"We don't understand our own brain. It has even been proposed that we can never understand it."

From where he sat now, across the room from me and just behind Mr. Fideles's line of vision, Jerry was making a motion as if he had a mop in his hand. That was our signal that Mr. Fideles was about to wax eloquent about science again.

Mr. Fideles turned his head suddenly and looked at Jerry to check whether he was still sitting. He was.

"This is not a scientific attitude, however. It leads to speculation of a very unscientific nature. For example, before we learned the specific functions of certain parts of the brain, there was wild speculation as to what some of them actually did. The brain stem itself — the most primitive part — has been called the reptilian brain. It does, in some ways, respond, and cause us to respond, as even a reptile would, to the environment. But does it really connect us in some *active* way to reptiles? Do we really, when this part of the brain is momentarily dominant, become again reptilian?"

Behind his back, Jerry was shaking his finger at me.

"Or take the pineal gland . . ."

"Somebody. Please." Jerry said.

Mr. Fideles whirled around. Jerry had his hand covering his face and was grimacing as if he was in pain. He shook his head back and forth. It really was like a dog. He looked like a dog whose muzzle had come loose and who was himself trying to get it back on with his paws. Mr. Fideles made a "stay" gesture at Jerry.

"The pineal gland has been a great source of unscientific speculation. It has been called the 'third eye,' appropriately, in a way, because it has all the attributes of an eye. It is actually sensitive to light. But why? It is located deep within the brain. What does it see from in there?

The philosopher Descartes thought it was the seat of all consciousness. Mystics give it strange powers. It has been thought to be the location of the 'mind,' an 'eye' into the universe, the place where 'insight' is located, or a kind of higher sight into the hidden connections of life forces, which communicate through it to us.

"By the way, I understand we have one of those people in our class — someone who's managed to focus his third eye on things. Someone whose brain understands these mystical connections more intimately than the rest of us. A new Saint Francis you might say, the first person since the last one to talk to the animals. Well, all I can say is good luck and don't forget to write."

Mr. Fideles didn't look anywhere near me when he said this, but my heart stopped when I heard him. I felt a kind of terror unlike anything I had ever felt. That passed, but a feeling of terrible shame that I couldn't explain came over me. Jerry gasped, and looked at Mr. Fideles with his mouth open. I looked at Jerry, then at Mr. Fideles, then at Jerry again.

I looked down at my desk the rest of the period. I didn't hear anything Mr. Fideles said. He went right on to the thalamus and other things, but I heard nothing. My heart was fluttering inside me.

What had Jerry done? Why had he told Mr. Fideles? After class, I left the room with my eyes on the floor.

"I didn't say anything," Jerry said. "I just said you knew some things about biology that the rest of us only guessed at. I didn't mean to tell him."

"Why did you say anything?" I said. "Why? Why did you do such a thing?"

"I don't know. He asked. He really did. He was asking about biology and whether he should keep me in class, and he asked me about you, whether you fooled around, too, and so forth. I didn't tell him much. I couldn't help it."

"Who else did you tell?"

"Some kids," Jerry said. He was looking at the floor.

"Jerry, how could you? You don't know what it's all about, even I don't, how could you talk to Mr. Fideles? I'm really fucked now. Now what am I supposed to do?"

"Don't do anything," Jerry said. "Don't mention it or anything. He'll forget about it. He'll think I just made it up."

"What kids?"

"I don't know. My gym class. I just got to talking and ended up telling the whole story. Once I got going, I couldn't stop myself. They thought it was amazing. I guess I was bragging for you. It is amazing."

"I know," I said. "Now everybody knows."

"It'll be all right," Jerry said.

31

It wasn't. He had really screwed things up. I found myself surrounded after school by a group of kids who wanted to know all about it. They didn't believe any of it, of course, they just wanted to hear my crazy story. I tried to shrug them off and keep going, but the whole crowd moved along with me. They were all yelling questions like Can you fly? Can you talk like a duck? They wanted to see me catch flies and eat them.

Finally, I stopped and as calmly as I could answered their questions. They wouldn't shut up while I explained, though. They kept making remarks and quacking and growling and stuff.

"It's not a joke," I said. "I don't expect anybody to understand, but it's not a joke."

They wanted to see me do it. They were laughing and telling me to fly or turn into a dog or some other animal. They kept thinking up weirder and weirder animals they wanted to see.

"Be a kangaroo."

"A koala bear.

"An aardvark."

"A duck-billed platypus. Let's see one of them."

I saw John Robbins standing at the edge of the group of kids with his hands folded across his chest looking at me, not saying anything.

"It's not a trick!" I yelled. "You want to know and I'm trying to tell you! If you want to know, listen!"

They listened for a minute as I told them about the

brain, and how we developed from lower species, and how our nervous system and brain contain remnants of the others. But when I told them I couldn't just do it on the spot like that, they started hooting again.

"What a fake," they yelled and other stuff like that. I was mad now, with all these morons hopping around scratching their armpits to imitate monkeys and daring me to turn into one.

"Don't get me mad," I said. "I can do it, too, when I want."

"Look out!" they yelled. "Don't get him mad. He's the Incredible Hulk." They pretended to scatter. "Run! It's the Incredible Hulk!"

"No it's not," I tried to yell. "It's not that at all. It's the opposite. I'm not atomic. This comes from inside! This is real!"

But they were all doing Incredible Hulk imitations in a circle around me. In my anger, I became an orangoutang, like the one in the zoo, and I sat, squat and fat, placidly spitting at the circle of them surrounding me. I heard Robbins saying, "Leave him alone," and saw him pushing them away. Then I was alone on the sidewalk.

The next day Robbins came up to me at my locker. He wanted to know what had been going on the day before. I started to tell him a little bit about my animals. He said he had heard some of that.

"But how did you get to be where I found you surrounded by creeps?"

I told him I had been trying to explain this thing I had about animals and they had started on me.

"Well, first," he said, "you shouldn't have said anything. It sounds like something you might want to keep to yourself. And second — you never let them get on all sides of you like that. Never. That way it always ends

233

up trouble. They be laughing at you like that — hey! That's when you let it slide. One on one — that's when you talk back."

He closed his hand into a fist and showed it to me.

"That's easy for you to say," I said. "You could probably take all of them."

"Maybe yes, maybe no. That's not the point. See, when you're black, you learn how to know what's a tease and what's trouble. 'Cause big as I am, there's still only one of me.

"But when it's a tease," he went on, "even when it's a hostile tease, most times if you laugh, too, and keep saying, That's right, that's right, you be okay. See, inside, you're still untouched by all that. But the other way, you end up getting hurt. Hurt inside and outside, too, sometimes.

"Look at yourself. What you did yesterday was nasty. That was some nasty spitting, man. You let them get you. You turned primitive, man. Worse than primitive. That was the act of an animal. A gorilla. See, you let them turn you into a gorilla."

"An orangoutang," I said. He just looked at me.

Then he wanted to know what it was really about. What all the jive talk about animals was.

So I told him. He asked questions as I went along, nodded his head, asked more specifically about the day before's orangoutang, then was silent for a minute after I finished. I thought maybe he understood. Then he pointed his finger at me.

"You," he said, "are making a mockery of your brain." He shook his head and left.

He caught me again after lunch. "Listen," he said. "We won't let them animals — pardon me — pick on you again. But I been thinking. How come this happens to you?"

I shrugged my shoulders.

"I mean you and not somebody else. I mean me for example. There's nothing special about you. You're white, you're intelligent, you do fine in school, you got a nice girlfriend. I'm the outsider. I'm the one people look at. I'm the one they're afraid of, the one sometimes they hate. I mean being black, different. I'm the one they feel threatened by. So you know who's the one that's really threatened. So how come you're crazy and I'm not?"

"I'm not crazy," I said.

Robbins put his face right in front of mine.

"You are, too," he said.

He caught me still a third time after school. Each time he had talked to me seriously, softly, without joking. To have Robbins mocking you was a lot worse than a bunch of stupid kids. The other kids just make fun of anything that strikes them — your complexion, your name, your socks. They're irritating, but when they get a rise out of you, it's really your fault. They're more like gnats than anything else. They swarm around your face, but they don't bite. Robbins, though, could mock you obliquely. I think that's the word. In other words, the other kids could taunt you, but Robbins could, like, put a mockery on you, like a hex or something. It's like a mosquito bite lasts a day, but a horsefly bite lasts a week.

So I wasn't happy when he started telling me some story about his crazy uncle.

"I never met him," he said. "A great-uncle, I guess he was, thought he could talk to the animals. This was a long time ago, now, before any of my family left the South."

"John," I said, "get out of my face." I wanted him to

235

understand in no uncertain terms that I wasn't going to let him get started with me. He could go on for weeks.

He put his hands palms-out as if to ward me off. Then he giggled. "Get out of my face, indeed," he said.

"You got it wrong," he said. "I'm not making fun. Listen. Every black person has somebody in the family who's crazy. Sometimes it's his own self. But this uncle, he was pretty crazy, but nobody bothered him. See, there was a power in that craziness. You bothered him, then later that night when you saw the snake by your back door looking to get in the house, or you noticed your own cow or pig looking at you funny, you left that man alone. So you see? I just know the story, and you and I don't live on the bayou where we would believe in that shit, but even if you just thought you were a alligator or something, you could do some damage around this school."

"John, don't be condescending, okay?" I said.

He shook his head. "I'm not saying it right. You're either crazy or you aren't. Later, maybe, for that. But right now you got some heavy things going on. I mean, you really feel those things. Maybe they're going to hurt you, maybe help you move your whole life on up. But my grandmother used to tell me that story about my crazy uncle, or about other people that did this or that, and I would say, But Grandmama, that was something. That person was somebody special. How come if he could do that, he was crazy, or how come, if it was some other man, if he was so strong or good to his family, or whatever else it was, he ended up dying of drinking, or getting killed. You know? And she'd say to me, Wings are just a burden if a bird ain't allowed to fly.

"I'm only saying, you might be crazy, you might not be. But you feel these things inside you, that's good. But there's going to be some trouble with the rubes. And I'm

236

on your side when it comes. I might be laughing, too, but I'll be there. Count on it."

That was one of the most surprising speeches I had ever heard in my life. I could only smile at him as he touched me on the shoulder and walked off.

32

There was a little field near the high school where kids went to have a fight. It was beyond school property, so you wouldn't get into trouble for fighting unless the people who lived in the house whose field it was called the school or the police.

Jerry had stuck up for me when he heard some kids talking about me. They had kept it up after he had told them to shut up, and he had pushed one of them into the lockers. So now he and the other kid were going to duke it out after school.

I hadn't been there when it started, but as soon as I heard about it, I grabbed Jerry and told him I was quite capable of fighting my own battles, but Jerry just shrugged me off. When I caught the kid in the corridor and tried to make him fight me, he said, "You can be next," and then walked away with his friends to meet Jerry.

There was nothing for me to do but back up Jerry. Somehow I was out of it, even though it supposedly was about me. It was between Jerry and the other kid now.

As we walked out past the school buses and toward the field, Jerry and I and a couple other kids with Jerry, and the other kid and four or five of his buddies, we picked up a bunch of other kids on the way. You can tell when there's going to be a fight by the way everybody is walking. As we passed, kids would yell out, "Is it a fight?" and someone would answer "Yes" and more kids would join in, even before they knew who was fighting.

When we got into the field, everybody made a circle, and Jerry and the kid pawed the ground with their feet to clear away the stones. They had their eyes on the ground while they did this, concentrating on the area they were pawing. They moved around and around while everybody else waited. Jerry had put his books on the ground. I went over and picked them up.

Finally, somebody yelled, "Let's go," and other people started saying, "Come on, let's get it on," and the two of them stood still and looked at each other.

Jerry stood with his arms at his sides, waiting for the other kid to start. The other kid had his head cocked to one side and was nodding over and over, as if he had heard everything about Jerry and that, looking at him now, he wasn't too impressed.

Jerry made a feint with his shoulder and the kid ducked and jumped back. There were hoots and snorts from the crowd. The kid did a similar feint, but Jerry didn't move a muscle. They stood there for a while just out of reach of each other, then both of them slowly went into a crouch. Nothing happened, and slowly they stood back up. Then the kid took a step closer to Jerry. They stared at each other. He went to shove Jerry in the chest and Jerry knocked his hands away. They stood for another minute, then the kid nodded at Jerry and waved his hand at him in disgust. He turned as if to walk away, then suddenly wheeled back around swinging. Jerry moved and just got clipped across the top of the head, then moved in and shoved the kid away. As the kid caught his balance, Jerry hit him a straight left jab, then another, then another. They backed off. The fight had started.

Jerry was popping him and popping him. The kid's face was really opening up. He was swinging, but it was Jerry who was connecting. Jerry hit him on the side of the head and he went down. Other kids were yelling, Stomp him and Kick him in the face, but Jerry waited until he got up. The kid's face was pouring blood. The front of his shirt was covered with it. Jerry kept twisting his wrists as if they were hurt. But he kept hitting him. The kid had big welts on both sides of his forehead, and wherever there wasn't blood, his face was all swollen. Jerry was boxing the shit out of him.

Then the kid charged. Even though Jerry hit him in the back of the neck, he dragged Jerry down. He had his leg between Jerry's legs and was trying to knee him. His forearm was in Jerry's face.

"Hey, fair fight," I yelled.

"Fuck you," the kid yelled back.

I could see Jerry was discouraged by the kid's getting him down. Jerry had been giving him a beating when they were boxing. Now he shook his head and the blood from his nose and face dripped all over Jerry's face. He tried to get Jerry in the mouth with his elbow, but Jerry kept moving his head. Then he started rubbing his arm across Jerry's face, trying to cut him with the rocks Jerry was lying on. Jerry got his hands around the kid's wrists and his leg up against the kid's stomach, and they stayed there for a while, neither one able to do anything. So the kid drooled spit in Jerry's face.

It didn't look like anything was happening. They strained and strained against each other with no movement at all. Finally, in slow motion, the kid began to rise. Very slowly, he began to tilt to his right, grunting the whole time. Jerry's neck muscles stretched like strings. His face was beet red. His arms trembled as he lifted the kid up.

The flip was instantaneous. Suddenly Jerry was on top

239

and the other kid was underneath. Jerry sat on him, struggling to free his wrists, which the other kid was now holding. Each time he got one free, he hit the kid in the face. The punches weren't that hard, though. He had no leverage. So he let the kid up.

Jerry was all cut up now, too.

The other kid looked a lot worse, but there were tears in Jerry's eyes. He wasn't going to quit, though. They circled each other again. Everybody watching knew what was going to happen next. The kid was going to try to kick Jerry in the balls and Jerry was going to try to take his head off when he did.

Then a voice came from the house. "Get out of here. Get the hell out of here." Some guy was coming toward us, waving his arms to scare us away. He walked right through the kids into the open space where Jerry and the other kid were standing.

"I've already called the cops," he yelled, "so get the hell out. I'm sick of you punk kids fighting in my yard."

Jerry turned to look at the guy, and the other kid jumped him. As Jerry started to go down, he swung his arm back as hard as he could. It sounded like a bat hitting a ball. An aluminum one, not the old wooden kind. The kid crumpled up, holding his face, and Jerry stood up to face the new guy.

"Oh, my God," the guy said. "What's the matter with you two?"

The other kid stood up. Something was broken, that's for sure. Either just his nose, or maybe his nose and his cheek. He kept turning his head to one side as if that would help.

"Goddamn kids," the guy said. "Look at you. Here come the cops. Now get out of here."

A cop car was pulling up at the edge of the field. Everybody started walking the other way.

"Get out of here before you get in real trouble," the guy said to Jerry and the other kid. They turned to go.

"But first, shake hands."

Jerry's eyes were still all teary, and he was breathing almost like he was crying. But he snorted in a kind of laugh and put out his hand to shake hands with the guy who had called the cops. The guy jerked his hand away and turned to go meet the cops. "Punk," he said to Jerry.

The other kid was already up ahead with his friends. He was walking between two of them, holding his face, and they were helping him walk. Jerry and I started walking at a different angle. There was only one cop. He was about thirty yards behind us, and as the group of kids split up he chose us to chase. We walked faster, but didn't run. He kept up, but didn't run, either. We reached the sidewalk at the other end of the field and kept going. We looked over our shoulders. The cop had reached the sidewalk, too. The distance between us had narrowed. He must have been running when we weren't looking.

"Paul," Jerry said, "turn into a car and get us out of here."

"I can't turn into a car," I said.

We both made exaggerated gestures with our hands as we said this, as if we were having a lively conversation and didn't even know there was a cop behind us.

"A horse, then. With a saddle. Or a cart. Something!"

The cop stopped and watched us walk away. He must have figured that if he got any closer, we'd start running, and he'd look foolish chasing us. He was right, too.

We went to Jerry's house. Jerry's grandmother lost her head when she saw him. His face had some real rake marks down the side, his hands were all cut, the knuckles from hitting the kid and the palms from the stones he had fallen on, and his clothes, of course, were shot.

"Don't worry about it," he said to her, but she was already too far gone. It was like telling a Superball to stop bouncing after you've thrown it against the wall. She was cracking ice out of the ice cube tray and running back to look at his face and shake her head, and running to find a washcloth, and yelling that it was the worst thing he had done yet, and on and on until she had him cleaned up. His hands stung, he said, but he didn't know about the scratches on his face until his grandmother put a washcloth on them. Then he yelled. They were deep.

"I would have boxed him," he said to me while his grandmother worked on him. He shook his head. "That's what we agreed on."

"You were slaughtering him boxing," I said.

"I just couldn't put him out. Still, that's what he agreed to." He shrugged his shoulders as if he was apologizing for what happened. "He should have stuck with it. He'd have been better off. He got what he asked for for jumping me."

He leaned back in his seat and shrugged his shoulders again. I couldn't blame him for acting this way. He had done quite a number on the guy. His grandmother put the washcloth and water and stuff away and sat down at the table with us. She was calmed down, too, finally.

"Oh, boys," she said.

"It happens, Grandma," Jerry said.

"Oh, oh," she said. She had her face in her hands and her elbows on the table and was shaking her head.

"You see," Jerry said to me, "Jews don't fight. Right, Grandma?"

"It's true," Jerry's grandmother said.

"That's how come they were held in such high esteem in Poland. Right, Grandma?"

242

"Ach," she said. She sat there for a while, then got up. "Ach, Paul," she said. "You want something?" She walked over to the window and looked out.

"Oh, boys," she said. "Come look. Two peasants."

We looked out the window. Two pheasants were strutting around at the edge of Jerry's backyard.

"Run for our life, Grandma," Jerry said. "It's the peasants. But you told me they carried torches and everything. I'm disappointed in these peasants."

"Not peasants," she said. "Peasants."

"Right," Jerry said.

"How do you say it?" she asked me.

"Pheasants," I said.

"Stupid," she said to Jerry.

She had made a bunch of cookies, so she went and got them.

"Take your pick," she said.

"And your shovel," Jerry said. He was all over fighting now. He picked up a cookie and rapped it on the table.

"You know how in the old country they used to heat up stones to bake bread and cookies? Ol' Grandma here does it the other way around. Bring me a hammer, will you, Grandma, I want to break one in half."

"They're good, aren't they?" he said to me quietly.

"Very," I said.

Jerry's grandmother came back out of the kitchen with two glasses of milk. She stopped at the window again to look at the pheasants.

"Grandma, you weren't a peasant in Poland, were you?" Jerry asked. "I mean, even after you were baptized, you still didn't live on a farm, did you?"

Jerry's grandmother was still looking out the window toward the woods.

"No," she said. "We lived in the town. My family had

a little garden. All the families had a little garden. Cabbages we would grow, and porows. Leek, you say here. Tomatoes, too, but not big like here. Little tomatoes like this." She turned around and showed us the top of her thumb.

"The dungcart would come down the street every spring and stop at each door, and the people would buy the dung to spread on the garden. Then the horse that was pulling the cart would drop more dung on the street, and the peasant man would put it in the cart, too, and sell it to the next one.

"Sometimes, potatoes, too, just a little patch to dig up one for the soup. My father would take a potato from last winter, with the eyes all growing out of it like this, and put it on a stick for me, and I would have a funny potato man to scare the other children with. And Jeddy — there was a plum tree, too, in the yard. That was the nicest thing. The children would yell at the birds in the summer to scare them away from pecking the plums. All the time I am asking your father, why not plant a plum tree here, it would be so nice. But he's getting the fruits and vegetables cheaper in the market, so why bother, I guess. So det's life, eh Paul?"

She came over to me and messed up my hair. "Anyway, Jeddy says you tink you're a dog," she said.

"Aw, Jesus," I said, looking at Jerry.

"You tink you Jesus?" she asked. "Det's worse. Jeddy, tell him he ain't Jesus."

"He knows that, Grandma," Jerry said.

"What about the dog?" she asked me.

"I don't think I'm a dog," I said.

"You sure?" she asked.

"Pretty sure," I said.

"You got to be sure," she said.

• • •

When I got home, my father was there. "I want to talk to you," he said. Jerry's grandmother. Jerry's goddamn grandmother had called.

"What's this about a fight Jerry was in?" my father started.

"Jerry was in a fight," I said.

"And you were there?"

"Of course I was there," I said. "I'm his friend."

"So you egged him on."

"I didn't *egg* him on."

"Don't talk like that to me," he said. "What was the fight about?"

"How do I know?" I said. "I wasn't there when it started."

"Don't give me that," he said. "You know very well what it was about. It was something to do with you."

"If you know all about it, why are you asking me?" I said.

"Goddamn it, I don't like your tone," he said.

And I don't like your face, I thought. Or your head, or your nose, or your arms or your belly or your feet or your clothes or your breath or your voice . . .

"Just what exactly is this crap you're pulling at school? You're an eccentric now, a mystic?"

"What did Jerry's grandmother . . ." I started.

"Jerry's grandmother, nothing!" he yelled. "All of a sudden you're a misfit — an oddball? What kind of pose is this? What are you trying to prove, anyway?"

There was really no way to stop him. What I needed was a Cap Chur gun — that's the tranquilizer gun they shoot animals with in order to tag them or capture them for zoos. The elephant is trumpeting away and shaking his ears, or the polar bear is up on his hind legs in a rage to squash you, then they suddenly get this peaceful look on their face, they stand still for a minute looking around, then crash! down they go, they roll over on their side, and sleep. My father wouldn't look bad with a tag in his ear, either.

"You better wake up," he went on. "Reincarnation, is it? Is that what you've been flitting around saying you believe in? Well?"

I didn't answer.

"You're the reincarnation of various animals? Some crap like that? Come off it. People are going to start laughing at you."

He started to turn away. "You know what you're the reincarnation of? Do you? A millstone. That's what."

That night I had a date with Karen. We weren't going anywhere. Her parents were going to be out, and we were going to study and listen to tapes. I got the usual look from my father when I left, as if I wasn't going where I said I was going, and wasn't going to do what I said I was going to do, and wasn't going to be home when I said I was going to be home. He always asked those questions: Where are you going? What are you going to do? When are you going to be home? Then when I told him, he always gave me the same look, as if whatever answer I had given him was so transparently a lie, and such a stupid one, that it actually made him feel sorry for me. Then, when I left, I'd see him staring at me with this combination of something like resignation and regret — the kind of look you'd imagine the father alligator gives his son when he realizes that the son has gotten too big for him to eat. Resignation tinged with regret, and maybe the little dot of an idea in his tiny brain that maybe there's still a chance.

Fuck him and his looks. There was a story Karen told me about some Greek or something who had to carry his father across the Alps on his back. I can tell you right now, if that was me that had to do that, first nice cliff we came to, See you, Dad.

As soon as I got down the street, I forgot about him. Karen wanted to study at the dining room table. I wanted to study on the couch. So we studied like that for a while, shouting back and forth between the two rooms. I was impatient to have her come onto the couch with me, but I didn't say anything. Gradually, I stopped answering when she yelled to me. Instead of coming in, though, she stopped talking.

I could see her back through the door. Her head was bent over her chemistry book. She was taking notes in her notebook. Every once in a while she'd shake her head to get the hair out of her face. Her hair fell over her neck and across her shoulders. I kept looking at her hair and her hand when she put it up to her face. I kept trying to study, but then I'd hear her shift in her seat. She was driving me crazy.

From outside, I could hear the spring peepers in the night. The little pipsqueaks were calling their mates. I stretched out on the couch. I tried to arrange myself with one leg stretched out, the other bent at the knee, and with my head resting at a slightly inclined angle across my arms so that when she looked through the door at me, she'd be struck by my unconscious natural grace. Every part of my body was tingling. She didn't look up, though. I couldn't concentrate at all. Lying there, I began to think about kissing her, touching her, pressing against her. She was about ten feet away from me, and I was dreaming about her.

When she finally came in, I pretended to be asleep. She knelt in front of the couch and put her cheek on top of mine, and we started to make out. My whole body was on fire. I rolled off the couch onto the rug with her and pulled us together. She wrapped her legs around me and put her mouth on mine.

She smelled wonderful, she tasted wonderful, she felt wonderful. Both of our shirts were off and our chests were together. She took my head in her hands and pushed me away a little.

"We should stop," she said. She was panting when she said it. I could feel how hot my own face was.

"No, we shouldn't," I said. We kissed some more. Oh, I didn't want to stop. It was all I wanted. It was all there was in the world to want. And it is all there is in the world to want. It's what everything is about. It's what your whole body wants, what it yearns for, what it tells you to do.

Mating. In insects, there is infinite longing and almost no other activity during his whole life by the male. He calls, he sings, he may even display; otherwise he barely eats or anything. Sometimes he has to fight, or he has to fly up and up and up after the female, and the great risks he takes, win or lose, are usually the end of his life. Think of bees. Of spiders. Or of the mayfly, who lives under a rock in a stream his whole life, then, in the course of one hour, hatches out of his shell, swims up through the frenzied, swirling, snapping fish that all the mayflies hatching have attracted, sits helpless on the surface until his wings dry while the fish suck down other mayflies by the thousands, struggles up into the air, flying finally, mates for an instant, then falls from the air, dead, back into the water.

I was willing for that to happen to me.

Or a salmon. There was a salmon inside me, swimming, leaping, straining against the current to get to her. We didn't stop then, but I began to feel a difference in Karen. She was trying to slow down. I kissed her harder and pressed myself harder against her. I kept trying to

248

unsnap her jeans but she kept her hand over the snap, even though she was still kissing me. She'd move her mouth to the side and say, No, then kiss me some more. Her tongue was like a needle touching mine. I didn't know what to do. Even if we didn't do it, we shouldn't stop. But each time we didn't stop just seemed to add a bit more force to the current I was swimming against, forcing me to swim stronger. Infinite longing — I had felt that while she was studying. Now I could feel her. Our mouths were still together, but our hands were having a separate battle. Finally, though, she meant it.

"We have to stop," she said, and tried to roll away from under me. As she did that, my hand finally unsnapped the snap of her jeans. She yanked herself away from me and sat up.

"You animal!" she said.

That was the wrong thing to say.

It hurt my feelings. She put on her shirt, then looked across at me. Her mouth and face looked all blurry. Her shirt was still open most of the way down. The infinite longing came back, along with an empty feeling in the pit of my stomach and an aching sensation a little lower down.

"That wasn't very nice," she said.

"It was," I said. I knew what she meant, though. My keeping it up after she told me to stop.

"If I can control myself," she said, "you can control yourself. How can I trust you otherwise? That's rape what you almost did."

"Rape?" I said. "Just because I wanted to more than you did?"

"You didn't want to more than I did. But I said no. I don't think we should. I don't think we're ready to. And then you tried to force me."

"I did not," I said.

"Maybe you don't know the difference, but there is one, between what you want and what I want. But you think you can make me want what you want by aggression."

"Wait a minute," I said. "I wanted you to want me, that's all. I stopped. There's a difference between that and trying to rape you."

"It's a very thin line. And you were about to cross it. In fact, I don't see the difference at all."

"Karen, there are differences. It wasn't the same thing at all."

"Aggression," she said. "It's men's instinct."

"It's one of their instincts," I said. "It's not the only one. It's certainly not the one I was feeling just now."

"I'm afraid it was. One is an extension of the other."

"No," I said. "Everything isn't an extension of something else."

"That's what I'm trying to tell you. Your feelings toward me are not supposed to be merely an extension of your other instincts. And your other instincts aren't supposed to be an extension of your feelings toward me."

"But they're not," I said. "I know there are distinctions. And differences. Why do you think I turn into animals? Because nobody pays any attention to the distinctions or the limits of things. Nobody shows any respect for people. Or reason."

"Well, don't paw me," she said. "I don't like it."

"We stopped," I said.

"Not when I said."

"Yes when you said. I thought you wanted to."

"I did," she said. "But I'm glad we stopped."

Then we made out some more, but sitting up, on the couch.

"Anyway," she said, "what you said just now didn't make any sense."

She let me touch her however much I wanted now, but didn't do so much touching of me. She just sort of lay back and let us be kind of mushed together. She seemed half asleep. Her eyes were closed, and she moved her head slowly from side to side, and she let me get on top of her again on the couch, but I wasn't sure what I should do. I sat up again, and so did she.

Finally, I got my books to go. Her parents would be home soon. I didn't feel like staying and talking to them.

"What can we do tomorrow?" Karen asked.

We decided to go to the beach if her mother would give us a ride to the train. The beach could be really nice in the spring. It was way too early for swimming, so there would be nobody there. Karen suggested a picnic.

33

"It's not just Good Friday," the guy on the radio was saying, "it's a Great Friday. And we have some great rock coming up for you after these messages."

A week had passed since Karen and I had gone to the beach. Jerry and I were riding around in Jerry's car trying to think of someplace to go. They kept playing songs about being crucified. They played this old John Lennon song that goes They're gonna crucify me, and this Dylan one where he says You would have killed Jesus, too, and they answer, You ain't him.

Good Friday was a good day for what had just happened to me. School got out at noon, and I was waiting outside for Jerry to bring his car around when they started. Two kids behind me began making animal noises. Pretty soon it was six or seven of them daring me to spit at them or bite them or something. None of them had been there the time I did spit, but they knew about it, of course, and some of the other things I had done had gotten around. Every time I told them to fuck off, they barked at me. Then they'd pretend to be serious for a minute and ask me to prove I could do what I said I could.

"You're the ones who say I can," I told them.

They kept it up and kept it up, in a circle around me. First one kid would come in close and try to scare me or something, then another kid would take a turn at it, then another. I didn't respond at all — didn't even blink at them.

They were like a bunch of blue jays who've spotted a cat. The closer the cat is to them, the louder they squawk. If the cat is asleep or not interested in them, they're very brave. They scream at it and dive-bomb it and fly right in its face. Cats sometimes chase blue jays not because they're really trying to catch one, or even because they're playing at hunting, the way they sometimes do. Sometimes the blue jays are just bothering them so much, they leap up the trunk of the tree to make them scatter, in the hopes that they'll get some peace. Of course it never works. After the cat misses — and especially when the birds realize that the cat isn't serious — they start harassing it for real. The only way for the cat to shut them up is to actually kill one. But at this point, it's impossible to get one. They've gotten each other so excited that they're alert to any move you might make. Unless you just lie there, absolutely still, letting them dare each other closer and closer, so close one of them actually gets a peck in on your head, while your eyelids droop heavier and heavier until your eyes are almost closed and all you are looking at is the thinnest slit of yellow light, waiting for the slightest disturbance in that yellowness.

Slap! One of them lay writhing at my feet. The others jumped back. Suddenly they were completely silent. I stared at them. The kid who was down jumped back up and ran out to the others. He had just been stunned.

I became aware of another presence outside my narrowed field of vision. I opened my eyes wide again. John Robbins was standing there behind them. He shook his head at me, and pursed his lips in a way that said no.

It took a minute for them to start making noise at me again, but by now they had gathered a lot of other kids around them. Still like blue jays, they formed a circle just out of my reach — just out of my range — and started to come at me.

"Nuts," one said. "Totally nuts." He pointed his finger at me. From a safe distance. "You are crazy."

"You are cracked," shouted another.

"Bonkers."

"Crackers."

"Bananas." They laughed. The noise was attracting more of them.

"Loony," chirped one of the new ones.

"Not tightly wrapped." Then they all started chiming in.

"Got a screw loose."

"Blew a fuse."

"Not playing with a full deck."

"Not rowing with both oars."

"Bats in the belfry."

"A guest in the attic." It wasn't even directed at me by now, they were just making noise among themselves.

"Bubbles in the think tank."

"A noise under the hood."

"The elevator doesn't go to the top floor."

"Flipped out."

"Cuckoo."

"Off his rocker."

"Lost his marbles."

"Tootsi-paz."

"What?" Everybody turned. It was Nino who had said that.

"Tootsi-paz," he said. "It means crazy in Italian."

"Tootsi-paz," everybody yelled. "Tootsi-paz. Tootsi-paz."

When they have a cat, the blue jays taunt it and taunt it until for who knows what reason, they suddenly quit and fly away. Maybe they just exhaust their repertoire of squawks. But when they come upon an owl, they try to peck its eyes out. The owl is a worse enemy than a cat. It glides in silently and takes them when they're sleeping. But an owl perches in the daytime. It can see as well by starlight as we can on a cloudy day, but during the day it sleeps, and has trouble with the light. It lifts its claws to protect itself, but with so many of them, it's best for it to just tuck its head into its shoulder and put up with a beating, which was what I was about to get.

Robbins stepped in between them and me. He didn't say anything, just looked at them. Slowly, they backed off. Then he turned and looked at me.

"Go," he said, whether to me or them I couldn't tell. Jerry's car finally pulled up and I got in. At the same time, they started to drift away.

"Listen," Jerry was saying. I was slumped in the seat with my feet up on the dashboard, pulling up loose threads from the seat cover.

"I'm the pariah around here, not you."

"Yeah," I said.

"I'm the Jew."

"Listen, Jerry," I said. "Has anybody ever called you that?"

"What?" he said.

"Jew. Or anything like that? Or treated you like that?"

"Sure," he said.

"Much?" I said.

"How much is much?"

"Well, what does it have to do with anything? What are you trying to say to me?"

"Well, I'm just saying — how come all this whatever it is about animals is happening to you? How come you're the one who's getting in trouble suddenly?"

"I don't understand," I said. "You're the Jew, Robbins is the black. Everybody keeps saying it should happen to them, because this, because that. Maybe you're just jealous."

"Paul . . ." Jerry said.

"No. You're saying this is something bad, that it's some kind of reaction to being an outsider or being picked on or something like that. Well, what if it's the other way around? What if my animals aren't a reaction to anything? What if it's not at all because I'm in trouble or unhappy or unpopular? What if I'm getting in trouble because of my animals? What if I'm just different in a way no one can understand and that's why they're giving me all this shit? You're so proud of being a misfit. So is Robbins so proud of being black. If you get in trouble for it, so what? Well, I'm proud of this, too, and if that makes me an outcast or a pariah . . . Oh, shit, Jerry, do you think I'm crazy, too?"

It was so confusing now. Only a few weeks ago, I had been so happy about it all, happy to let anything happen that could happen, happy to follow any direction my instincts wanted to take me in. And my friends, too, had seemed to think it was as terrific as I did. But now, it

255

seemed like I was on the defensive all the time. My own friends — the people who were supposed to understand me best. Even Karen.

It had been beautiful that day at the beach. The day was sunny and hot, but at the beach there was a wind off the ocean, so walking along the shore you had to keep your sweater on, but when you found a protected spot tucked in among the dunes, you could just lay there and soak up the sun.

Karen had brought a huge picnic lunch, with cole slaw her mother had made, and ham sandwiches and potato chips, and hard-boiled eggs, raw carrots, and some cake that was delicious even though the frosting all came off in the foil when we unwrapped it. She brought a blanket, a couple of books, and her notebook that she writes her thoughts in. She even remembered suntan lotion. The whole thing weighed a ton. I tried to carry it more than she did, but we traded off a lot.

We got there at low tide. We found a place back in the dunes and left our stuff, then took our shoes off and walked through the mud flats and around the rocks that the tide had left exposed. The water was freezing when it touched our feet, but in the pools and in front of the sandbars, it was warm. We walked a long way up the beach, all the way to where the beach itself turned pebbly, then back again. You could tell the tide was coming in. It was pushing things up the beach — pebbles, shells, seaweed — and leaving them there as the wave receded, then just as they began to roll back down again, a new wave would pick them up and carry them up a little farther. A whole line of seaweed and crab skeletons and shells marked where the tide reached at its highest.

Later, we ate back at the spot we had found in the dunes. Karen had snuck some wine from her parents and put it in an empty tomato juice bottle. That's one thing that had made the pack so heavy. By now the wine was hot. All the food was hot from the sun. After we ate, I took my shirt off and stretched out on the blanket, while Karen took out her notebook and began writing. She said she was going to describe the beach. Then she lay down, too, and we did some nice fooling around. We got a little sunburned, too.

But then, when we went for another walk along the beach toward the end of the afternoon, she said, "There's something we have to talk about, and I don't know how to say it."

You should never start talking to somebody like that. My heart immediately tried to crawl up out of my mouth and jump into the ocean and swim for it. Abandon ship, it said. I was just waiting for her to tell me it was all over. I didn't know why she was going to do that. She had seemed to love me so much back on the blanket. She had seemed so passionate. But everybody knows that's also the way you are after you've decided to break up.

"Paul, I'm worried," she said. "About you. These things that come and go. You know what I mean?"

I said I wasn't sure what she meant.

"I mean these passages. I mean these things . . . what you feel . . . these things that take you away from me. These things that you feel that are different . . ."

What in the world was she talking about?

"You don't understand, do you?" she asked.

I shook my head. She took a deep breath and launched into it. "I mean your imagination," she said. "Your flights into animal identities. I mean those times when you seem to lose touch with reality."

She looked at me to see how I was taking it. I looked back, not able to say anything. She looked down at the sand and continued as we continued walking. She didn't look again at me as she talked.

"I don't mean what you feel isn't real," she said.

"Not what I feel," I said. "What happens to me."

"All right, what happens to you."

"What I actually do. You've seen me."

"All right. Whatever. I've seen you. But I don't know what I've seen." She said some other stuff, I don't know what, and I stopped correcting her. I had no more to say.

"Paul," she said, "I don't mean that there isn't anything to it, or that you don't feel it, or that it doesn't make you act in a strange — in an extraordinary way. You think it's a great power, but I'm not so sure. It's strong feelings, it's anything you want to say, but it's — I don't mean they're not real, exactly, but they're not."

"What are they, then?" I asked.

"They're, I don't know, fantastic flights of fantasy, wonderful, imaginative journeys, momentary escapes from reality. So powerful that for an instant they *are* real, not just to you, but to everybody who sees them. But they're not reality. And if you don't learn what reality is and what it's not, you'll go . . . go . . . ."

"Crazy," I said. She was silent.

"So what's reality?" I asked. "High tide, the pretty sandy beach, the waves, the surf, the smooth blue water covering everything? Is it? Or is reality low tide, like this morning when all the mud flats were exposed and the crabs were crawling around, and all the scum was floating in the pools, and wherever you stepped, little things with shells cracked under your feet? And all the barnacles exposed on the rocks and the sand fleas swarming around the seaweed — and the giant worm we found hidden in the seaweed? Huh? Which one is real?"

258

"Oh, Paul," she said. She tried to take my hand. I wouldn't let her.

"I'm not afraid of reality," I said. "I'm not afraid of the reality underneath things, either."

"But I love you," she said. "And I'm not afraid, either. But I'm afraid it's not all what you say it is. Here's what I'm afraid of. I'm afraid you're indulging yourself in this to the point of taking something that does exist in you — that is real in some way — and letting it take you over. I'm not afraid of your imagination. I'm just afraid you won't be able to keep the real parts and discard the unreal ones."

"What do you want me to do?" I asked.

"I don't know. Talk to somebody besides me about it."

"You mean like a shrink?"

"No, not necessarily. Just somebody. Just to help see what it's all about, how much really is real, what you should do with it."

"What about you?" I asked her.

"It doesn't happen to me," she said.

"No. I mean would you rather be with somebody else, some other boy that this didn't happen to?"

"No," she said. "Absolutely not."

And now here was Jerry of all people telling me I wasn't normal.

"Look, I'm not saying you're crazy," he said.

"What are you saying, then?"

"Paul, look. You've got the La Brea tarpits for a mind. It's pretty amazing in there, but basically it's a swamp. And while you're busy excavating all these bizarre creatures, the whole thing is turning into coal."

"Some friend," I said.

"Some friend?" he said. "I stood up for you, didn't I? You think I'm jealous? You think I really want to spit at

259

people? Or catch flies? Or turn into a squirrel? Better a squirrel than a nut, I guess."

He had parked the car at the end of my street.

"Some friend, huh? A friend is someone who's loyal, right? Who really cares about you?"

"That's right," I said.

"Who sticks up for you? Who defends you if you're attacked? Right?"

I nodded.

"Who's on your side no matter what, and puts up with all your faults, and tries to help you out when you're in trouble? Right?"

"I guess," I said.

"Is that the kind of friend you want? A friend who underneath everything else really loves you? Do you want that kind of friend?"

I nodded again, looking down at my hands.

"Then buy a dog," Jerry said.

I took my stuff and got out of the car. Jerry got out his side.

"Aw, come on," he yelled. "Where are you going? Don't walk away."

"What do you want me to do?" I asked.

"I don't know. Decide some things. Figure some things out."

"Sure," I said. I turned to go.

"Don't you want a ride?" he called. I shook my head.

"Well, wait a minute anyway. Don't leave me here. Give me a hand with the car."

I had forgotten about the car. There was something wrong with the starter. Whenever Jerry turned it off, he had to crawl under the engine and whack the starter motor with a hammer, then get back in and try to start it. Sometimes it took four or five tries like that. It was much easier if there were two people, one whacking the starter, the other turning the key in the ignition.

"You're on your own," I said. "Just like me."

"You asshole," he yelled. "It better start."

Now what? The La Brea tarpits. People *are* animals. Let them think whatever they want, let them close their minds off completely to everything around them and everything inside them, but that's what they are. You can see what their inner being is — the instincts beneath the surface — just as you can see their resemblance to other animals. Not only that, but animals are better than people. They can see better, smell better, run faster, bite harder, even think quicker in most situations. Chemicals and bulldozers — those are the only things people have over animals. And guns. And it's their human nature, not their instincts, that lets them kill and destroy and poison everything. Animals don't have wars. Except ants. If my brain's a swamp, what's theirs?

So what's wrong with letting the animal nature emerge? It is in there. What's wrong with seeing the animal nature in other people? They may try to bury it, but it's in them, too. They're the ones with the La Brea tarpits for brains. They're the ones who are letting their animals suffocate in the swamp, never to rise again. They're the ones whose instincts are extinct.

They think they know everything. Sure they do. They don't even know what's a person and what's an animal. They divide everything up — classify everything. This is a predator, this is a parasite, this is a herbivore, this is a scavenger. These animals are territorial, these are nomadic. These mate briefly, these mate for life. These are solitary animals, these have a highly developed social structure. These are harmful, these are beneficial. None of that applies to humans. They can be all of those things.

So what am I, harmful or beneficial? I'm neither, god-damn it, I just live here. A parasite or a predator? Depends on who's doing the talking. Animals don't fit into categories that neatly, either. The glutinous hagfish — what Jerry's been calling his grandmother since we read about it in biology — is that a predator or a parasite? It rasps a big hole in the side of a large fish, crawls inside the body cavity, and eats away the viscera. What's the difference between that and a hookworm? Or a motile amoeba? The amoeba probably thinks it's a predator, too.

Maybe what I am is the canary in the coal mine. And I'll have to die for them to notice there's something wrong here. They wouldn't care. In my book of the great zoos, it quotes a veterinarian on diseases in birds: when a sick bird is brought to you for treatment, there is only one thing to do, send the owner away, go to the nearest pet shop, and get another dickey bird. Nice. That's what they'd do to me, too.

No. That's not the way it was going to be. Let them turn on me. All social species have their outcasts — those animals that have been driven from the herd or pack. The rogue elephant, the rogue lion, even the rogue baboon or chimpanzee. He hunts by himself, sleeps apart from the rest of the tribe, wanders through their territory and others, and becomes dangerous. The others may start by scorning him, but soon they fear him. If that's the way it was going to be, then so be it. A rogue male.

But what was Robbins's part in all this? Had he been keeping them away from me or me away from them? They were the pack. I was the outcast. Was he the one who finally drove me out? There can even be more than one rogue male. They can band together, hunt together, protect each other. Isn't that what Robbins had said before? And Jerry? And what happens to Karen?

By now I had reached Ken's house. Ken was out on his front lawn throwing up. I waited to see if he was okay. There is nothing in the world you could compare to the sight of a dog throwing up. The way they stand there looking at the spot where the puke will land, with their mouth stretched open twice as wide as it should be, as if it was pried open with a stick, just patiently waiting for it to happen, then making that hacking sound in their throat that makes you want to retch, too. Then they puke or they don't, but in either case, they just start up doing whatever they were doing before as if nothing had happened, even go back to playing with you, running around, jumping — until they decide to throw up again, stop, look down, hunch over the spot where they're going to let it go, open their mouth, and start making that sound.

I watched Ken doing that on the lawn. Finally a little bit of green stuff came out of his mouth and fell in a puddle between his front feet. He smelled it, then trotted over to me.

"Ate some grass," he said.

"You know," I said, "as long as I live, I'll never understand why dogs like to eat grass and puke it up."

Ken made a huge hacking sound again, then seemed to feel better.

"Listen, Ken," I said. "Would you be willing to talk to me with somebody else present? Just enough, you know, to prove it really does happen?"

"What!" he said. "Certainly not. Never." He looked away from me and kept looking away.

"Just once." I said.

"No."

263

"But why?"

He turned and looked at me again. "Because you they'd try to cure," he said. "Me they'd put to sleep."

34

Imagine a bright, sunny day with a blue sky and a warm breeze, and just a few little clouds way over by the horizon. You take a walk, or you play a game, or you just lie back in the grass, happy to be alive on such a beautiful day. But all this time a huge thundercloud has been growing and growing and slowly covering the sky, while you didn't notice anything at all. Suddenly just its edge touches the edge of the sun and the whole world is threatened by darkness. That is what my animals were doing to me. Everything seemed sunny, but all the time the whole sky was being engulfed by a gigantic black cloud. It seemed like only a pinpoint of light was left to be saved.

Nothing especially terrible or spectacular had happened. I hadn't turned into something and not been able to get back to myself again. I hadn't hurt somebody or done any damage the way Robbins seemed to have been hoping. I hadn't stopped seeing Karen and Jerry hadn't stopped being my friend. We hadn't talked about being crazy again. In fact, everything seemed to be back to normal. I didn't tell Jerry about incidents anymore. I did tell Karen when something happened, but we wouldn't talk much about it. And I tried not to let anything happen when I was with them, though I think it was probably luck that nothing did. It was true that I was out of control. I didn't tell either of them about the times I just wanted to strike out at any living thing that darted across my path. The times when anything small that made a quick motion hypnotized me. Even bugs. I never told about the time there was a cat on the sidewalk in front of me and I suddenly wanted to get it in my mouth and break its back by shaking it, or that as I got closer it broke into a little trot and so did I, and that when it saw that, it took off across the street and just missed getting run over.

It just seemed like I was scared all the time, or mad all the time, or horny all the time, or miserable all the time. It seemed my animals were taking up all my time and leaving me no time to be myself. Without Ken, I had no one to talk to. And he wasn't talking anymore.

Jerry and Karen both had a kind of air of expectancy about them. They obviously had talked to each other about me. And now clouds, clouds in the shape of animals — like when you lie down on the side of a hill and watch them move across the sky — were gathering over my head.

I didn't want to go see the school shrink. He was a maniac. I don't know, maybe he was good at drug counseling. That's what he did mostly. Kids would get into trouble with drugs, then run to get into the drug counseling program before their parents were notified or before they were suspended from school so they could say they had already been getting help and what they did this time that got them in trouble was what they had been trying to get help for all along. Sometimes it worked, sometimes it didn't.

"That's where to start," Karen said when I talked to her about it. "Maybe he'll send you to someone else better."

"He'll think I'm on drugs," I said. "He'll assume it. Especially when I start talking."

"Should I come with you?" she asked. I said no, but when I went, she waited outside.

I did it when school started again after Easter vacation, which I had spent most of reading and watching TV in my room.

I hung around in the guidance waiting room, looking through the Careers booklets until Mr. Halpern, the school counselor, opened his door. He looked around the room. I was the only one there. He looked at me. He pointed his finger at his own chest, saying, "Me?" I nodded yes, and he waved at me to come into his office.

This guy, Mr. Halpern, had the original crusher hand-shake. You got that when you first went in. When you left, you got the Brother's handshake, thumb versus thumb. Sometimes you ended up grabbing each other's wrist and holding on. That was either his idea of a Modified Brother's or else a Modified Scout's. What it really is is the mountaineer's grip for pulling another guy up over a ledge.

I saw him two times. The first time I was nervous, I guess, because each time I described something that had happened, I started laughing. He would smile and say, "Why do you think that's funny?"

Of course he assumed I was taking drugs. He started out, "I'm not going to give you a big moral lecture about drug use. I'm sure you've heard all that before."

I shook my head.

"No?" he asked. "You've never heard that before?"

I shook my head again.

"Not even from your parents?" he asked.

"Oh, from them," I said. "Sure. But I'm not here for that."

"For drugs, you mean," he said.

"That's right."

"What are you here for, then?" he asked.

"For what I said."

"Yeah, but what was that again? I don't think I get it."

"Me either," I said. "Why do you think I'm here?"

"Hey," he said. "Don't get smart, okay? You come here, I treat you straight. I expect you to treat me straight." He sat back in his chair and flexed his triceps. He always wore short-sleeve shirts so you could see he had big arm muscles. That was supposed to impress us adolescents. Big deal.

He couldn't get it straight that I didn't take drugs. He kept trying to put what I told him into the context of drug flashbacks. He kept asking if I had ever done pot, if I had ever done PCP, if I had ever free-based. He got mad when I said I hadn't even heard of some of the things he came up with.

"Just don't bullshit me, okay?" he said. "Just don't bullshit me."

"This isn't going to help," I told Karen after the first time. "For one thing, he's obsessed by drugs. He can't believe I don't take drugs. He even asked me if I ever sniffed contact cement."

"What is it?" Karen asked.

"I don't know," I said. "Some kind of cement, I guess. You ever see anybody get high sniffing the sidewalk?"

"Look, I'm sorry," she said.

"And second, you get stigmatized just walking in there. By him, no matter what he says, and by everybody else who sees you. I can't go back there."

"What does he say?" she asked.

"I'm supposed to see him again Thursday," I said.

Karen waited outside on Thursday.

267

"I'm supposed to go to some clinic," I told her after. "A regular psychiatric counseling clinic."

"Good," she said. "That's better than here."

35

"As a teenager," the lady was saying, "you are trying out different identities, almost like trying on different clothes, to see what you will look like. That's what being a teenager is about. It's not surprising that you're a bit mixed up. It's a very confusing time. But that's how we grow.

"Your sympathy and understanding of animals shows that you are a sensitive person. These new feelings you have can sometimes seem quite scary — the awakening of sexual feelings, the conflicts between your desire for independence from your family and the wish to still be protected by them, your own perhaps confused feelings of desire and tenderness. These conflicts are all a normal part of the process of becoming a man."

"So what does all that have to do with turning into animals all the time?"

I had been there an hour and a half, the first hour filling out forms, being told that everything about my visit would be kept totally confidential if I wanted it that way, and then waiting for my appointment. I had to tell them twice that I wasn't there for the VD clinic. It must have been the word "animals" on the referral the school shrink gave me that made them think that. Then this lady came and got me and brought me into her office, where we sat in two leather chairs and I explained, as clearly as I could, what was the matter with me.

She took a breath and went on. "Well, of course, you don't really turn into an animal. I'm sure you don't believe that literally. But you feel overwhelmed by some of your feelings of tenderness, of sympathy, of love for other people, which seem threatening to you, and in your anxiety at feeling such strong emotions, you are transferring them to less-threatening objects, in this case, animals. Loving animals is not bad. In fact, you might say that learning to love, and to feel protective instincts toward an animal — a pet dog or cat, for instance — is preparation for the loving relationship you will eventually develop with another person. Do you see that?"

"I guess so," I said. "But I don't know if it's really that."

"Well, let's see if it's that. For instance, the last time you experienced these feelings you call 'turning into an animal' what happened?"

"I turned into a dog."

"Okay. Now why did you do that? Was there a dog you felt sorry for? Or felt some attachment to?"

"Yes. There was a dog that was being mistreated."

"What, exactly?"

"Yanked down the street by its leash. Then it got slugged a couple times when it didn't keep up."

"Well, that certainly fits in with what we've been saying. People can be mean, your relations to them are ambiguous, but here, when you see a fellow creature mistreated, you instinctively reach out to it. And what did you do when you had put yourself in that dog's place?"

"I bit its owner," I said.

"You did what?"

"I turned into another dog and bit the owner. Then the other dog got in a fight with me and I ran away. You know how loyal dogs are to their owners. I guess I shouldn't have interfered."

"I don't believe you," she said. "You didn't really bite the owner."

"Yes I did. Really."

"And then what?"

"I took off around the corner and came back as me again."

"And?"

"The guy was hollering to a cop about finding the dog that bit him because I had broken the skin and he was afraid he'd have to have rabies shots if they didn't catch me."

"I see," she said after a pause. "Look. I think I'd like to refer you to our resident therapist. She might be able to help you more than I could. I'm more a sort of general counselor. I work more with kids whose problems are less . . . less . . ."

"Loony," I said.

"No, no," she said, "that's not what I meant at all. I mean I deal usually with kids whose problems are more normal. I mean their problems are more normal, not that they are more normal.

"In fact," she said, talking a little faster, "you seem quite normal to me. But your problem is a little different from what I'm used to dealing with. That's all."

She gave me a big smile. I lolled my tongue out of the side of my mouth and laughed like a crazy. Jerry could do it perfectly, but I had never been able to get it right. It was good enough for her, though.

"Deep breaths," she said. "Slow, deep breaths."

I just sighed. I was pretty miserable.

"Let's go back out to the reception area and make that appointment," she said, and beat me out the door.

• • •

I hadn't told my parents about going to the clinic. Karen knew, of course.

"What did they say?" she wanted to know.

"They told me I was a teenager," I said.

"That's all?"

"That and they want to see me again."

"But what did they say?"

"They said I bit the guy on the leg because I'm confused about my feelings. It's just part of growing up."

"You bit somebody?" she said.

"Yeah, didn't I tell you that?"

"No."

"Well, I'm not sure I'm going back. I mean how would you feel if you went to the doctor and said I'm sick and instead of helping you he went Aargh and ran out of the room?"

"Is that what happened?"

"Approximately."

"Did you bite somebody at the clinic?"

"No, no," I said. "Forget it. It happened a long time ago."

"When?"

"Couple weeks. But now they want me to see somebody else."

"Another counselor?"

"A veterinarian."

"A dog obedience trainer," she said.

"Maybe a lion tamer," I said.

"Ooh, I'd be so proud," she said and squeezed my bicep. She was pretty funny sometimes. But she really wanted me to go back.

The day before I was supposed to return to the clinic, Mr. Halpern spotted me in the corridor.

"Hey, how's it going?" he hollered, then came over

and we had a short thumb wrestle. "How they treating you over at the clinic?"

I said okay and that I was supposed to go back again the next day.

"Who've you been seeing over there?" he asked.

I said I had seen a counselor and now was going to see a therapist.

"A real good buddy of mine works there," he said. "He's good people. They all are. Trust them." He pointed his finger at me when he said trust them. It looked like he was telling me to sit. I watched him walk down the corridor. He sort of rolled back and forth as he walked, and with the walk and his sleeves rolled up, he looked like Popeye on the poop deck.

You had to sign in to the clinic, then wait until you were called. I was waiting when this man who had been sitting on the other side of the room came over to get one of the magazines that were on the table, then sat down next to me. He nodded to me, so I nodded back.

"You an outpatient?" he asked me.

"I guess so," he said.

"Me, too," he said.

"I'm proud," he said after a minute. He looked at me. "I'm proud to be an outpatient. Aren't you?"

"I don't know," I said. "I never thought of it that way."

"Well, think about it," he said.

"You got your certificate?" he asked a moment later.

"What certificate?" I asked him.

"The certificate that says you're sane," he said. I looked at the receptionist, but she wasn't paying any attention. "I've got mine. It's a good thing to have."

"I'll bet," I said.

"You don't have one?" he asked.

"Not yet," I said. "I didn't know I needed one."

"Hhm," he said. He looked at his magazine. "I don't know," he said to himself. "I don't know about that."

Finally they called me.

The therapist seemed nice. All she did was ask questions the whole time. She asked why I was there and who had referred me. She asked me in what way I thought they would be able to help me. When I said I wasn't sure, she said that might be the first thing we should try to figure out. There was no way, though, that I was going to say we should get rid of my animals. Control them, understand them better, learn how to utilize them — tame them — sure, but not just get cured of them. She thought "understand them better" was okay. That might be a good place to start, she said. So she asked me to repeat the story I had told the first counselor.

"Very interesting," she said. "How did you feel during the time you were a dog?"

"Mad," I said, but she didn't get it.

"Mad," she said. "How mad? By the way, is there something wrong with your hand?"

"I hurt it in gym," I said. I had landed on it in gym doing a flip on the mats and had twisted my wrist. I was opening and closing my hand while we talked to try to get it to loosen up.

"It's a bit distracting," she said. "Does it hurt a lot?"

"I can't even make a fist," I said.

"Why do you want to make a fist?"

"I don't. But I couldn't if I wanted to."

"Are you angry now?" she asked. "You did say fist. Do you want to punch someone?"

"No," I said. "That's just how much it hurts."

"I see," she said. "When you get angry, do you want to punch people then?"

"Sometimes," I said.

"Let me ask you this," she said. "Do you ever get angry and then discover your hand is hurting?"

She was much better at it than my father, but I knew a trap when I heard one being set. She couldn't have had more practice setting them than I had evading them. She asked a lot of questions about school and home. At the end of the time, she said, "Do you think your home situation could have anything to do with it? I mean with both parents in the home, sometimes there is a lot of tension. There can be a buildup of resentment. Nondivorced parents often have conflicted children."

"Ball four," I said.

"What does that mean?" she asked, smiling.

"It means you're trying to get me to say something I don't mean by tricking me. Like making me swing at a bad pitch. But I won't, so it's ball four."

"It's a kind of sports metaphor?" she asked.

"Right," I said.

"No," she said, "I'm not trying to trick you, especially not into saying something you don't mean. I'm wondering, though, whether it isn't time we told your parents about this. Don't you think they have a right to help you if they can?"

An appointment with my parents. Exactly what I needed. Too bad I couldn't dress them up in Big Bird costumes, or as one of those two-person horses. That would blow their minds down at the clinic.

"Think I'm nuts, huh?" I'd say. "Well, I'd like you to meet my parents, Mr. and Mrs. Big Bird." Then my parents could sit there and act as normal and concerned as they wanted, but nothing would help. The more normal they acted, the more crazy they'd seem. Pretty soon the therapist would be asking me questions about them. "I only do these things to please them," I'd say about my

274

animals. Then my father would throw up his hands the way he does, but all you'd see is a crazy man flapping his Big Bird wings.

I was almost home. I passed Ken up on his porch. When he saw me, he put his head down on top of his front paws and watched me walk by.

I didn't want to tell my parents, especially my father. I didn't want a repeat performance of the time Jerry got into the fight. Of course maybe it wouldn't be that way.

"Dad, can I talk to you about something?"

"Sure, Beaver, come into the den. Now what's troubling you, son?"

"Dad, I've been acting like different animals lately, and I'm not sure what to do about it. Wally says I'm crazy."

"Oh, Beaver, is that all it is? It's a perfectly normal thing for a boy your age. Why, when I was your age, we used to turn into animals all the time." Et cetera. Sure. My father was going to handle this about as well as Mr. Cleaver would have handled Beaver's whacking off.

"What!" he said. "What are you telling me? What's this again?"

I wanted to show him, to do it right in front of him. That was the real problem with the whole thing as far as I was concerned. I hadn't learned how to make it happen when I wanted to.

"This is the crap you were peddling around school about yourself? This is how far it's gotten? To seeing a psychiatrist? What are you trying to prove? You're whacko? Is that it? You want everybody to think you're some kind of . . . of what? Some kind of visionary or something? Weird? Different? What are we now, so sensitive, so something'd by the world that we're too delicate to function in it? Huh?"

"Dad," I said. "I know some things . . ."

"You know nothing!" he yelled.

I knew the thing I'd do if only I could. There's a certain species of termite whose soldiers have a 'glue squirter' for a head. If they meet an enemy, glue squirts out from their head and sticks the enemy to the spot. A little glue between the mandibles wouldn't hurt either, in this case.

"You know nothing," he yelled again. "You're a perfectly normal, average boy with nothing wrong with you. You're trying to make yourself out to be weird when you're not. You're a faker all the way. What do you think you are, a 'sensitive artist' or something, somebody us boobs, us 'normals' can't understand? You're an artist, all right. A bullshit artist."

"I didn't say that," I said.

"What'd you say?" he yelled.

"I didn't say anything like that. I said the therapist wants to talk to you."

"The therapist! The quack."

"Richard," my mother said. She tried to put her hand on my father's arm.

"No," he said. "Enough is enough. And I've put up with more than enough from him. I don't have to put up with this." He turned to face my mother. "I don't have to encourage it. I don't have to participate in it. I don't have to take pride in the fact that my son goes to a shrink. A *therapist*, I mean. Let him go if he wants to go. Let him pay for it, too."

He walked out of the room. My mother stayed, looking down at the table in front of her.

"Your father's upset," she said.

"How can you tell?" I asked. "He seems his usual self to me." A total prick, I thought to myself, a real asshole, a fascist.

"We'll talk to the therapist this week," my mother said. "We'll see what she thinks we should do. I know your father will want to do whatever he can to help you."

"I can see that," I said.

My mother made a big sigh and got up to finish making dinner. I sat there. My cheeks began to burn. I clenched and unclenched my fists, not caring how much the hurt one hurt. The tears started rolling down my cheeks. I got up before anybody saw and went to the bathroom and washed my face.

Later that night I heard them arguing in their bedroom. They were trying to whisper, but I could hear them fine.

"Nobody in my family was ever crazy," my father was saying, "and I'll be damned if I'm going to let him be the first."

"Are you saying it comes from my side?" my mother said. "The only crazy one in my family was me for marrying someone so stupid."

"Oh, is that so?" my father said. "How about your brother Paul that we named Batso in there after? Forty years old and his greatest achievement is his collection of Grateful Dead records. And being a fruitarian. Not just a vegetarian now — a *fruitarian*. Until his colon stopped working — WHICH he blamed on the pesticides, not on the fact that he ate nothing but fruit mush for a year."

"Stop it," my mother said. "Tomorrow morning we're going to call the therapist and make an appointment to see her. Then we'll find out exactly how serious this is, and we'll decide how to deal with it. Maybe it isn't as serious as it seems right now. Maybe we're letting ourselves get upset over nothing."

"Nothing!" my father said. "The kid thinks he's a mutant!"

"He's a troubled child," my mother said.

"A mutant," my father said. "A troubled mutant."

"He's a good boy," my mother said.
My father said nothing, at least that I could hear.

36

My parents had an early afternoon appointment to see the people at the clinic. When I got home from school, they were in the living room talking about me.

"Shock therapy," was the first thing I heard my father saying. I froze.

"Richard!" my mother said.

"Not for him," my father said. "For me."

"Oh, come on," my mother said. "They don't give shock therapy anymore."

"Well, I want some," my father said.

I stepped into the doorway. My mother was shaking her head at my father, and my father was shaking his head at nothing.

One of the best ways to bug your parents is to turn into a fly and buzz around the room. Flies buzz in a sort of large figure-eight pattern. In fact, a fly is a little like a racing car on a track in midair. It goes at full speed away from you, banks the far turn, and comes racing back. The sound it makes is F-natural. F-flat if the weather is cool. Flies are also tireless. They never quit.

My parents tried to brush me away at first, but I kept coming back. When my father finally became so annoyed he got up to swat me, I landed on the inside of a lamp shade. Calmly rubbing my front legs together, I watched him trying to sneak his rolled-up newspaper down between the shade and the light bulb without breaking anything. When he was finally ready to strike, I flew away.

At first my father couldn't find me, so I had to go back and buzz him some more. Once I had his attention again, I flew over to the curtain. He swatted the curtain as hard as he could. It didn't hurt at all.

"I think I got him," he said. I waited a second, then began buzzing again. My father started chasing me around the room, leaping up in the air and swinging the newspaper like a wild man.

"It's only a fly," my mother said.

"No, it's not," I said. "It's me, your son."

My father looked startled. He looked at the newspaper, then looked around for the fly. He looked at me.

"What do you want?" he said.

"I want to know what happened at the clinic," I said. "What they said."

My father took a deep breath. He threw the paper on the coffee table.

"Sit down," he said. "Let's have a talk, you, your mother, and I."

My father did the talking. He was very calm, not angry at all, very serious. He tried very hard. Unfortunately, he didn't make any sense. He told me I was too passive, not aggressive enough, that I let things happen to me instead of going out and making things happen. At the same time, he said, I was trying too hard, being too much of a perfectionist, and getting too upset when I didn't do something perfectly. He said my mother and he loved me very much, that I could trust them, but that I couldn't rely on them to make my decisions for me. That this. That that. He went on and on. He was like in math, where two parallel lines recede to infinity. You kept thinking he was going to come to a point, but he never did.

They told him at the clinic that I was passive-aggressive with something else wrong, but that I wasn't schizophrenic.

"You're not schizophrenic," he said.

"Am I going to keep going to the clinic?" I asked.

"Oh, yes," he said. "Your mother and I agreed that that would be best. They're going to give you an evaluation, which they'll give us the results of, and then decide on the best type of counseling for you.

"I wish you had come to us sooner," he said. "Maybe this would be all over by now."

My next appointment at the clinic was switched to Wednesday so I could have an evaluation by Dr. Gimmealobotomy or something like that. A long name, anyway. He was a regular doctor, I guess, because he started out by checking my reflexes and my blood pressure and my heartbeat. He made me close my eyes and touch my finger to my nose. Then I had to stand on one foot, then the other foot, with my eyes closed. He scratched the bottom of my foot and asked if I could feel it. He shined a light in my eyes, I think to make sure my pupils dilated. Then I read the eye chart and he checked my ears.

"All normal," he said. He sat down behind his desk and I sat in front of it. He put his elbows on the desk and looked across at me. They must have cut the legs off my chair or something, because when I put my elbows on the desk, they were about at the level of my neck.

When he read the evaluations on his desk, all I could see was the edges of the paper. I couldn't read the words at all from that angle, even upside down.

He skimmed the reports. "Gets along well in school . . . two siblings . . . no family history . . . no diabetes, no rheumatic fever . . . He presented as an intelligent, articulate sixteen-year-old boy with appropriate behavior."

He looked up at me after reading that, as if that said something. I presented as? I thought that's what I was. Did he mean I presented myself as a sixteen-year-old boy instead of presenting myself as a monkey or a giraffe? Which would have been inappropriate behavior, certainly. Presenting is what mandrills do, it's like displaying, only they present their purple and yellow assholes to you, which is appropriate behavior for them whenever they feel like grossing you out. Anyway, if his question was why I didn't do that, he didn't ask it.

"Physiologically, neurologically normal," he said. "Drugs, sex, alcohol, family problems — nothing. I don't understand. Kids today . . . the problems they have . . . you have nothing. There's nothing wrong. You're a nice, well-adjusted, successful boy. What do you want to turn into a bird for? You have nothing to escape, nothing to prove. This is no way to get attention. Steal, do bad things in school, take a lot of drugs. Even your father — I met him. No big deal. A nice man, but he's not a doctor or anything, somebody you have to compete with or prove yourself to. So come on. You can keep coming here if that's what you want, certainly no one's going to turn you away. But you're going to have to snap out of it by yourself, that's all I can see. Well, what do you say? Can we shake on it?"

He stood up and put his hand out. I stood up, too, and we shook hands.

I kept going to the clinic, though, no matter what the doctor said. In fact, when I tried to get out of it by saying he had said I could, it turned out that that was not what he wrote down. He had recommended that I see a real psychiatrist, which is what I got switched to.

"Identity problems, eh?" he had said the first time I saw him. "Well, you've come to the right place." And he rubbed his hands together. I had been going there for more than a month now, ever since just after Easter. This day was my third time with him.

I always felt depressed going there, and embarrassed in the waiting room, especially looking around and wondering how many of the other nuts had a Certificate of Sanity like the first nut had.

My parents had had to tell Jessica and Luke something. They told Jessica that I was a little mixed up about school and stuff, and that sometimes it could be a big help to talk to somebody. Jessica knew what a psychiatrist was.

They told Luke I was very interested in animals, perhaps too interested, like some kids get real interested in, well, animals, and don't pay attention to other stuff. Like in school, when kids get too interested in one thing they are doing and the teacher has to help them settle down and go on to the next thing, even if the thing they like is a good thing to do, like coloring or learning about animals.

From then on, Luke told me anytime he saw an animal, or learned about animals in school. He would watch closely, too, and make sure he had everything right when he told me something. You can imagine how it made me feel, though, knowing that he was trying to help me. My mother had told me that he had asked her if it was okay to talk about animals or if it was better not to. She had said it was okay.

"I saw two birds fighting on the way home from school," he said one day. "They were on a branch all hooked together, then they fell off and almost hit the ground."

He flapped his arms to show how the birds had been flapping their wings.

"But they didn't fall on the ground, because they were flying at the same time. Were they fighting, Paul?"

"Well, it depends," I said. "Were they the same kind of bird?"

"I think so. They were the same color."

"Same size?"

"I don't know. Yeah. They were the same kind, I think."

"Well, were they both males, or was one a male and one a female?"

"What's a male?" he asked.

"A male is a boy bird and a female is a girl. If they were both males, they were probably fighting, but if one was a male and the other was a female, they probably weren't. See, the males fight with each other to protect their nest or their eggs, or to protect the female. But the male and the female don't fight."

"Which one's the boy and girl again?"

"The male is the boy and the female is the girl."

"Why don't they fight?"

"Well, they don't," my mother interrupted. "They're a family together."

"Are they married?" Luke asked.

"Yeah," I said. "So if it was two males you saw, you're right, they were fighting. But if it was a male and a female, they were doing something else."

"What?" Luke asked.

"Hugging and kissing the way birds do," my mother said.

"Oh, Mom," Jessica said. She had been listening.

My mother raised her eyebrows. "Do you have a better explanation?" she asked Jessica.

So Luke was very proud of how well he had observed the birds, especially how long he had stood still not to disturb them, and proud of being able to tell me stuff about animals. He was very serious about it.

But this day was one of my counseling days. Who did I find sitting in the waiting room when I got there but Andy Espada. He gave me a big smile and moved his books so I could sit next to him. He didn't seem embarrassed about my finding out that he came here, too. He seemed really glad to see me. I felt sort of sheepish about it, like I had found out a secret about him, and he, of course, had found out the same secret about me, but I said hi.

"What'd they get you for?" I asked him. That did embarrass him. I realized that you probably weren't supposed to ask. Like maybe Andy kept turning into different molecular structures or something. Wouldn't that be a coincidence.

"Oh, anxiety, I guess," he said. "Insecurity. Feelings of inadequacy. You know. What are you doing here?"

"You can't guess?" I said.

"Oh, yeah," he said. "That's very interesting. In fact, I mentioned you to someone I know where I take some courses. He thought it was very interesting, too. He said I should bring you with me some time. He'd straighten you out, he said."

"Who's this?" I asked.

"He's a professor of genetic ethology. A zoologist, really."

"Ha!" I said. "You know what Jerry wants to do?"

"Jerry Raynor?" Andy asked.

"Yeah. He wants to perform an exorcism. Exorcise all my animals. He says all we have to do is say their Latin names backwards and they'll leave my body.

"Oblongata medulla," I chanted.

"That's part of your brain!" Andy said.

"Whoops," I said. "I need that."

"That may be where the animals live," Andy said.

The shrink was standing by his office door waving for me to come.

"Did you really talk to a zoologist about me?" I asked Andy.

"Not purposely. I don't know how it came up. He did think you were very interesting, though. I didn't tell him your name or anything."

"That's okay," I said. "Doctor Lugosi is calling. I'll see you later."

"Let's review where we are," the psychiatrist said. "One day you talk to animals, another day you perceive other people as if they were animals, a third day you believe you yourself have become an animal. Now this isn't logical. There's no consistency here. Now which is it?

"You see," he went on, waving his finger in the air, "these are three separate types of delusions, each well documented in the medical literature. But a combination of them is unheard of. I want to go back to the dream you told me."

The phone rang in his other office. He had two offices, one with a desk and some files, and other with just chairs and a table. I think he was the head of the whole clinic.

"Excuse me," he said. "I'm sorry for the interruption. This isn't supposed to happen when I'm seeing someone." He went to answer the phone.

I had made the mistake of telling him about a dream I had had about wolves. In the dream it was late at night and I was alone in the house — in our old house — sleeping. I heard a sound coming from the woods behind the house and woke up, in the dream. I looked out my bedroom window. There was a bright full moon, and standing at the edge of the woods were all these wolves, a whole pack. The young ones were wrestling and chasing each other, and some of the adults were standing while others were sitting on their haunches. One of them stepped forward from the trees into the backyard and looked up at the window and saw me. He and I looked at each other. The other wolves seemed restless like they wanted to go, but the one wolf continued to look at me. It almost seemed as if he wanted to talk to me. All the wolves were silver-colored in the moonlight. I got up and went downstairs and went to the sliding glass door in the back. I remember I had on underpants and nothing else. Nobody was home but me. The wolf came up from the edge of the woods and walked up to the outside of the glass. We looked at each other through the glass. The wolf was me, a wolf, looking in at myself, a boy. As soon as I opened the door, one of us would go in, or one of us would go out, to join the other. That's how it ended.

The shrink found it extremely interesting. I thought it was pretty good myself, so when I woke up at that point, I sat up in bed and replayed it in my mind so I wouldn't forget. Still, I had dreamt it about a year ago, maybe more. I knew it had something to do with something, but everything has.

I didn't like the psychiatrist, though. He didn't take me seriously. I mean he was serious, but it was himself he took seriously, not me. I mean it would have been pretty good if he could have said, "I'm not interested in you, I'm just interested in your mind," you know, like the opposite of what you can never say to girls.

"There was, of course, a famous case history of a man who thought he was a duck," he said to me when I first told him my problem. "His personality was quite unstable, it goes without saying, and one time, evidently, in a moment of anxiety and depression, he had found relief in contemplating these creatures, and ended up by identifying himself with them."

The thing is, he didn't find that interesting because it might have something to do with me. In fact, he said it probably didn't. He found me interesting because I might have something to do with it.

Now I could hear him on the phone. "My own Sybil!" he said. "My own Wolfman!"

That did it. Well, I thought, you're not getting famous off me, and I walked out of his office, out of the clinic, and kept on going. My own wolfman. I wasn't his own anything. The best thing would have been to turn into a wolf in his office like he wanted and rip his throat open. Then they would find him dead in there and start a manhunt for me. That's what would happen in the werewolf movie when the psychiatrist thought he knew so much about everything.

Then they could hunt me down with torches with the villagers all crossing themselves and some innocent little girl being my friend, and the wise old professor who's seen cases like this before and who knows that if he can't find me and cure me in time, then I must be killed.

I didn't want to be hunted with torches. And I didn't want to be a freak that some doctor writes a book about.

I had to stay out until five-thirty. That was the time I usually got home from the clinic. I could hear my father yelling before I even opened the door.

"Family counseling!" he was yelling at my mother. "I'm supposed to get *my* head shrunk because *he's* crazy? They're trying to milk us, that's all they're doing. They're quacks! Snake oil salesmen! Family therapy! Are they going to say it's my fault?"

I stood in the hall, making no noise. Maybe my mother would shoot him.

"Well, maybe it is my fault," he said more quietly. "Maybe I've been too harsh with him or something.

Maybe I should have been more understanding. Maybe I should try to be kinder. Maybe we should do more things together."

"Here, fella!" he called. Wheet, wheet, he whistled. "C'mon boy. Here. Let me rub you behind the ear. How 'bout a nice biscuit. Let's go for a walk."

I could hear him walking around. "Holy shit," he was saying.

"All right, son, how 'bout you and your ol' Dad here joining the 4-H Club together. Let's raise champion guinea pigs. Let's you and me go fishin'. Let's go dig the worms now, but you can't eat any till we get there. Ho, ho. Mother of God. What's going to happen to us?"

I closed the door I had been holding open. My father heard it and came out and looked at me. "So you ran away from the shrink," he said. Then he walked right by me, opened the door, and left.

37

I went with Andy on Saturday to see his friend. I really felt this was my last chance. Everybody thought I was nuts, I thought I was nuts, and I was beginning to have feelings that I knew were bad. I was beginning to feel a longing for the forest.

Andy chattered away the whole way there. I guess nobody had ever come with him to his class or his lab before. He really hoped we would have time to see his lab space. He said he had his own table and cabinet and access to the computer terminal and everything.

We met his friend in the cafeteria. He shook my hand and looked at me with an amused expression.

"So you're the specimen, eh?" he said. "The missing link. All the links, according to Andy."

Andy had called him his friend, but he was pretty old. I had to try not to look at his nose. He had big tufts of hair coming out of his nostrils. The hair was either growing down out of his nose or growing up into his nose, you couldn't tell. But I had already decided I was going to talk to this guy and tell him everything. He didn't have to believe me, he just had to answer me, just say what the connection between a human and a rat is, for instance, or how humans and dogs usually communicate. He could tell me I was out of my head for doing such things, as long as he could also tell me something about how I did them. Something to balance the kids and the shrinks and my parents, something that would help me hold them off. And hold off my own slipping feelings.

Instead, he decided to tell me I was wrong about evolution. He had listened to my stories, just nodding his head and going hmmpf. He looked right into my eyes the whole time, which made me look back at him while I was talking, instead of looking down or around the way you usually do. Sometimes I'd find myself looking into his nose, which made me bring my eyes back up. He didn't ask if I thought these things *really* happened, or whether I felt an affinity for animals. Sometimes he'd nod and say something like, "Yes, that would be right, there's a structural affinity there," or else, "No, no, that's not correct, the mesopodialia aren't that well developed yet."

Finally, he looked over at Andy. "No," he said. He raised his arms. He turned back to me. "You're wrong," he said.

He accused me of Lamarckism. Here I was, totally out

of my head, evidently, and he's telling me Lamarck's ideas about evolution are all wrong.

"You can't acquire characteristics just because you want them," he said. "You can't adapt just because you should. To apply Lamarck's own example: the protogiraffe stretching its neck to reach the leaves. You see?"

I didn't.

"Well, it's beside the point, anyway. It's not your case, really. Unless you wanted to pass it on.

"But look. You seem to think you're not a whole person, but just a bunch of layers of other things. Do you think these animals have colonized you? Certainly not — we'd be talking about bacteria, viruses, steroidal protein strings. Look. If there had been any logical order to the things you became, for example, first a protozoan, then a sponge, then a flatworm, a mollusk, and so on up through amphibian to primate, I could see some point. We could say, as some biologists do, that the development of the individual reproduces the development of the species. But this randomness. One day a cat, the next day a rat . . . It has no basis in science."

He was beginning to get excited, even mad at me.

"Actually, it was Haeckel who proposed such a system of correlation between species evolution and embryonic development. But young man, he was proven conclusively wrong fifty years ago! Ontogeny does NOT recapitulate phylogeny! You must know that. Everybody knows that. Evolution is radiational, not linear! You're not part frog, part snake, part human. So you have a pineal gland, so you have embryonic gills. You're still not descended from any of them. Oh, boy. Don't they teach you kids anything in school today?

"So in a strictly taxonomic sense, son," he said with an ironic nostril flare, "you're off the wall."

"Taxonomic?" I said. "You mean you're going to stuff me?"

"Kid," he said, "you're full of it already."

He was really rolling now. People at the other tables were turning to look. I could feel my face getting red.

"And if you're so smart, let's see you turn into something that isn't bilaterally symmetrical. Something with radial symmetry, like a coelenterate. Any coelenterate. Well, why not? Because you're not descended from them, is that it? No, it isn't. It's because you never heard of them. You're not descended from dogs and cats, either, but you know all about them. Whatever the hell you're doing, it's coming from your mind, not your brain." He tapped his head with his finger. "Here's the real trick. If you have developed from other animals, they are probably extinct. You evolved out of earlier versions of man. If you want to do something, become one of them. Become a Neanderthal."

I looked at his nose. "They're not extinct," I said.

"Listen to me, snotface!" he yelled. "Be a dog. Be a cat. Who cares! You are of no interest to me."

"That didn't work out too well, did it," said Andy after the guy left.

"Well," I said, trying to think of something to make Andy feel better, "he didn't say I was crazy. He said I was stupid."

"Most of his work is with slime molds," Andy said.

"That's why he was disappointed when he saw me," I said.

As soon as I got home, my parents left for the shrink's. They had a family counseling session with him. They would be gone the rest of the afternoon and then were going to go out for dinner. I was supposed to baby-sit

291

until they came back. My mother told me what she had left for our dinner and what I had to do.

"You be good," she said to the kids. My father didn't say a word before they left. Something must have been going on before I got home. The other kids didn't say good-bye or anything, just stood and watched my parents leave. I went to my room. I just stood there for a while, looking at my desk and my stuff, at my radio, at my books, at my baseball glove.

Luke and Jessica both came into my room. They sat on my bed without a word. I was about to tell them to leave, when I realized they were scared. They were scared for me, and because I was their big brother, they were just plain scared. Luke seemed terrified. He stuck really close to Jessica, actually touching her as they sat on the bed. They just looked at me.

I couldn't think of anything to say. I think Jess had planned something, but she didn't say it if she had. I think she had also planned some dramatic gesture like taking my hand like she had seen on TV, but she didn't do that, either. They just looked at me with frightened looks.

I felt so tired. All I wanted was to go to sleep. I started to tell them to get out so I could lie down, but I suddenly burst into tears. As soon as I did, so did they. We were all huddled up together, all three kids. I was on the floor with Luke in my arms, my face on the bed next to Jess's leg with both her hands on my forehead, all of us crying.

The three of us must have gone to sleep like that. When I woke up, I had no idea how long we had been lying there, but Jessica and Luke were still sleeping. It was almost dark outside, with just a little light slanting in through the corner window. The apartment was still. There was still no one home but us.

I got up very quietly so I wouldn't wake the kids up.

The hallway was dark. I went to the bathroom and looked in the mirror. I didn't look like I had been crying, but my eyes still felt like it. I brushed my teeth and washed my face.

I put the french fries in the oven and made hamburgers from the stuff my mother had left out. The sun was still coming in through the kitchen windows. The kitchen seemed golden in the light. Outside, the whole world seemed bathed in that color, as it streamed through the new leaves of the trees.

Jess came in.

"Why don't you set the table," I said, "for the three of us."

She did it without saying anything. I sliced some raw carrots so we'd have a vegetable and put the milk and ketchup on the table. Jessica went back to wake up Luke, so he wouldn't be alone when he woke up, she said, then they came back. Luke looked sleepy, but not sad or scared anymore.

We watched TV while we ate. I kept wanting to tell them that everything would be all right, but every time I started, a big lump would come up in my throat, and I knew I would start crying again if I tried. After a while, we did talk about the program we were watching — a wildlife program — and Luke asked what time Mom was coming home, but we didn't talk about what had happened in my room.

When my mother and father came home, they snapped on the kitchen light, and my mother said, "What are you doing in the dark?" The light was really startling. We must have looked like three owls suddenly caught with a flashlight.

"I guess we forgot to turn on the light when it got dark," I said.

"Did you eat by the light of the television, too?" she asked.

"It wasn't that dark yet," I said. "It must have gotten dark while we were eating."

She cleared the dishes while my father carried Luke to bed. He had fallen asleep in his chair. I got another glass of milk and took it to my bedroom. Before Jessica went to hers, she opened my door and looked in and waved. I smiled at her and she smiled back. Then I went to bed and cried some more.

38

I'll fly away. I'll fly away home. The words had been singing in my ears, in my mind, for weeks. That's all I could hear now, all I could think of. The song had a thousand different tunes. Sometimes it was harsh, with a hammering beat, an angry, hating song that I'd fly away from there, fly so far they'd never find me. And sometimes it had a simple, happy tune, like flying away home was the easiest thing in the world to do, and I'd do it in another minute or two, and it would be fun. And sometimes it was the saddest melody in the world, and those same words were sad, too.

I'll fly away. One bright, fine day when morning comes, I'll fly away home. And then sometimes, maybe most times, it seemed like a call, like a beautiful song coming from a faraway forest, or even from the sky, saying, Fly away, come on, take wing and fly away home.

Home. Where would that be? Where would I end up if I ever could fly? What would happen to me? Would I be in some forest? In the jungle? Sometimes the song seemed to come from some far-off place like Brazil, some place I had never even seen.

"Fly!" they yelled. "Fly away!"

It was the last day of school, school had just gotten out, and they had me surrounded. It started with a couple of them feeling good about the end of school and making fun of me. By the time we got outside, there were about fifteen of them yelling and pushing me around on the sidewalk. I started swinging back, but somebody pushed me from behind and I fell. My hand was cut and sand and little rocks had got in the cut. When they saw me starting to cry, they began to move in. More and more kids came, all yelling different stupid things, until they all began to be yelling the same thing — Fly! Fly! Fly! There must have been fifty of them.

Suddenly Jerry and Karen were there with me in the middle of the circle, trying to pull me over to Jerry's car and take me away. But I pushed them off and stayed in the middle.

I heard someone saying, "Leave him alone. They called his father to come and get him."

Robbins wasn't there. Robbins said he was like me, that he could feel things that hurt, too, and he said he'd stick by me. Where was he, then?

"Fly!" they yelled.

Someone threw a rock. It skipped by and hit a tire on Jerry's car. A kid ran into the middle of the circle waving his arms as if to frighten me into taking off. Then I could see Robbins pushing his way through the people. He was knocking them out of the way and waving his hands at me to tell me he was coming.

And then I flew.

The air above the trees holds you up. The warm air,

rising from the ground and from among the branches of the trees, carries you up with it, too. The first few yards are the hardest — you push against the air, you feel pressed down by it onto the earth. The ground clings to you. But you shake yourself free of it, pushing it away with your legs, you struggle upward, heavy, awkward, you stumble, push again, your body still clings to the earth with all its weight, and then up again and you feel the air flowing beneath you, air pushing you up, not down, carrying you — pulling you now — up and up, even with the highest branches of the trees, then clear of them and you are free.

I could see them on the ground, the circle with Jerry and Karen in the middle, all looking up, then I could see the cars on the different streets around the school, could see all the treetops moving in little circles in the breeze, as I soared, my back hot under the sun, and the wind making my eyes all teary, but carrying me higher and higher in wider and wider circles.

Where was home, then? Where did I fly? In the air, with the sun on my back, did I drift until my real wings grew strength and carried me to the forest I had dreamed of? Did I fly and fly until my strength was gone and I fell back to earth lost and alone? Did I just circle around with no idea of what to do until some stupid kid got over his gaping and brought me down by plugging me with a rock? Did I fly at all?

Oh, yes. And none of that happened.

I did fly home. I flew home to my house where my mother and father and brother and sister lived. I didn't perch in a treetop or scare my mother to death by looking in at her from the second-floor window. I just landed in front of the building and sat on the steps and waited for my father to come home.

He came up the street at about two hundred miles an

hour. He hit the brake and came right over the curb onto the sidewalk as he stopped. He jumped out of the car.

I felt so sorry for him. His face looked so desperate. He started running toward the front door, then saw me and stopped. I was standing up, looking at him.

"Dad, I'm all right," I said. He grabbed me and put his arms around me, pulling me tight against him.

"I'm all right," I said over and over, "I'm going to be all right."

He was holding my face down against his chest and rubbing my head with his hands.

"It's going to be all right. I know it is. It's going to be all right," he was saying.

Then Jerry and Karen came screaming up in Jerry's car. Behind them another car stopped. I couldn't see who was in it. My father took me back in his arms. I could feel him waving them to go away. "It's all right," he said, trying to say it loud enough for them to hear, but they couldn't have. Jerry and the other car drove off, leaving my father and me standing together.

My father and I sat down on the steps. He kept his arms around me for a long time. The tears on our faces dried from the breeze. My mother came to the door and looked at us from inside.

It was such a sunny day. Everything seemed like it really would be all right. My father took some deep breaths and let them out.

"I don't know what to say," he said. "Do you?"

"No," I said.

"Maybe nothing," he said.

After a while, he said, "Did you remember to bring your report card home?"

"I think I dropped it somewhere over Old Orchard Road."

He nodded. "We could drive over and look for it later," he said.

My mother came out and sat down on the other side of me. She put her arms around me and drew me toward her for a minute. Then Jessica and Luke came out and sat on the step below us. So we all sat there.

Every once in a while one of us would go inside to go to the bathroom or to get something from the kitchen to bring out for all of us, but otherwise, we all just sat together on the steps for the rest of the afternoon. It was about the second or third day of summer — the first day, really, since school was just over. The mailman came by, then some little kids came and stood there with us for a while, asking us why we were sitting there. Then my mother went in to start supper.

ABOUT THE AUTHOR

JOHN LEVERT makes his home in Natick, Massachusetts, with his wife and two children. He received a Fellowship in Fiction from the Massachusetts Artists Foundation for his work on this novel, his first.

Bantam Offers Zindel

Pulitzer Prize Winner
Paul Zindel